In The Midst of Fire

A Novel by Sierra Kay

ISBN: 978-0-9848477-7-8

In the Midst of Fire

Sierra Kay

Cover by Art on the Loose, Chicago

Since my friend told me that I can't dedicate this book to Diet Dr. Pepper ® (even though without that sweet elixir this book wouldn't have been possible), I will dedicate it to a few of the grinders that keep me on my toes.

Chris P., my dear friend and #1 dynamo. She packs more work into 24-hours than most pack into 24 days. You conquered 2016 like a champ.

Naleighna Kai, fellow author and editor. I'd run out of space adding all the roles she plays. Plus, every time I sneeze, she has a new book. Motivation.

Erika P., the event designing guru. One morning, I opened my eyes, and she was on a major network in Chicago. Round of applause.

Chelle, the boss lady. I don't know how she does all that she does, but she makes it work.

Ms. Gail, my line editor. Any mistakes that appear are mine, and it means I was working without the benefit of you-know-what. If I could make eye drops to see all that she does, I'd be rich.

To the other tremendous women, I've been fortunate enough to walk beside. A few have made their transition. Some I talk with often. While others, I talk with rarely. But I could call any one of them (the live ones) day or night, and the only question is, "What do you need?" That means something.

And, that includes the wee ones. For the record, this is still grown folks business, but you know I love you.

Thank you for your love, friendship and inspiration.

Book One

CHAPTER
1

March 2009
Greenview Avenue
Chicago, Illinois

Seraphina Brooks Glen bit her lip, trying to ignore the stab of uncertainty that filled her as she looked up at the four-story brick structure in the affluent area of Lincoln Park. Chase Glen, her new husband, was paying the cab driver, which gave her scant seconds to view her new home. Husband. The taste of the word was foreign on her tongue. But a quick glance at her left hand confirmed everything that had transpired within the last three days.

That, plus the frenetic energy sparking through her system, pushing her to smile, skip, dance; might this be happiness?

The cars on the tree-lined street were parked tighter than a 60-year-old virgin. Each tree had a small fence keeping the flowers from flowing onto the sidewalk. By far, the well-manicured yard in front of Chase's house was the most impressive that she'd seen. The plants and flowers flourished in a riot of color that was unlike where she'd been born. In her neighborhood, the dry, cracked dirt couldn't sustain a worm, much less a flower.

Seraphina took deep breaths to calm her nerves, while whispering to herself that she belonged.

Chase opened the black wrought-iron gate and placed his hand on the small of her back as he guided her up the stairs. "Welcome home, my angel."

He opened a wooden door with a glass-etched oval in the center, which led into a small foyer. A gasp echoed throughout the space as she turned to the spacious living and dining room areas. Seconds later, she realized that gasp had escaped from her own lips.

Chase virtually beamed.

Get it together, Seraphina.

"Be right back."

Seraphina turned, focused on the way she had just come from, only to find that the bulk of their luggage was still on the sidewalk. Her new husband felt safe enough to leave their luggage on the curb?

That, in itself, spoke volumes. Try that in the hood and your polka dot bra would be a new hat for some homeless dude.

Seraphina's legs moved into the living room on their own volition. Her whole apartment could fit in this living and dining room. She was sure of it.

Turning to her right, she glanced down the hallway that led to the kitchen. Well, damn. This is some HGTV stuff, for real. She spun around as her heart pounded harder than a House music baseline. This was arriving.

This was a home, something her bastard of an ex-boyfriend had told her she'd never have. Six months ago, Michael McNair told her she wasn't good enough, right before he beat her so badly that she lost consciousness and five hours of her life.

Seraphina closed her eyes, fighting that soul-crushing memory; but the tentacles of pain wrapped around her mind once again. Six months ago, she woke up in the John H. Stroger Hospital with a dry, scratchy throat and the desperate need to cough. Even in a semidelirious state, she realized coughing was a bad idea. The incessant beeping from a heart monitor was so irritating that if she had more strength she'd yank the cord from the wall.

As she drifted in and out of consciousness, voices belonging to people she couldn't identify floated in and out of existence. She refused to acknowledge them, refused to open her eyes, refused to face this new reality.

In the Midst of Fire

She knew as sure as that beeping monitor that the soul that she'd been nurturing in her womb for the past four months was gone. So what was the point of opening her eyes?

That's what loving the wrong man could do. The wrong man could suck all semblance of hope like the devil yanking your wretched soul into hell. And Michael McNair had been the wrong man. Yes, he was fine. Yes, he had swag. Yes, he was the shit in the neighborhood gang, the Kingdom Knights. Yes, all the women in the hood had been jealous of her.

But then, they had always been jealous of Seraphina, starting with her hair—long, thick, and straight with no need for chemical enhancements. It ended with her deep dimples that only required her to compress her red lips for them to appear. She'd had many fights growing up, most of them to protect herself, others to protect her virtue.

Ever since she'd left her mother's womb, it seemed she was always fighting someone for something.

She scanned the Lincoln Park home that would be her saving grace and her first thought was …"

Finally, peace.

CHAPTER 2

Seraphina had progressed from fighting with fists to fighting with weapons a long time ago. When someone came for Seraphina, they'd better be ready to kill her. So far, no one had been ready—except Michael.

She had witnessed firsthand the violence that he inflicted on other people. His temper was quick and violent. Once, he had punched a man, who had accidently stepped on his kicks, so hard that he'd broken the man's jaw in two places. At the time, she stood by so amazed and proud that this was her man. He knew how to handle his business. She had gotten used to the blood oozing from his victims.

That's why her preferred weapon was a knife. Something about blood called to her, seduced her like Michael's slow, baritone whisper.

However, when Michael had turned on her, kicking her repeatedly in the abdomen, she realized that it was *other people's blood* that enticed her. Her blood, her baby's blood running down her legs, hadn't brought on the usual shiver of excitement. Instead, the sight broke her down to the same whimpering mess she saw in her victims. While on his apartment floor, Seraphina had tried to tighten her legs, compress the flow with her hands—all to no avail.

Her baby must have known that this world wasn't for her. Or was it Michael? The baby realized that Michael would not be the type of father with a soft voice or a soothing hand when it cried. No matter. Her baby was now back in heaven waiting on a mother who could protect it, waiting for a mother who didn't love a death dealer, waiting for a mother who deserved the blessing a baby could bring.

The hospital door opened again, and this time the steps were slower, heavier. The cadence was one she recognized. She had known Vincent Curtis since kindergarten. He was her best friend, her protector. He loved her even when no one else did. Her mother apparently had a one-hour limitation on love, if the men going in and out of her bedroom were any indication. Never any love for the little girl she'd given birth to. Two years ago, when Seraphina was twenty-three, her mother up and left. Whether the egg donor that gave birth to her was dead or alive wasn't something Seraphina lost any sleep over— it or her. That's how close they were.

Vincent was different. He wanted to be her everything, but so had Michael at some point. She'd seen the violence in Vincent too.

The kind of depraved acts required to keep on this side of the grave, broke something inside of them, allowing them to kill without thought and yet sleep well through the night. Allowing them to understand that their forest was full of different kinds of demons than were told in the fairy tales.

Not being able to hold it any longer, Seraphina coughed. *Oh, hot shit and damn.* The pain that spiked her skull and shot through her body was like someone had split her in two. The searing burn through her abdomen was sudden and intense. Tears gathered in her dark brown eyes as she gasped trying to fight for air.

"Sera?"

Vincent's voice was tentative, cracking.

All she could do was moan a reply.

She heard him, felt him shift his weight. "Do you want me to call someone?"

Seraphina let out a breath and croaked, "No." Taking another deep breath, she was able to put some strength into her efforts this time, "No."

The crunch of a 6-feet 3-inch, 300-pound man landing on an old vinyl chair was unmistakable. She blinked her eyes open, startled by the onslaught of light. Finally, she managed to ask him to turn the main light off.

The swish of clothing signaled that he had complied. Soon, she opened her eyes again to a much softer glow from her bedside lamp.

After playing possum for the better part of the day, she was going to have to face how wrong her choice of man was. Laughter from doctors and nurses in the hallway didn't seem to fit with the somberness that being in the hospital required.

Turning her head toward Vincent, she whispered, "My baby's gone." She wanted to be more emotionless about it; but the current situation, and everything that had led up to it, had stolen every ounce of bravado. Her eyes betrayed her with every tear streaking down her face.

Vincent's gaze searched the floor as if the answers to all of life's problems were etched into the white-and-black-speckled design.

Sera's eyes narrowed on him. A woman didn't know someone for this long and not know when they were hiding something.

She swallowed another cough. "What do you know?"

Vincent drew his hands through those shoulder-length dreads. "The doctor was talking to the nurses. Your insides …"

Gritting her teeth, she demanded, "Say it."

"You should know," he ground out, dark brown eyes flashing with a recognizable kind of anger. "Michael won't make it through the night."

"You'll be the first person they look at, V. It's too soon."

Vincent finally met her eyes and smirked, "It won't be me. Remember that genius kid, Ninja."

Ninja was never in the game. The Kingdom Knights used him every now and then, but he had been smart enough to secure a college scholarship. Everyone knew that was his path, until his brother started selling and using. Then Ninja came back a year ago with a wealth of knowledge about science and police procedure. He was the reason most of the Knights were out of jail.

He used his brilliance to cover up a multitude of crimes. Hell, he had cursed her out for leaving fingerprints in the blood of every violent episode she'd had. And it took balls to curse out a woman who was holding a knife dripping with someone else's blood.

"Vincent."

In the Midst of Fire

Vincent snapped to attention, then barreled ahead with his story. "Michael killed his lying, stealing brother. He's the man Ninja's looking for. One call and he's all taken care of. It's a brilliant plan, Ninja—"

"Vincent!" Seraphina clamped her teeth and tried to breathe through the pain. She didn't want to hear about Michael, Vincent, or the dead brother. She wanted to know what Vincent knew about her insides.

"Chère, I'm sure the doctor will be here soon.". Vincent turned towards the door as if willing the doctor to appear.

Sera banged her hand on the mattress, cutting off a pain-generated curse word. Vincent was as frustrating as a dripping faucet. "If I told you once, I've told you a thousand times, we're not French. Tell me what the hell you know!" Her pillow was already soaked. She wanted to roll on her side, but the strain on her abdomen was a perfect reminder of why she shouldn't.

She turned her head towards him. This wasn't her Vincent. *Her* Vincent would have just given it to her straight and kept going about the conversation. This had to be bad, real bad.

"Your insides," Vincent began, gesturing to her abdomen. "Well, you can't have any more …"

Sera filled in the last word. "Kids. I can't have any more kids."

The shimmer of tears in Vincent's eyes said it all.

Sera turned away from him and put her focus on counting the holes in the ceiling tile. Her heart rate slowed as anger set in, hardening her arteries, removing all remnants of the emotional weakness that put her in the hospital in the first place. Every second another shield slid into place. "No Ninja," she said in a voice so cold she could barely recognize it as her own. "Michael is mine."

Walking to her bed, Vincent used the pad of his thumb to wipe a tear from her cheek. "No, ma petite; he's mine."

That day, when Seraphina closed her eyes to get comfortable with the shields that would keep her from ever being this hurt again, she opened them in the hospital. That was then.

Today, when she closed her eyes, she opened them to see Chase Glen, the stranger that she married on a whim, walking back through his front door. *If you're going to marry a stranger, might as well be a rich one.*

As soon as he dropped the bags onto the marble floor of the foyer, she jumped in his arms. "Baby, it's beautiful. I haven't even seen the rest, and I can tell it's wonderful."

She kissed him as she slid down his body. Footsteps trotting down the stairs caused Seraphina to pull back and make her way into the living room. The children.

"Dad?" a female voice inquired.

The girl slid to a stop at the bottom step, causing her brother to run into her back and bump her into the living room. Without speaking, the two looked at each other, frowning at this new addition in the house.

Sera assessed them through their silent communication. The girl was tall with a medium build. Her natural hairstyle was achieved with the help of a decent colorist. She wore a pair of ratty jeans and a Lenny Kravitz t-shirt.

The boy was slightly taller than Chase, but had that "look" about him. His hair was cropped close to his head; he had thick eyebrows and eyes that were now even narrower as they focused on his sister. He wore a button-down shirt and a pair of high-end jeans, whose special discoloration was created in the lab and not from too much washing or sitting. He was a younger version his father—a pretty boy who'd be pulling women for the rest of his life with no effort whatsoever.

"Hey there." Chase said with a laugh that barreled through his chest before pushing through those kissable lips. "Enough of that twin telepathy. I want to introduce you to Seraphina."

"You can call me Sera."

The girl extended her right hand. "Hi, Sera. I'm Giselle." As they shook hands, Giselle turned Sera's hand over to view the sparkling four-carat diamond wedding ring. The girl raised her left eyebrow and blew out a slow breath. "Well, it looks like you're a bit more than a guest. Might your last name be Glen now?"

Sera stiffened at the accusation that laced her tone.

The boy's mouth dropped open. He snapped it shut, and his jaw rippled underneath the skin of his chin. He exhaled, shifted a gaze to her sister, then held out his hand. "Hawk." He too turned her hand for a better look at the ring. "Well, Dad. It seems like you struck the jackpot in Vegas."

He was more welcoming than his sister, but there was still an underlying accusation in those words.

Chase laughed again, his merry eyes twinkling with pride. "Yes, I did. Let's sit for a bit," he said, gesturing towards the orange leather couch.

Again, the twins shared another silent communication before complying with their father's wishes. Sera settled next to Chase. Something about having his arm around her brought a stability that had escaped her for most of her twenty-five years. After the original shock of seeing her standing in their home, the twins stared without blinking.

"It's an amazing story really," Chase began. "I go all the way to Vegas and find someone as beautiful and wonderful as Sera. She was born and raised in Chicago, too. A few miles from here—right, Sera?"

"Yeah, not too far," Sera replied, trying to keep her voice level. She hadn't exactly lied about where she used to live, she just didn't bother to disclose everything. In relationships, who discloses everything?

Giselle leaned forward. "And out of curiosity, what year did you graduate?"

Age? They were worried about age? Sera almost laughed out loud. She thought for sure a bank account or pedigree would be their first question; especially, given the fact that it was obvious privilege was as much as part of their life as milk and eggs.

She relaxed a bit more, crossing one jean-clad leg over the other. "I'm 25 years old. I know that's young, but you'd be surprised at how much your dad and I have in common."

Hawk's dark brown eyes opened wider than the shades covering the matching lamps on the end tables. "Dad? Really? That's more than fifteen years?"

Giselle's hands curled into fists. "Well, did you know each other before Vegas?" she inquired, her gaze falling to that wedding ring again. "Dad just left on Thursday. I mean, were you drunk? What happened? How can you get married in four days? She doesn't even know—"

The caution in Hawk's eyes caused Giselle to stop mid-sentence. Chase stiffened under the weight of those words. The silence stretched out and engulfed them until taking small inhales of breath became a labored thing for Sera, as though a hand was pressing down on her chest and wouldn't let her go. She looked between the Glens. She shifted her gaze so that it took in each one of the Glens.

"What? What don't I know?"

Chase relaxed again and rubbed his hand down Sera's arm. "You know when you're in love."

The twins whipped their heads to stare at their dad as if he had grown another head. "Love!?!"

Chase grimaced and then stood, pulling Sera up beside him. "Yes, love," he confirmed; but there was something in his tone that brought Sera up short. "It was instant and liberating."

The heat of his gaze nearly seared a hole in the shield on her heart. She'd have to be careful. She concentrated on trying to figure out all the emotions crossing his kids' faces—shock, anger, resignation.

Hawk's cell phone buzzed as Chase continued, "And you guys are going to go on with your own lives soon, so ...."

Hawk shrugged, extracted his cell from the shirt pocket and looked at the caller ID. "I have to take this."

Chase lifted his hand in an effort to pause Hawk. "Wait, Hawk. I had hoped—"

"Yeah, welcome to the asylum, Sera." Hawk raced out of the room, but yelled back over his shoulder, "I hope you enjoy your stay."

Chase watched his son's retreating back for a moment before shifting his gaze to Giselle, whose solemn expression signaled that something wasn't quite right in the world of everything Glen. "Why don't you whip up something for dinner?" he suggested. "We can get to know each other better."

Giselle nodded. "No problem, Dad. You could do steaks on the grill, and I'll handle the sides. We have some asparagus, maybe a bit of risotto."

"Risotto?" Sera quipped.

Chase chuckled, "Giselle is addicted to *The Food Network*."

As Giselle rushed from the room as though a burning fire were nipping at her heels, Chase pulled Sera into a hug. "See, that wasn't that bad. Was it?"

Uneasiness settled into the seat of her soul. If growing up in the hood taught her anything, she knew when she was being watched. Instead of responding to Chase's baited question, she angled her head toward the back of the house.

Hawk had the phone to his ear, but he was watching them intently from the upper level of the steps. Giselle peered out from the edge of the dining room.

They didn't look pissed anymore. If she had to sum up their countenance and expressions, it would be—sad.

Maybe it was because their father had mentioned love. Did that word, applied to her, mean that their father would have less to give to them?

Sera didn't know anything about the three wives that came in between his first love and the "love" he claimed he felt for her.

She didn't know at the time that they weren't worried that she was using him for his money because he didn't have any left.

Sera didn't know that their lives were falling apart and his wedding was just another boulder on the crumbling structure that was his family.

She didn't know that one day she'd be awakened by the pounding of the sheriff's department, expecting their immediate departure from the premises; and with it, all hope for the kind of future that she'd been promised when she stood in front of an Elvis impersonator and pledged her life to Chase Glen.

CHAPTER

3

The television in the living room competed with squeals of crying babies, anger spewing from shouting parents, and rebellious tirades of cursing teens. The endless symphony of the projects drove Sera from the kitchen into the semi-quiet of the bedroom. Drowning in the ocean of desperation that seeped from the ceiling and bled through the walls brought a sadness that was hard to shake.

Sometimes, when reflecting on her peaceful time with Chase in Lincoln Park, she wished she had never left the projects. Then she would never have known that life could be better. Coming back to Burnham Park made her want to scream every hour of every day. Coming back made her want to cut somebody, anybody. Her hand shook with the need to inflict the type of physical pain to match her emotions.

Sera turned the tight corner, past the requisite last supper poster that black churches must give out as often as Mormons put Bibles in hotel rooms. The only disciples that crossed her neighborhood had Gangsta in front of their names, and forgiveness was never on the menu.

She stalked through the doorway of the kitchen and leaned her head against the refrigerator. Chase came to mind. Most days she wanted to kiss and kick his ass at the same damn time. This is what a trip to Vegas led to—a whirlwind wedding, where Chase charmed her panties, ring finger, and common sense; leading her to believe she was as close to happily ever after as a woman from the hood could get.

Forty-three years old with smooth skin, which even today was often described as red-bone, and soft hands that told of his pampered life. His voice didn't rise, his breath never reeked of alcohol, and even the thought of the feel of his body next hers caused her creamy love to come flooding down.

Seraphina had been raised in a household with a rotation of men who viewed women merely as places to blow their load and their temper when you tried to deny their not-so-welcome requests.

She felt cherished in Chase's arms. But she couldn't stay in his arms 24/7, and the rest of her world wasn't welcoming at all.

She covered her ears to protect them from the sudden pounding on the neighbor's door. The firm, harsh beats sounded the same as the sheriff's that had roused her out of her sleep in her Lincoln Park home, and had rousted her out of a life that she had barely settled in to.

The staggered rhythm of each blow against the door snatched her back to the memories of the last day at her dream house.

She was asleep, wrapped in Chase's arms, when the sheriff's deputies and their moving crew tried to knock down the door with their fists.

"Chase?" she whispered.

After a short pause, the ringing and pounding started again. His kids came to the bedroom door.

"Dad." Giselle's voice was barely audible, but it was the way she plucked at her shirt sleeve that alerted Sera to the fact this wasn't an ordinary visitor. "It's the sheriff."

Sera's gaze fixed on her stepdaughter. "What?!!"

Her mind couldn't process why the sheriff would be at her house—not this house, at this hour. And from her place in an enormous master bedroom, it sounded more like a drug raid than a courtesy call. What was going on?

"Chase?" she whispered, afraid to voice anything more than that.

Chase's steady smile, one that smoothed over every concern, was gone, replaced by a look so uncomfortable it caused a stab of worry in her heart.

"Baby, I didn't know how to tell you."

The ruckus continued.

Giselle tossed a disgusted look at her father before running out of the room, down the stairs, evidently on her way to open the door for their unwanted guest.

Chase jumped up from the bed, grabbed his robe, and ran to chase her down.

Hawk looked at Sera and gave her the most unwelcomed news, "We're getting evicted. You may want to pack your bags. Giselle and I have been packed for months."

Sera stilled the anger that whipped through her, quickly scanned the room trying to figure out what she wanted to pack, while still trying to wrap her mind around the reason for such a hasty action.

By the time Sera focused on the door again, Hawk was gone.

Heated voices from downstairs spurred her into action. She jumped into yesterday's clothes, ran to the closet, and grabbed up the first set of garments she could put her hands on.

Chase came back in the room and closed the door.

Sera kept slamming items into Chase's Louis Vuitton duffel, as she glared up at him. "Chase?"

Chase bent down in front of her. "Listen, I had some tax issues a while back, and a few other money problems. So I have to give up everything. I just . . . just wanted a little time with you without"—his gesture took in everything around them—"all of this."

Packing tape ripped from a holder downstairs, sounding eerily like the tearing of her heart. This had all been a lie?

"Where will we go?" Sera hated the tremor in her voice, the sign of weakness that she had never shown to anyone but him.

"You still have your place, right?"

Cringing, she did a mental tally of what that place looked like right about now. It was definitely a better sight than being outdoors, sleeping on the lawn. She gave him a slow nod.

"We'll just stay there until we're on our feet again," he supplied, trying and failing to give her his signature smile. "I'm a bit money-broke, but I have a few dollars. It'll be fine. You'll see."

In the Midst of Fire

No, he would be the one to see. Chase didn't know that those few miles between their places were across the proverbial tracks. His place was Tiffany's. Hers was Target—no, Wal-Mart; no, Dollar Store. Her place was "the projects," a building nestled in the center of the city's elite, where exclusive addresses mingled with a sturdy brick fort that stood proudly as if it has been vaccinated against gentrification. It was a world she never wanted to set foot in again.

"Chase, I live close, but my place is smaller than this."

"I'm sure it'll be fine," Chase murmured, while he turned the combination to the safe hidden in the wall behind the bedside table.

"I mean *much* smaller, like … Burnham Park Apartments."

Chase froze. The color practically drained from his face.

Sera pulled Chase beside her and tried to block out the noise outside the door. She monitored his reaction, seeing the disbelief and confusion in his expression. Right now, she had no idea what he was seeing from her.

Chase caressed her cheek, but it didn't make her stomach flutter as usual. "It's alright. I'm no better. Every woman I've married had money. This house belonged to my first wife." He chuckled, "Obviously, I'm horrible with money or the sheriff wouldn't be downstairs."

Even as the words were falling out of Chase's mouth his facial expression still told a different story.

"Dad?" Giselle yelled.

"Give me a minute," he shouted back, then grabbed Sera's hands and lowered his voice to a whisper. "I won't always do the right thing or say the right things, but I love well. I can love you very well. I don't care where we are. Please, just hang in there with me. I—"

Pounding on the bedroom door interrupted anything else he could say. Sera glared, believing that his children were on the other side. Here her husband was pouring out his heart, and those heathens interrupted. And it wasn't the first time.

They were always around with their whispers and secrets—always interrupting, questioning, and watching. Another thing Chase had failed to mention when he sealed her future with a ring. What man doesn't let his future wife know that he has a little baggage back home?

This time Hawk hollered, "Dad! Open up. We need to get out of here."

Chase rushed from the room, abandoning any further explanation, hurrying to console his kids.

Sera debated whether to get close enough to eavesdrop. The debate ended in three seconds. She edged her way towards the door, at first only hearing faint mumbles. Opening the door a crack, she was able to make out snippets of their conversation.

"Dad, this is why you don't marry for money," Hawk whispered, his voice tight with anger.

Chase leaned in, saying, "We were staying at the same hotel. She was spending cash like I was. It's not like I could ask her. I mean, I've done really well in the past."

Sera heard a disgusted snort came from one of the twins, then Giselle sighed, "Dad, with your divorce record and the sheriff downstairs, clearly you haven't done well.

Giselle rubbed her forehead. "This is too much. All you have to do is—"

"It'll be fine," Chase soothed. "We'll stay inside most of the time, and I'll just keep her under control. A month tops."

Hawk's dark brown gaze arrowed in on his father. "What about after the month is over?"

Chase answered with a smile in his whisper, "I have a backup plan. There's a widow that I've been seeing."

The two children groaned their disappointment. Hawk's open glare matched Sera's anger. Giselle's cheeks grew red.

"It's not right just yet," Chase said, obviously ignoring his children. "And I have to find a way to get out of this relationship with Sera. But a month with her is not a hardship. If she had real money in the bank, this would've been a match made in heaven."

Sera slowly closed the door, praying they didn't hear the soft click. She stumbled over to the unmade bed. So, that's all she'd been was a paycheck—and a bad one at that. Even the children knew it.

On autopilot, she left the plush comfort of the designer bedding and packed the last of her clothes. The more she stuffed most of important of her belongings in the duffel, the angrier she became. How had she gotten everything so wrong?

She was going back no better than when she left. Now Chase was going to dump her for some dowdy widow, simply because she had more money. Like hell! If she was going to Burnham Park Apartments, they were all going back to the projects. They'd stay there until Chase's ass got them all out—her included. She'd be damned if they were going to use her this way and get away with it. Hell no! Not this time.

The door to the bedroom opened, and the trio was on the other side, bags already completely packed, looking as innocent as they could manage.

Those spoiled brats were on to their father's schemes? They could have warned her. Their concern for her pain and well-being had come a little too late.

Raised in luxury. The only people that Chase actually loved. Well, a few months at her place would show them a bit of appreciation for the finer things.

"We'll all go to my place. It's nowhere near as beautiful as this," Sera said, gesturing to indicate the opulence around her.

Chase smiled with the same lift of his talented lips that had reeled her in three months ago in Vegas. "But we'll have each other."

Sera walked over to him, beckoned for the twins to come closer before embracing the three of them. "Yes, we'll have each other. That's all that matters," she confirmed right before vowing, inwardly, that she'd cut all of them off at the knees before they'd walk out on her.

The vibration in her jeans pocket snapped Sera back to her present circumstances. She glanced at the text message and nodded before slipping the cell back into place. Those twins would learn that no matter what age, children should be seen and not heard. And she knew the best way to silence them. Maybe forever.

CHAPTER 4

Chase's eyes blinked open as he tried to reconcile where he had been to where he was now. All the moves he had made, all the women who had loved him, all the energy he had poured into never being poor again; and here he was, sitting in a different project—poor, again.

The floor creaked as Sera made her way to the bed. Even now, his heart sped up when she sauntered toward him. In Vegas, he quickly sensed they were kindred spirits.

It wasn't just her deep-chocolate, smooth skin, coupled with rich brown eyes, framed by long lashes that didn't merely close, but swept together and apart. He had dated beautiful women—beautiful rich women, models, actresses. He had enjoyed women immensely.

But more than a pretty face and tight, young body, Sera understood the layers that he didn't show anyone, the layers that she had herself. These layers were forged by growing up around the best and worst the world had to offer, places the devil himself would give a wide berth. Places like Shelton Homes on the far south side of Chicago, where his grandmother raised him, between those struggling to survive the best way they knew how and those who languished in poverty, needing no more than the crumbs that government provided.

In the Midst of Fire

His grandmother helped him survive in a place where the wrong tone in your voice, the wrong word, or a long look at the wrong woman could get a man hit, cut, or shot; a place where schools more often served as glorified day care centers instead of institutions of learning.

Chase closed his eyes, picturing his grandmother with her high cheekbones and full lips paying homage to the beauty she had once been. Her buxom frame was normally planted in a reclining chair near the front window. Occasionally, when she laughed, that sparkle of spirit would light up her entire being. But then there came a point where those same dark brown orbs were dim with worry. He hated it when she worried, even though she had every reason to.

She had lost her daughter, his mother, to the streets—killed right before Chase's tenth birthday. Rumor had it she was beaten to death by her pimp. Chase's father's name was anyone's guess. So her grandson's fate in life had already been determined.

One night he eased his way into the house after a night of street running as she called it, hoping she wouldn't be awake. He froze at the simple words, "Hey, Chase."

He ran to the bathroom, calling out, "One sec. I really have to pee."

He finished his business and quickly hopped into the shower. His grandmother's sight wasn't what it used to be, but her sense of smell was keener than those K-9 dogs the police trotted out every now and again. Thanks to his new line of work, he smelled like he'd been rolling around in a cannabis field all night.

On his block, everyone had a job. No matter how much he tried to resist the pull of the streets, it really wasn't much of an option if survival was the ultimate goal. Those who did something different were looked at with suspicion. The hood didn't take to someone who stood out more than any Chicago neighborhood. And survival was always his top priority.

Chase, who was more sensitive than tough, wasn't good at much; but he did have a freakish green thumb. Thank God. It kept him off the streets and in the labs growing all types of weed. The smell, though, was overpowering by the time he left and quickly drenched him in a scent that would tell his life story minutes before his actual body made it into a room.

When he rushed out of the shower, he dressed in a fresh set of clothes, sealing the old ones in a zippered storage bag and took a seat at the kitchen table across from his grandmother. His grandmother kept the radio tuned to the gospel station, as if the continued praise would dispel the devil that had taken root in the projects. That and the creaking of her recliner was Chase's morning wake-up call and evening lullaby.

She gave him a lengthy once-over, taking in the polo top and jeans that she starched and ironed so stiffly that it crackled when he sat down. "Chase, baby. Why are you always running to the shower every time you walk in?"

Chase smiled at her observation. Instead, he reached out for her hand and drew it to his lips and whispered, "I have to look good for my favorite girl."

"Sell that shit to someone else," she snapped, narrowing a steely gaze his way. "What's going on? You smoking now?"

Chase shook his head. "I promise, Grandma. I don't do drugs. You know that. I've kept up my end of our deal. My grades are high. I stay out of trouble. "

She took a few moments before nodding as though that explanation was satisfactory, when even he knew that it wasn't nearly enough. "And I might be your favorite girl; but if it was another girl, then you'd shower *before* you left, not when you came back." Squinting, his grandmother assessed him with those rheumy eyes. "Are you messing around with one of these loose girls? You too young for all that. Don't be bringing no babies up in this house."

Chase's smile widened as he leaned back in the wooden chair. "Well, the ladies do love me, you know, Grandma. But I got you. No kids up in this house."

"You don't get it," she despaired, taking a sip of chamomile tea from her favorite porcelain cup. The delicate vessel had come from a china set that she unearthed at a garage sale.

"These fresh little girls pretend like you all on the same plane. Then next thing you know she's tossing her pills and poking holes in condoms, thinking a baby will fill the hole in her heart." She placed the cup gently onto a saucer before her wrinkled hand reached out to grasp his. "I know for a fact not having people, having family, has put a hole in your heart."

Chase's heart warmed. "But, Grandma. I have you and that's all the people that I need."

Showing a perfect set of dentures, she brushed her hand across his cheek. The familiar feel of calluses from years of cleaning other people's homes caused a sting of sadness and loss. All he wanted to do is give her an easy life. And he was failing at that.

"That's true," she whispered. "I do love you something fierce. I hate I can't give you a better life than this."

"Grandma, this is fine," he replied, trying to keep his voice level. He needed her to believe he was alright; when in actuality every time he left the apartment, he signed the cross and sent a prayer to a God he was never sure he actually believed in.

She laughed and the sound didn't have a single drop of mirth. "This isn't fine. I worry myself crazy every time you take one step out that door. I worry that someone's going to beat you senseless or shoot you dead."

Chase grasped her hand and held firm. "But they haven't and they won't."

She bit her bottom lip and rasped, "My mother's father up and left before the doctor managed to slap her on the ass. You never knew your dad." Lifting her right hand to God, she added. "Have mercy on my soul. Promise me this—if you ever make it out of here, you keep going," she warned. "Even if I'm here, don't look back. Living in the projects should be a bump in the road, not a lifetime sentence for each generation." A soft smile touched her lips. "Branch out. See the world. Experience shit."

"Grandma, there's nothing wrong with our life," Chase retorted, unable to keep the fierceness from his tone.

With a dry chuckle, she scratched her head; the salt and pepper braid that wrapped around her head like a crown shifted with the movement. "Son, if you don't see there's better out there, then I surely did something wrong."

"There's nothing in the world better than you, Grandma," Chase insisted, and inwardly he believed that. Years in the neighborhood had taught him loyalty was as fleeting as honest money. Love and loyalty made a man soft, vulnerable. When everyone else was thinking about their next move, he better be thinking about yours, too; or his next move might be six feet under, like his grandfather. He had borrowed money from the wrong people trying to get his grandmother out of the projects. The loan was the kind of money that was supposed to be paid back with hefty interest. In this case, the payment and interest ended up with a bullet in his grandfather's gut.

Shaking her head, she conceded, "Fine, I'm the greatest; but I'm old and won't be here forever." She leaned in so there was a mere few inches between them. "If you have the opportunity, leave this place far behind and never look back."

Before Chase could utter a word, his grandmother held up a hand. "Promise."

"But Grandma, you're gonna live for—"

"Promise!"

Flinching from the harshness of her tone, Chase gave his word.

Twenty-four years later, as Chase touched the concrete walls of Sera's two-bedroom apartment, which bore an uncanny resemblance to his grandmother's place, he was confused. How had he wound up right back where he promised he'd never return? And with his kids.

Two generations—failure, big time.

CHAPTER 5

Sera's hands shook with equal amounts of anger, disbelief, and the desperate need to destroy something or someone. Taking the knife from the sheath in the small of her back, she spun the tip on the dining table and watched as it slowly whittled into the wood.

She hated waiting. Somehow, this was worse. She was waiting for Vincent. He'd been her first call when it became apparent the Glens had to leave all their valuables for the tax auction. Now, as incredible as it sounded, even to her ears, they were living in her old two-bedroom apartment in Burnham Park.

For minutes at a time, she thought it was a dream. She couldn't be back in a place she'd left to move on up like the Jeffersons in the reruns she grew up on. Yet, she was. Where was the sunlight? the expansive space? the hardwood floors?

Now, there was darkness, dingy carpet, never-ending noise, and oppression. She couldn't breathe this air anymore. Yet, she had to find a way to make it work.

Thank goodness she hadn't given away her place. Women raised in the projects know one basic rule—you don't give up subsidized housing. The government takes years before they find out the resident don't need it anymore.

Vincent cleared the members of the Knights who had taken up residence out of her apartment without her having to say a word.

And though her body was begging for sleep, she'd walked over to his building next to hers, desperate for a connection that would get her back under the Knights' protection. She grimaced when she looked down at her handiwork. Damn! She was fucking up Vincent's table.

Sera leaned back against the soft brown leather of Vincent's dining room set, pulling a coaster over the scratch. Tension was crawling up her neck and into her temples, leaving a throbbing ache that wouldn't go away. V knew she hated waiting, especially to hear his version of *I told you so.*

The bedroom door opened and NuNu, a 5-feet 8-inch Knight walked out with a gut so round that his body must have transferred the fat from his nonexistent ass. He was the type of man who would stick his piece in a girl's snatch whether her answer was yes or no.

He was fearless, which was useful to the Knights; but the man had as much brain power as a cockroach high on weed. Even now, he was leering at her and nodding like he'd ever have a chance.

Men like NuNu required no room for interpretation. His memory should be just a wee bit longer.

Sera smiled, whipping her knife before he could draw the next breath, barely missing his ear as it embedded itself into the drywall.

NuNu stepped forward.

Sera rose up to her full 5'1" height. She wasn't scared of NuNu.

Vincent placed his hand on NuNu's shoulder. "You're lucky she decided to miss."

NuNu chuckled, but he never broke eye contact with Sera when he muttered, "Later," before leaving out of the front door.

Vincent slid across from Sera, who had reclaimed her seat at the table. She inquired, "So tell me what business do two grown men have in the bedroom."

Bursting out laughing, Vincent leaned closer. "Join me and see, Chère."

"We …," Sera started.

"… aren't French," Vincent ended, chuckling more. "Pretty girl, did I ever tell you about my Creole grandmother?"

In the Midst of Fire

Gritting her teeth, she quipped, "If you have a Creole grandmother, then mother was a genius inventor."

Vincent leaned in, whispering, "Hell, the way those cats followed her around, she may have been."

Sera paused. She didn't like to be reminded that her mother was a whore, whether it was true or not. "I need a job."

"Oh, *now*, the happy homemaker wants to work," he taunted. "Before, you were too good for us." All signs of humor disappeared when he added, "The Knights do have memories—long ones."

Sera knew Vincent was going to make her work for it; but damn him, he could've given her something. She'd put in ten years and had sliced men to protect the Knights' territory before the rest of them were even a speck in their daddy's crotch. "I can start at the bottom."

Vincent raised his eyebrows, indicating that his interpretation of starting at the bottom was a bit different from hers. He walked over to his kitchen. "Water?"

"No," Sera spat. "I don't want any damn water." Seeing Vincent's grin, she clamped down on her temper, but the tremor in her hand reminded her how close to the surface that temper was.

She couldn't afford to lose her shit. He was an ass, but an ass she needed. She regulated her breathing, as Vincent made his way back to the table and slouched in his seat.

"Are you going to leave him?" Vincent watched her closely, his expression impassive.

Sera lifted her head. The implications slammed into her all at once. She'd be damned if Michael was going to be right. She was going to keep her husband and those damn kids. Her plan was already in motion. "No. He's my husband."

Smiling, Vincent leaned in so that they were mere inches apart. "Has he ever seen your knife work?" nodding to the wall, where her knife was still hanging a few feet from the bedroom door.

"V, there was no need for that where we were."

Sera closed her eyes. Vincent has always wanted one thing that, before now, she was unwilling to give.

This one thing could guarantee her easy entrance into the world she left with a laugh and a curse.

Before she could even wrap her mind around the ideas good and tight, Vincent was already saying, "No way."

Standing up, she edged around the round table locked on Vincent's intense gaze. "You sure about that?" She straddled his lap and leaned over to nibble at his earlobe. His heartbeat pounded against her breasts.

Vincent hissed. Then he pushed himself away from the table, and lifted her off him.

"When you come to me, it's not going to be because you owe me a favor," he snarled, those fierce dark brown eyes ignited in anger. "It'll be because you can't imagine your life any other way, but waking up beside me every morning."

Sera tried to part her lips, but Vincent clamped them shut with his fingers.

"And I won't even tell you I told you so." Vincent took two steps back. "You do know the Lily Whites that you brought with you are going to be a problem. Knights will look at those kids and wonder why they aren't in, too. Well, I can probably get around old ass Chase and possibly Giselle; but Hawk?" Vincent shook his head.

Sera lowered her eyelids to hide any thoughts hidden in her eyes. She wouldn't be able to rejoin the Knights without her new family. They were a package deal. The street wouldn't trust her unless they felt they could trust her family. Well, hell, sacrificing one wouldn't be so bad. Hawk would just have to deal with it.

"What do you need me to do?"

Vincent's lips edged up, showing a set of gleaming white teeth. "Well, Michael's job is still available."

Michael had been head of security in their neighborhood. It didn't sound like much, but the responsibilities were much deeper. He knew everything that went down, sometimes before it happened. He knew when to show up and when to disappear, when to handle a situation and when to turn away.

Nothing happened without Michael McNair's knowledge. That had made him the keeper of the secrets, which also made him both feared and revered.

As she weighed all her options, she looked over to the man who had always taken care of her. It was Vincent who kept her alive for six months after she left the hospital. He showed up every morning, forcing her out of bed, making her walk the block with him, allowing her to unleash her anger on anyone that the Knights needed to send a message to.

Yet, the ferocity of that violence soon made Vincent realize that her mind wasn't healing with her body. That's when he sent her on an all-expense paid trip to Las Vegas.

The day after she boarded that flight to Sin City, she received a message at the Aria Hotel that Michael had tried to outrun a Metra train and ended up dead. Shame. His death freed her in more ways than one.

That night she met Chase Glen, a man who exuded wit, charm, and was so handsome that one smile flooded her basement. He represented everything that Michael, the Knights, and even Vincent, was not.

Sera rose, laughing as she dragged a reluctant Vincent into a hug.

Poetic justice.

CHAPTER
6

Thanks to her friend, Ninja, Sera was able to track down the trifling widow that her husband planned on leaving her for.

Now, standing outside of a large, airy townhouse that was almost an exact replica of the one the sheriff's department had forced her out of, Sera smoothed down her form-fitting skirt, then walked up the steps to ring the bell of Mrs. Catherine Knight.

With each step, Sera remembered how desperate she had once been to be a part of this neighborhood, this life. How she watched out of her window at the women jogging past in the morning with their slender bodies, sometimes pushing strollers, but often alone.

Sera herself didn't jog and didn't see the benefit of taking up the sport just to make some friends in the neighborhood. During the day, she would sometimes hang around the Starbucks on North and Wells, watching the chess players battling for hours at a time, hoping to become a regular.

The baristas knew her; but outside of that, she was still an outcast. Even with new clothes, hair, and nails, she didn't fit in. She felt like an imposter pretending to be right for the role of Chase's wife.

And as much as she would deny it, she had been lonely. During the days when Chase went out for some meeting or another, she wandered around the home that might as well be a mausoleum, for the lack of warmth the living areas displayed. Now, one of the women who hadn't reached out to make her feel welcome was trying to "reach out" to her husband in a way that was more friendly than was proper.

She had chosen a black pencil skirt, black open-toe heels, and a purple tank—a suit jacket away from looking like a businesswoman. Summertime in the Chi was no time for extra clothes. She'd melt before hitting the end of Mohawk Street and would be funkier than a high school boys' locker room after a football game.

As Mrs. Knight opened the door, Sera assessed the competition. The elegant woman had her sleek silver hair done in an elongated bob style. Her body wasn't exactly full-figured, but she was definitely knocking on the door. She could use a few sessions at the gym, but she hid it well with loose-fitting clothes. The padding around her cheeks and her neck gave her away. Even with all that, Mrs. Knight was drenched in floral perfume and class. Bitch.

Sera smiled. "Mrs. Knight, I'm Sera Glen."

Dismissal already easing into her eyes, Catherine Knight responded with a cool, "And why should that matter to me?"

"Sera Glen," she added, widening her stance, "Chase Glen's wife. May I come in?"

Mrs. Knight's face gradually reddened, before she stepped aside and allowed Sera to enter the marble foyer.

Ninja had been thorough with his investigation. He had a list of all of Mrs. Knight's assets down to the penny. This woman was old money. She had her own business, stocks, bonds, the whole suite that all those investment commercials said wealthy people should have.

Mrs. Knight indicated with a flourish of a pink-manicured hand that Sera should take a seat on a massive white leather couch. Sera scanned the house that was similar to her old one in layout, but polar opposite in style and size. Clearly, this woman was without a man. Sera had never seen so much pink in a grown woman's house in her life.

Sera wanted to hate her. She wanted to take the tight ball of stress that was in her stomach and use it to propel a cut straight into Catherine Knight's abdomen. But there was something about this woman that reminded Sera of herself; maybe it was the broken look in her chocolate eyes when she learned of Sera's identity.

Hell, could she really fault Mrs. Knight for loving Chase? The first night he'd brought her home while she was in the en suite shower, Chase set up a picnic—candles, wine, and Oreos.

"This is about the extent of my cooking ability," Chase admitted with a charming grin. "But your first night home should be special."

Sera smiled as he gently fingered the strands of hair that escaped her ponytail. He leaned in and gently kissed her lips, soft and gently, dispelling any fears of his feelings about her. He pulled her closer to him. As they broke apart, they wrapped their arms at the elbow and fed each other Oreos.

Laughing, she exclaimed. "An Oreo picnic? You're a nut."

"Maybe. Or maybe I know how special you are, and I want you to know both in word and actions."

Chase pulled a remote from beside the blanket on the floor and turned on music with the flick of a button; the soft stirring music of Toni Braxton filled the room. He helped her to her feet, and they swayed to the music. Halfway through, he dipped her. Her anxiety settled. In that moment, she understood—the songs, the poetry. She lived her whole life with this anger, this drive. Now, for the first time in her life, now she had peace.

"Didn't know the old man had moves like that, did you?" he teased.

Sera gazed at this man. How had this happened? With all the people in the world, all the men that pushed up on her, how did she wind up in that perfect moment with him. "Oh, I'm well- acquainted with your moves." She had kissed him then. Kissed his lying, cheating lips before she realized that's what they were.

Even now as she sat across from Catherine Knight, knowing of his betrayal, there was something soft and right about that night that she wanted to capture every day of her life. And she'd fight up to St. Peter and down to Lucifer to keep her family together, to prove she was worthy of being loved.

"Mrs. Knight, I know you're familiar with my husband."

Mrs. Knight's hands tightened in her lap. She paused to let the sentence hang, as the chirping birds outside of the window filled the silence. Sera was aware of the sound of a game show playing on a television not too far off.

In the Midst of Fire

Mrs. Knight nodded, "I'm familiar."

"Well, I recommend you get *un*familiar." Sera's smile disappeared and was replaced by a cold glare, as she tossed the marriage certificate on the chrome and glass coffee table. "Quickly."

"I didn't know he was married," Mrs. Knight admitted, her wide eyes scanning the document, while her hands gripped the edges of the page.

"Well he is. And now he lives with me, in Burnham Park."

Mrs. Knight's hand came to her collar, grasping a set of imaginary pearls; the kind of pearls that appeared on the necks of rich women. Ones that loving fathers gave their precious daughters. Not her father, though. Whoever he was.

"I'd hate for there to be an issue between us," Sera continued in a tone that normally made her enemies quiver.

Mrs. Knight swallowed hard and nodded.

Sera stood and smiled again. "I'm glad we had this chat."

Mrs. Knight rose from the couch with a slow elegance that belied her fleshy frame. "Is there … What should I say when he calls me?"

Sera gazed at her now ex-nemesis. "Don't answer." She turned to make her way to the door, but said over her shoulder, "But you can call him next Saturday night."

Catherine's perfectly arched eyebrows drew in as she asked, "Why then? And say what?"

"It's a surprise. And, you can tell him Sera said it was over."

Mrs. Knight placed a hand on Sera's shoulder. That was normally enough for her to cut a bitch. All that pink must have been seeping into her pores, making her soft.

"Mr. Knight, my first husband, had a lady friend on the side—actually, more than one," she hesitated as if struggling with the admission still. "It was never my intention to be that for some other woman. It's not a good feeling."

The distant television became the primary sound in the room. Sera paused and fought the emotions generated from that one kind statement. "Thank you for that. And you're right." She searched Mrs. Knight's eyes for a hint of deception, but she saw only sincerity and sadness. "It's not a good feeling at all."

CHAPTER
7

Chase tried to sweep all thoughts of the past from his mind. Sera inched up to the bed, situated herself near the pillows, and said, "Hey, sweetie."

He looked up at her soft expression and, for a moment, a sliver of guilt about his upcoming plans eased past her ribs and settled as a cramping pain in his heart. His children didn't deserve the lessons that this neighborhood would give them. And even so, he was torn. "Hi, my Sera."

As she sat on the bed, he casually placed his hand around her hip. She snuggled closer to him. They sat in silence for a while, each lost in their own thoughts; and he wondered if she had the kind of regrets that weighed on her like a 50-pound barbell. It was impossible to tell, because hood life fit her curves like one of those tube dresses she wore.

Chase broke the silence with, "Where are the kids? How are they adjusting?"

He knew better than to ask that question. They were scared. They had to be. Hell, he was scared. With all the noise, loud shouting, phantom gunshots, and poorly concealed gun exchanges, they had to wonder why everyone wasn't patted down and hauled off to jail.

Although he had grown up in similar surroundings, it had been years since he had actually driven through the hood, not to mention live here.

"They haven't left the apartment since we moved in," she responded, avoiding his gaze. "You'd think someone was waiting for them around every corner?" she added, with more anger than what was warranted, while extracting her hands from his. "It's not that bad."

Chase gave a slow smile. "They're not used to the neighborhood."

"They'll be fine," she shot, and then bounced up and down on the bed, bringing his attention to the way her breasts jiggled. "So, guess what? There's a Blaxploitation cinema fest on cable tonight:. *Dolemite. Five on the Black Hand Side, Foxy Brown* ... ."

Laughing, Chase responded, "I don't know how someone as young as you are can be into those films so much."

Sera gave a little half smile. "It could be our date night. I'll even wear that dress you like."

Chase rubbed the curve of Sera's ass, his hand lingering on the parts of her that were as familiar as the veins lining the back of his hand. The dress in question was the one she was wearing when they'd met in Vegas.

Versace, Louboutin, every piece of clothing that touched Sera's skin whispered a level of class that was in stark contrast to the narrow closet stuffed with wire hangers that held them.

Chase should have recognized all of the signs, for he too was what people could consider "polished ghetto." Maybe subconsciously that's what drew him to Sera in the first place. Imposters, the both of them. They were users of people on a level that allowed them to upgrade their lives from the ones they were born in—even if only for a short time.

Now, as he lay in the bed in an apartment he had never wanted to see the likes of again, Sera shook him to get him to answer her question.

"Let's definitely make it a date night," he answered.

Sera nodded and walked towards the door. When she had her hand on the knob, she paused. "We could be happy here—all of us, together." When Chase didn't respond, she added. "I can make us happy. It doesn't have to be like this."

Chase grinned at her naïve thoughts. "You're the flower that blossoms in my heart every morning," he whispered. "I can't ask much more of you than that."

He was used to women blushing and ducking their head when he complimented them. He used to at least rate a kiss.

Sera was different. She searched his face. Obviously, she didn't see what she was looking for, because her eyes glossed over with a dimness he'd been seeing all too much lately.

Chase walked to the bedroom window, which gave a view of the gentrified building across the street. This block was merely one mile from the lake that it made it worth it for the monied to move across the street. But, this particular housing project was so deeply rooted, its foundation may have hit the earth's core, making it too difficult to move its inhabitants anywhere.

So killers live across from accountants, the hypes across from the doctors, the hood rats across from the corporate pimps and whores. *That's city living for you.*

That made it even more nerve-wracking. It isolated the destruction. Going after the wealthy would bring the wrath of the police that no one wanted to see. So the residents in the building he now called home tended to turn on each other. That's why he had to get his children into some place, before this area stripped them of the protective sheen of the high life.

Hearing commotion on the street, Chase leaned down to see men unloading furniture, apparently shouting instructions. Evidently, another lawyer-doctor-corporate grunt, or whatever was moving in across the street.

Chase placed his hand gently on the screen, itching to reach out and touch the life that was once his. That was before everything fell apart, leaving his family shattered in the aftermath. He tried not to think about how life had snatched him back from the kind of success that would have had his grandmother cackling with glee.

Another glance across the street, and he tamped down his jealousy. He could have purchased one of those condos easily. Hell, there was a time when he could have purchased two or three without breaking the bank. However, back then the last thing he wanted to see when he looked out of his window was the projects—so even if he could, he wouldn't have. At least not here—for that reason alone.

Funny, now he would sell a kidney to be across the street, looking at the projects instead of peering out on someone's high-styled life from inside them. He wondered who was moving in, who was starting a new chapter on such a high.

Inching away from the window, he turned to block out the reminder of how far he'd fallen.

Hawk and Giselle weren't prepared to handle half of the things that could go down in these buildings. Actually, with twenty-four years of distance between him and the time that he lived with his grandmother, neither was he. The difference is Hawk and Giselle didn't deserve to be here. He, with how completely he'd failed his family, was an entirely different story. He deserved whatever the projects dished out.

For not protecting Rose, for not protecting her legacy, for not protecting her children, he deserved to sit here and rot away until the good Lord saw fit to take him. Knowing the depths to which he had sunk and the women he had used, God wanted no parts of him. That's why God ensured that, even with all of those best laid plans, he still ended up in hell.

CHAPTER
8

Giselle propped her feet on Hawk's legs and leaned back against the leather couch while they looked at college volleyball on the television.

The twins had moved a week ago from an insulated, and safer, existence in the Chicago neighborhood of Lincoln Park to Sera's place, merely three miles from where they had been raised. Those few miles made one hell of a difference. Giselle and Hawk had been sliding closer to hell's fire ever since.

"Giselle! Hawk! You aren't going to lay up here all day," Sera yelled, as she exited the kitchen.

Giselle and Hawk glanced at each other from the couch cushions they had claimed on the day they arrived. It wasn't exactly their dream to be stuck in the two-bedroom apartment on Sedgewick Street, which reeked of bacon grease and weed.

And where, anger seeped its way in and embedded itself in their spirit, causing the members of the Glen household to start snapping at each other for no good reason.

The tan carpet was matted flat with mysterious stains speckling its worn pile. The white walls could also use a good wipe-down. The only acceptable things in the place were the two leather couches, which appeared to be newer than anything else in the apartment.

"Giselle, Hawk! I need you to go to the store," she snapped.

Giselle and Hawk looked at each other, then to their stepmother. "Is it safe for us to go to the store?" Giselle questioned.

It was a simple question, but a valid one. The twins had become worried after the multitude of hard stares that had focused their way when they moved into Sera's place. The weight of the stares added a heavier burden to each box and every suitcase they brought into the apartment.

Sera's gaze narrowed on them for a moment. They were dressed in the kind of clothes that bespoke subtle wealth.

"I was raised in the building next to this one," Sera said in a tone so icy it caused Giselle to shiver. "And I survived. They know you're mine. And that means something around here."

Giselle glanced at Sera's petite 5 feet 1 inch frame. To be that small and have survived living in a building riddled with bullet holes meant Sera had to know something. Giselle was the exact opposite of Sera. Giselle was a few inches less than 6 feet of well-proportioned breasts and hips.

Her vanilla skin was the opposite of Sera's chocolate; and natural cinnamon twists contrasted sharply to that long, silky hair Sera prided herself on. Yes, no telling what the woman had done to survive or the mistakes she'd made along the way.

Sera handed over a list. Giselle gave it a quick glance, and a flash of irritation filled her. The items scribbled on that paper included nothing that was worth endangering their lives to bring home. Something was off.

"We're not going out in that hell for this," Giselle declared through her teeth.

"You will if I say so," Sera shot back.

Hawk stepped forward, putting a few inches of space between them. "I'll go."

The fact that he volunteered to take the trip through the violence-ridden courtyard for a simple errand wasn't surprising. Giselle had noticed the increased restlessness in him since they moved in.

He wasn't used to being in such a small space for an extended period of time. He shared Giselle's vanilla complexion, but he was 6 feet 3 inches of solid muscle. Unfortunately, none of that muscle could stop a bullet; and the array of gunshots that filled the air was as good of a warning as any other.

Sera's gaze narrowed even further, a vein throbbing at the base of her temple. "You'll both go."

"Giselle is fine right here," Hawk hedged.

Sera threw money in Giselle's direction. "I said you'll both go."

Hawk stepped forward and opened his mouth to protest, but Giselle grabbed his arm. The muscle under her grasp tensed. "It's broad daylight, Hawk. I'm sure it's fine."

He whispered a series of instructions as he left the apartment and went out on the landing. "Move fast. Don't look anyone in the eye. Don't respond to anyone. Just walk; and if something happens, run, fast, back here." He grimaced and glanced back in the direction they'd just come from. "I had hoped to lie low until you left for college. I guess that was too much."

Fortunately, thanks to a 4.3 GPA and a 32 ACT score, Giselle had earned a full academic scholarship to Lexington University, outside of Philadelphia. Hawk had never worried about his grades that much, and standardized tests even less. So when the bomb dropped that their dad had to use all of their money, including their college funds, to stay out of jail after years of suspect tax practices, it left Hawk without options. He had been accepted to Lexington University as well, but without money to see it through, he was stuck.

Now, he was scrambling to find money to support his college dream, without scholarship-worthy grades, without grant-worthy tax returns, and definitely without a rich, connected father to grease any wheels.

However, Giselle had been counting the days until she could leave. Now she wished she could blink past the summer into the fall and right into school. Living under a tension blanket with her depressed father, restless brother, and a stepmother, who had been fuming since the four of them had graced the threshold of apartment 2B, no one was more ready for school than she was.

The minute they left the apartment, Giselle felt the eyes. She heard the hushed whispers and noticed the smirks and nudges as they passed. Looking across the street, Giselle was amazed at how high-end condos could even exist on the same block with the fort that was Burnham Park Apartments.

If only she could tear off a piece of that luxury, taste it, and savor it, to remind her of what life had once been and what it would be again as soon as she graduated from college.

"Hawk?" Even the one syllable wavered, as her nervousness took her vocal cords hostage.

"It's fine. It's only two blocks away," he replied, picking up speed. "So I heard you talking to your new roommate. What is she like?"

"Awesome. Kim, that's her name," Giselle appreciated the change of subject, "Her family runs this karate camp in the summer. They have a dojo and everything. Do you know she's training for the Olympics?" she babbled, quickening her steps to match his. "She invited me to come down early. The camp is in the Poconos. She says there are so many people in and out, they'd barely know I was there."

Hawk smiled as he surveyed the concrete landscape around them. "You should go."

Giselle disagreed. "Dude, I'm not leaving you one second sooner than I have to. You can still come with me. We'll find a place off campus. It'll be great."

Hawk's smile faded. "This is your time. You did the work. You got the grades. You studied while I was out kicking it." His voice paused. "You got the scholarship while I was daydreaming. There's no way I'm going to let you drag me about campus on your coattails."

Giselle scoffed. "You're my brother. You'll be by my side, not riding coattails."

"Well, anyway," Hawk replied, reiterating, "Go. Get the hell out of here."

Giselle shook her head, "Not without you."

Hawk sighed. They'd had this discussion before. He tried to get her to leave right after graduation, stating that if she started early, she'd end early; but she'd dug in her heels. "Plus, I don't want to leave Lizzie."

Giselle drew her head back and looked up at her twin. "I thought you weren't allowed to talk to her."

Just the mere mention of his girlfriend caused Hawk's already tight muscles to stiffen more. Giselle felt his turmoil as clearly as if it were her own. Lizzie's mother wasn't a fan of public and messy IRS audits and had forbidden

Lizzie to see any Glen—Hawk specifically, as if the sins of the father would translate to the son.

Hawk nodded as he slowed down. "I'm neither confirming or denying . . . "

Fear. Giselle felt it percolating through Hawk before she followed his gaze to a group of males in front of them. The group was leaning against a vacant building's wall and broken down cars that littered the area. She reached for Hawk's hand; and he gave it a gentle, encouraging squeeze. Only a half a block to their destination and now this. She didn't know what to do. Flee? No, the guys weren't blocking the sidewalk. They could make it.

As the twins worked their way closer to their destination, one by one the boys pushed off from the wall.

Shit! We should have fled.

"Hey, man."

Hawk pushed her a half step behind him and answered, "Hey."

"You Sera's boy?" asked a guy wearing baggy jeans that were slung so low on his slender hips it was amazing they stood up on his lanky frame. He had cold, assessing eyes that missed very little.

"Sera's my stepmom."

The guy smiled. "You know Sera's a member of The Kingdom Knights?"

Hawk continued up the street, but the guys who had been acting as if they didn't have a care in the world a few moments ago surrounded them, effectively blocking their path. Giselle scanned for the police or someone, anyone who could help if things turned ugly. Instead, the rest of the people on the street were avoiding her eyes and scurrying away to whatever hole they had crawled out from.

She hated that she had left her phone at home worried that it would get jacked on the street. Now she had no way to call the police. She mentally hit her head against her palm. Maybe someone else would call. Doubt crept in faster than Speedy Gonzalez on uppers.

Checking out the boys surrounding them, she was met with one pair of cold, flat eyes after another. Except the one that stood closest to them, the apparent leader, he gave her a curious glance before focusing on Hawk.

Flexing his fist, Hawk inquired, "What does that mean?"

The leader that Giselle now referred to as Alpha encroached on Hawk's personal space. "It means, you have to be what she is."

"Look, fellas, I don't want any trouble," Hawk said, keeping his focus on the boy. "We're heading to the store and home. That's all. We don't want to join a club or gang or anything. We just want to handle our business and go home."

Alpha, lips curled into a sneer, circled them. "That's the thing. You don't walk these streets without reppin' something. And Sera said that you'll rep what she's reppin'. So . . . " He spread his thin hands as if the meaning was obvious.

Hawk eased his hand out of Giselle's and pushed her slightly back. She took that to be significant and inched back a few more.

Alpha noticed the shift and raked his eyes over Giselle. "Don't worry. We'll just jump you in, right quick." Then his smile widened. "Sis, here can help you home."

Giselle turned and took two steps. Someone grabbed her from the back. She screamed. Hawk turned towards her and yelled, "Nooo," before one of the guys snapped Hawk's head back with an upper cut to the jaw.

Her head snapped back as well, as she was screaming and squirming, trying her best to get loose so she could help her brother.

The scene before her played out in the type of slow motion seen in B-movies. Hawk fell to the ground and was kicked and punched repeatedly while trying to cover his vital organs. Even when his blood splattered the pavement, they kept going at him.

Giselle kicked her captor in the knee, forcing his grip to loosen. She slipped away, running towards Hawk, almost making it; but someone grabbed a fistful of her hair, pausing her abruptly in mid-flight, and then threw her on the ground.

"Help! Someone help!" she screamed, then put every ounce of movement into bucking her assailant off of her.

Unfortunately, she was no match for the weight on her legs, or the knees on her arms, or the strong hands that were greedily groping her breasts.

"Please. No," she cried, though she wasn't expecting anything or anyone to stop what was happening in broad daylight on the streets of Chicago.

When she heard the pop of the buttons of her blouse, she struggled harder, scraping her own cheek against the concrete as she whipped her head from side to side. She could still hear the grunts and groans of her brother and smell the sweat and testosterone oozing from the pores of her tormentors.

Suddenly, the weight on top of her was lifted. One minute she was imprisoned in hell, and the next minute she could breathe again.

"I told you. She's off limits," The Alpha growled. "And I don't like repeating myself."

As she tried to push herself away, even if it was a few inches, someone mumbled, "Dude, come on."

"Sera said no. So. no. Or you can explain to her what the hell you're doing." Alpha's voice was as menacing as her attacker's touch. "Are you on board, or do I need to make a call?"

The musky male scent of her attacker assaulted her senses, causing a burning in the back of her throat, as whatever meager fare they'd had for lunch wanted to resurface. She felt him lean in closer as he grabbed her chin. "Look at me."

Giselle glared at him, determined not to appear to be a victim to his touch or his tone. Sporadic breaths caused her chest to shudder. Her attacker roughly grabbed her crotch and growled, "One day, this will be mine. Hell, to be one of us, this will have to be all of ours." Leering, he gave her one more once-over before sauntering off after his crew. "Promise you that."

CHAPTER 9

Hawk groaned as he tried to assess the extent of his injuries. For the second time in his life, the sound of Giselle's worried voice snapped him into consciousness. The first time was when a driver shattered their car and their lives by killing their mother. This time he was downed by the neighborhood welcoming committee, invited into their world by the woman who had ensnared their father.

He made an attempt to sit up, but only managed to ignite the pain that shot through several areas of his body. Slowly, he blinked his eyes open only to be met with Giselle's dark brown eyes drawn together by the worried crease in her forehead.

"Take it slow." She gently rubbed his brow with the back of her hand. "It'll be okay."

Giselle helped him sit up, then leaned him against her while he contemplated the next step to getting off the concrete and onto his feet. As he stood upright, a wave of dizziness hit him; his body swayed in a small circle before committing to a solid position.

Hawk took a good look at Giselle. As his gaze drifted from her worried eyes down to her shirt—or where her shirt would be if it still buttoned—anger bubbled in his blood, pushing his pain back just a bit.

His breakfast returned to the back of his throat. Giselle was tying the two parts of her shirt together, which, while still a bit slutty, was much more appropriate than walking down the street with her bra hanging out.

Blood pounded in Hawk's ears. All he wanted to do was lie down somewhere … soft. With the Knights skulking around the block, he definitely didn't have the time for that.

He had to protect Giselle. If he got beat into this gang, what would they do to Giselle? Beat her, rape her, run a train on her? He wasn't so sheltered that he hadn't heard things. Giselle could not, would not, endure any of those things.

The best way to do that was to get her to the Poconos with the roommate—now. He grabbed his cell out of his pocket. One of the punches or kicks had rendered it useless.

"Come on, G."

Hawk tested both ankles. The left was tweaked a bit, but he could still walk. They passed the grocery store that had started this madness and headed for one of the few pay phones in the area.

He put in a call to Lizzie. With everything else going on, he hated to put this on her doorstep; but she was one of the few people in his life who always came through—without hesitation.

"Baby, I need you to meet me and Giselle at Phil's gas station." The pause signaled that she was deciding whether or not to argue. He didn't have the time or patience to fight with her, not today.

Rubbing his throbbing temple, he tried again. "Listen, we were jumped today."

The gasp on the other end signaled another layer of stress he'd brought into Lizzie's life. He turned away from Giselle and lowered his voice so only Lizzie could hear. "I need you to bring the money. I have to get Giselle out of here."

"I'm on my way." Lizzie disconnected before he could utter another word.,

Lizzie was going to be pissed off and conflicted. On one hand, she was going to take one look at him and fly into protection mode. On the other, that money was too important to her to give it away.

In the Midst of Fire

Hawk sank onto a steel bench next to Giselle and waited the ten minutes it took for Lizzie to roll up. When her Range Rover skidded to a stop and she hopped out, tears were shining in her worried hazel eyes. He wished he had someone, anyone else, to call; but even with the communication ban between the two families, Lizzie still considered Giselle to be her best friend. And the woman was Hawk's life. It wasn't in her to leave them stranded this way.

"Oh my God, Hawk. Who did this to you?" she shrieked. "We have to call the police!"

Hawk shook his head. "No police. This is gang activity that we're talking about. That'll only make it worse." As Lizzie inspected him for other injuries, he asked Giselle to give them a few minutes.

Giselle inched closer to the gas station that served hoopties alongside Hummers and beaters next to Beamers. She kept her focus on the sidewalk like concrete was the most interesting thing she'd ever seen.

The minute Giselle was out of earshot, Lizzie snapped, "What are you doing? You know the only money I have is for the abortion. Travel roundtrip to my cousin's house is going to cost a mint."

"I'll pay you back, with interest if I have to,'" Hawk pledged. "Even if I have to sell my blood plasma to do it."

Lizzie looked off into the distance as a turning car honked at a pedestrian. "You never wanted me to get the abortion anyway."

Hawk's teeth clenched at the censure in her voice. "That's true," he agreed, placing a hand over hers. "I want you to have our baby. That's no secret." He glanced at Giselle, whose back was against the building as her eyes darted around at every sound. "But ask Giselle what happened to the buttons on her shirt. Ask her what they plan to do to her. Then talk to me about choices."

Lizzie followed his gaze to Giselle. "This isn't over."

Hawk snorted, "I didn't think it was."

Lizzie and Giselle helped Hawk into the back of the truck. He never realized how bad the roads in Chicago were until every dip and pothole caused a level of pain unknown in eighteen years of his life. The curse words flying through his mind were for Streets and Sanitation as well as the mayor.

From the north side to downtown Chicago, and still there were patches of horror that made him struggle to keep his eyes dry. If someone passed him a pint of whiskey and a leather strap to bite, he'd probably kiss their feet, if he could bend, of course.

Taking Clark Street south, the condo buildings and storefronts soon gave way to the downtown office buildings and a Chicago skyline that appeared as if it was taken from a tourist map.

As they rolled to a stop at Union Station, where Amtrak allowed passengers to escape the city for better pastures, Giselle hopped out of the car.

"Where are we going?"

Lizzie and Hawk's gaze met in the rearview mirror. Lizzie shook her head as she slid out of the driver's seat. Hawk moved much more slowly, but managed to get on the sidewalk. Giselle rushed to his side, and they made their way into Union Station. After a few minutes, they stood in front of the ticket booth, where a dour-faced woman gave him a once-over and frowned.

"I need one on the next train to Philadelphia."

"One?" Giselle parroted. "*One* ticket?"

Hawk ignored Giselle until she hit him in the shoulder.

"Son of a—ow."

Lizzie beckoned for Giselle to step away from the booth. As Hawk finished the transaction, he sifted through every conceivable excuse to get Giselle on that train—without him. He came up empty.

He was tired, hurt, and was breaking his own damn heart, sending his sister off to the east coast. They were supposed to have days, weeks . . . at least a couple of months. Not hours. Not minutes. Surely not seconds. Yes, this was bullshit. But it was necessary. She had to see that, right?

And that was the hard part. Getting Giselle to agree, when she was a stubborn pain in the ass most days. She was used to getting her way, but today he had to make sure she got the hell on a train. Philly, Pittsburgh, Texas. Shit, he didn't care which way, as long as she was far away from here.

He turned to face his sister, who had been by his side every day of his existence. The disheveled hair, her damaged shirt—all of which meant he couldn't protect her. It wasn't just about the injuries he had sustained today, Giselle had a future, and he had to push her towards it.

In the Midst of Fire

The sting of unshed tears caused him to blink, forcing one out of his eye and down his cheek. His throat tightened to the point where no words would come. He focused on the ground, mentally tracing the speckled pattern of the tiles. Looking in Giselle's eyes hurt too damn much.

Hearing the confident march of people committed to their destination, reminded him that Giselle had somewhere to be. The overhead speaker announcing departures and arrivals urged him to make her be steadfast in the decision to leave.

Clearing his throat, he croaked. "So, here's some money for you. "

He turned and snatched Lizzie's phone from her hand as she shouted, "Hey."

"I know your phone is still at the house. Take Lizzie's phone. Get your roommate's info from your e-mail. Make your way to that karate camp." Holding her hands tight, he added, "If you're careful, the cash will last until you start school. Then your scholarship will kick in. You should be fine."

Giselle took two steps towards him. "And what are you going to do?"

Hawk closed his eyes against the pain reflected in his twin's dark brown orbs as he responded, "Survive."

A passenger jostled him, causing him to flinch from the sudden flare of pain. Giselle moved closer and took his hands in hers. "Come with me. We'll make it, together. You don't have to go back."

The hope laced in her voice was almost as painful as the thought of being separated from the one person who had shared nearly everything with him—even a womb, even a mother who had long since died, leaving them to a father who made poor choices in women, and even poorer choices with money and life. "Giselle, your future is secure. You worked hard for that."

Giselle touched her forehead to his. "I can't leave you, not here, not like this." Lifting her head to look over his shoulder, she addressed Lizzie, "Make him come with me."

Hawk manually turned, "Don't do that," he pleaded. "Don't put Lizzie in that position."

A shudder ran through Giselle's body that transmitted to his. "I can't do it without you."

"You were going to do it without me in August. What's the difference between August and June? Two months."

Giselle touched her fingers to his. "Two months took us from Lincoln Park to Burnham Park."

His heart cracked like the peanut shells at a ballpark. Did Giselle hear it? Did Lizzie? Did they know how close he was to breaking down?

"Giselle, do it for us," he whispered. "Show Sera that she doesn't get to win. Show her what real Glens do. If the block gets really hot—"

Giselle snorted at his attempt at slang.

"I'll find a way to get out of there," he promised. "But I can only do that if you're safe."

"But—"

Hawk shook his head. "Promise me, on mom's grave, that you will finish college, that you'll do us proud and live your life fully, on *your* terms."

He was running out of the strength needed to keep fighting Giselle on this. "Nod your head, Giselle. Please, for me."

Giselle took a moment, an array of emotions flashed across her expressive face, but she finally complied.

They walked, practically shuffled, to the gate. Lizzie slid her arm around his waist. All signs pointed to the fact that he might not survive this sojourn into the hood, especially if Sera had her way. This might be the last time he would see his sister.

When she turned for her last wave, he smiled. She smiled back. He needed that—her smile. He closed his eyes to burn it into his memory.

However, as she walked through the door to the platform, he felt the weight of her despair crushing him. Or was it his? It was impossible to tell. He pulled Lizzie into a hug. No matter how much it hurt, he needed something to sustain him as the train pulled out. Then he turned. He had to get to the business of survival. He could only hope that business was good.

CHAPTER 10

Sera looked out of her window, keeping a close watch on the activity in the alley. Ninja walked by, glancing up without breaking stride, as he continued on toward his apartment on the far side of the complex. It was done; no going back now.

If she was going to keep her family together, they had to stay in the projects. She handled the Knights' security. Her crew watched the block, made sure the drug trade ran smoothly, and greased a few palms if need be. Here, status talked; but she was the one making the money.

It wasn't the kind of money that Chase was used to, but she couldn't make big money unless she was directly involved in the drug trade. Her job was enough to keep them living better than she had growing up.

Chase was still a loose cannon. He exuded charm and needed money. If she let him loose on the women of the north side, he would upgrade her by latching on to some golden-egg-laying goose with that generational money. It wouldn't take much. Then she'd be no better most other females in this hellhole—another wrong choice, another failed opportunity.

Now, she was a married woman and was determined to stay that way. If he left her side, it would be in a pine box. That part of her plans she'd definitely keep to herself.

First she had to take away his options. With Mrs. Knight out of the picture, one down, and now number two was complete. Hawk was now one of the Knights. Whether he wanted to be in a gang or not was irrelevant, she needed him to be.

Sera wanted to laugh out loud, but that would require answers. Energy zinged under her skin. She needed to do something or she'd explode. Or maybe a good explosion wasn't a bad idea.

She went into the bedroom and crawled into bed with Chase.

He gave her a gentle smile. "Penny for your thoughts."

Sera lowered her eyelids and ran her leg in between Chase's thigh. "No way would a penny cover these thoughts."

Chase leaned over and gave her a kiss.

Inwardly, she growled. This was affection. She wanted sex—hard, fast, exciting. She was way too ramped up for the type of slow afternoon lovemaking that Chase always defaulted to.

Sera bit his lip until she tasted the saltiness of warm blood.

"Ouch!" he flinched to the point of pulling away.

Sera's eyes narrowed, giving her that patented look, which left men panting—one that signaled she was waiting, ready. She placed her hand on his chest and pushed him back until he was lying flat atop the black satin comforter.

Continuing to rub her leg up and down on his, she leaned forward and took control of the kiss. She attacked his mouth, kissing him hard and fast; then she sucked his tongue into her mouth like she was sucking his dick.

After overcoming the initial surprise, Chase tried to get enough leverage to take over. Sera merely smiled into his mouth, giving another slight nip.

Chase pushed up on his elbows without breaking the kiss, then pushed Sera onto her back. He pinned her arms above her head and laid his body on top of hers. He adjusted the intensity of the kiss. Every time she pushed her lips into his, he would draw back. She bucked, but was unable to get traction to change their position.

She growled her frustration, tugged at her hands, but they refused to move. As his eyes narrowed to slits, he smashed his lips against hers, grinding her lips into her teeth. Welcoming the pain, she sucked his tongue into her mouth.

By the time he pulled back, they both were panting. Chase released her hands and commanded. "Stay." Sera grinned and, with their eyes locked, she lowered her hands down an inch. He punished her with another kiss, placed her hands above her head again, and with his nose flaring, insisting "Stay."

He caressed her sides and she arched her back to guide him towards her breasts. As his hand's journey reached the bottom of her white Chicago Bulls t-shirt, he pulled it up over her head. He unsnapped her front clasp bra and demanded, "Take it off."

Sera quickly disposed of it and opened her arms out for him. He pinched her swollen left nipple until she winced. "Hands over your head."

She returned to the original position. Chase unsnapped her pants. By this time, Sera was aching; she wanted his mouth on her breasts; she wanted his hands below. Her body temperature was so high, a soft sheen of sweat covered her smooth skin. She wanted it even higher.

Sera yanked her pants down and whipped them on the floor. She smiled as he crawled back up her body. He finally turned his attention to her breasts. He sucked on the left one while toying with the right. Her hands itched to draw down to his head. So she did.

He immediately shifted his focus by using those long, tapered fingers in her core; but it wasn't enough. She squirmed with need. She needed his mouth, his hands, every inch of him on every inch of her.

She snapped her hands back up and gave him a contrite, "I'm sorry."

Chase tilted his head. "Really? Are you sure?"

Sera opened her eyes, giving him what she hoped was an innocent expression. "Yes. Yes."

Smiling, Chase turned his attention again to her breasts. However, impatience had already set in. His hand, his mouth, the scratchy feel of his clothes against her bare skin led to the slow, arduous journey of a man who had nothing more than time.

She groaned as she lifted her hips in rhythm with his hand, hoping that he'd get the hint.

"Please."

He stopped. "What did you say to me?"

"Please, Chase. I need you—in me." Whimpering, Sera said again, "Please."

Chase tore off his shirt and jumped out of his pajama bottoms.

"Say it again." He demanded.

"Please."

Chase punished her mouth while he toyed with his erection against her entrance.

Sera couldn't do a thing with her hands, because it would cause him to stop. And if he stopped right now, she would cut his ass so deep that she could use his blood for lubrication.

As Chase popped his tip into her, she tightened her walls around him and lifted her hips. His breath caught. Sera smiled.

Chase slammed all the way into her, and they both gasped. She reached around and pulled him towards her. As they pounded each other, she bit his chest. He growled and kissed her again.

The comingling of their body heat caused a heavy layer of sweat where chest met chest. Drops slid down her side onto the bed sheet, and she didn't care. They continued to pump and grunt.

Chase stopped and grabbed her legs, pushing her knees up to her shoulders. He slowed their pace, as he leveraged himself on top of her. She punched into the mattress in frustration. He ground himself into her.

Sera sighed with pleasure. Part of her wanted the pounding, but this felt so damn good. So she wound her hips to match his cadence. Now that they weren't chest to chest, the cool air caused her nipples to pucker.

He lifted her legs straight up in the air and filled her completely, almost digging out her uterus. She hissed with a bit of pain and pleasure. She felt her body elevating. She relaxed into his stroke, as each one brought her closer and closer to completion.

After a few minutes, he opened her legs, leaned down between them, and slammed her at an amazing rate. She tried to match him hit for hit, but she was already in the beginning of an orgasm. Her right leg shook as her body lifted off of the mattress and she cried out.

Pumping a few more times, he shouted his release and fell on top of Sera. As she attempted to regain her breath, she smiled.

From Vincent getting her a job, to dealing with Mrs. Knight, and now Hawk becoming a Kingdom Knight, everything was falling into place. No way was some dried-up old money going to compete with her twenty-five-year-old body and her determined mind. She dared them to try.

CHAPTER
11

Chase heard his name and sat up in bed. Hearing it again, he threw his pajama bottoms on and ran into the living room. "What the hell? Where is Giselle?"

Hawk lifted his chin resolutely, even as he looked down into Chase's eyes. "Gone. She couldn't stay here."

Chase's mouth dried up as the realization of what those words meant hit home. Tears sprang into his eyes. Life had turned on a dime, just like that. He'd forgotten those hard lessons he'd learned over the years—ones that caused his soul to bleed, scab over, and bleed again. He'd forgotten how friends were there one day and gone the next, how his wife was there one day and gone the next; and now his daughter, just like that. All of this happened while he was distracted with his situation, his life.

Looking at his son, he couldn't believe the bruises covering his face, the winces of pain as he shuffled from one foot to the other. His demeanor was so different from Hawk's normally loose-limbed swagger.

"She's gone? How? What happened? And what happened to you?"

Sera moved from the sofa and came to stand by Chase's side. Hawk glared at her, but before he could utter a word, Chase's cell rang. He glanced at the screen, realizing he had to answer. This was his future calling at the same

In the Midst of Fire

time that his past was being whipped around by a hurricane. Why didn't his children trust him to get them out of this little patch of trouble? He had before.

Holding up his finger, he mouthed, "business call."

Hawk was shaking with anger as his focus stayed on Sera, who eased herself into a relaxing position on the couch. Even with his heart beating overtime, he pulled himself together enough to take this important call.

"Hey, baby. How's it going? I was just talking to the kids. Can I call you back?" Chase's words rushed out as soon as he closed the bedroom door behind him. Actually Kid. Kid, because the other had just . . . left.

"Are you sure you're not talking to your wife?"

The chill in Cathy's response froze his fingers on the phone. How the hell? Shit. Think. Think. "Baby, what are you talking about? We run in the same circles. You haven't seen me with a wife."

There is no way Cathy had seen him with Sera. And if she had, no way she would've assumed that he was married. Of all the angles and scenarios he ran, Cathy finding out about Sera wasn't one of them.

Cathy chortled, the sound was lacking the softness she normally held. "Really. I don't run around in Burnham Park normally, but that seems to be your modus operandi."

Anxiety danced a jig on his eyeball, causing a headache like he never experienced. Racking his brain to figure out how Cathy had found out and also how to save the situation, Chase implored, "Listen, I can explain. It's not what you think."

"You made me the other woman," she whispered, her tone broken and low. "Knowing how my ex-husband cheated on me, how it . . . oh God . . . it changed me. You were supposed to heal me, not cause this … not hurt me more. But you made me the other woman. You forced her to come to my house to try to save your marriage." Cathy's voice cracked, and the sound of it put a stab of pain through his heart. "How could you do that to me?"

Chase closed his eyes, taking in what her words actually meant. Cathy was the sweetest woman, soft and gentle like a lilac. She was the perfect person for this next chapter in his life. Her softness in voice and body was a balm, easing all aches. He could be happy with her. He needed to get his plan back on track, fast. That required a more personal hand.

"I'll come over and we can discuss this." Chase pleaded, as he paced back and forth across the room. "I love you, Cath. Don't do this to us."

"Don't do this to us," Cathy taunted, the words so icy he was surprised his ear wasn't suffering from frostbite. "I wonder if that was what my husband said to his first mistress. You know it's that first one breaks you down the most."

"Cath," he started, without knowing the right words to reply to such a heartbreaking diatribe.

"Chase."

The silence extended between them to the point that it became louder than his heartbeat. "Chase, men like you don't get it. You have a pretty face and smooth words. You're fun. Women flock to you. And you don't know when to say no."

"I only want you, Cathy."

"You had *her* and you were about to use me!" Cathy cried out, taking several deep breaths before she continued, "Men like you break women like me. And honestly, I deserve better." Her broken streams of breath came right before her voice shook like someone talking through tears. "Goodbye, Chase."

She didn't understand that his heart was breaking, too. He had lost everything—his daughter. He doesn't know what the hell happened to his son, but he'd bet his Gucci loafers that it wasn't an accident.

Somehow, Sera had changed his whole life; his whole trajectory wasn't just off—it was nonexistent.

He stumbled back into the living room, where Hawk and Sera were engaged in a staring contest. "Son, where's my Giselle?"

Hawk snapped his focus from Sera and put it on Chase. "She couldn't stay here." Using his good arm to emphasize his injuries, "It's too dangerous, so I got her out of here. I had to protect her." He leveled an angry glare at Sera, who seemed unruffled by his actions. "She's someplace safe."

Shaking his head, Chase implored, "Who did this?"

Hawk grimaced, as though struggling to let an answer cross his lips.

"Tell me. Sera knows people. She can help," Chase said.

Hawk's dark brown eyes doubled in size, followed by a facial expression that gave Chase pause.

He looked over at Sera, who stood with her arms crossed, as though merely a spectator in this family drama. Her body language was off—almost defensive.

Sera had her demons, sure. Her anger was powerful and deadly. But to hurt his kids? To hurt him through his kids? To fuck him while his children were deliberately placed in danger? *His* Sera?

He couldn't begin to comprehend the mind of someone who would do that. Not Sera. He surely wouldn't marry that kind of mind. No way.

"Where is she?" Chase repeated.

Hawk sneered, "Somewhere that no one will find her, somewhere the streets can't touch her."

"I could've fixed it," Chase conceded after a lengthy silence. "I could've fixed everything. It would have been all right."

Hawk stared his father down until Chase broke the gaze. The bullets of Hawk's anger pierced his skin, and the pain of three sudden losses dropped him to his knees—Giselle, Cathy, and hope.

Chase lowered his gaze to the carpet, summing up the past few hours. "Sera," he began, putting his focus on the silent woman. "What's going on? What are you doing to us?"

Sera snapped her head around to look at him as if he'd lost his mind. "Me? How did I become the bad guy?"

She left her spot near on the arm of the couch and stalked towards him.

"I'm just trying to take care of my family, the family that was supposed to be living in Lincoln Park." She gestured towards the far right wall. "You want a bad guy? Look in the mirror, babe. I didn't lie about our finances. I didn't make the sheriff bang down the door. I'm not the reason your life fell apart."

Chase ignored the truth of those words, and he reached out for Hawk, who merely tossed him a disgusted snort. "Son?"

Hawk gave him a look that was filled with so much disdain that it punched him in the gut. He shuffled towards his bedroom as Chase struggled back to his feet.

Sera ambled over and whispered, "Is this all you are?"

Blinded by temper, Chase reached up and grabbed Sera by the neck. She choked, pushing her foot against his chest until he released his hold. They both scrambled to their feet, panted, and circled one another.

"Who was the call from Chase?" She folded her arms and shifted to her version of a Superwoman stance, but with a malicious smile. "Cathy, maybe?"

"You bitch!" he snarled. "You ruined everything."

"I was supposed to be living in luxury, not this two-bedroom hovel," she countered. "Did you think I was just going to let you leave me after using me this way. Did you?" She picked a candle off the table and threw it at him.

"My children deserve better than this," Chase spat.

Sera stopped, confusion clouding her face as she made a point to strain her neck, scanning the room. "Children?" she taunted, with a curl of her lips that looked almost feral. "Looks like you're missing one to me."

Chase lunged, anger clouding every other emotion. Sera skirted out of the way, circling the coffee table. "You should be happy. Your precious daughter is safe. You all tried to make a fool out of me. All three of you! You know that's usually cause for someone to get cut."

"How?" Chase's voice rose an octave. "*How* was I making a fool out of you?"

Sera's nose flared as she threw a couch pillow at him. "I heard you."

Chase halted in the path of trying to get closer to her. He frowned, trying to picture what she was getting at.

"The day the sheriff showed up," she added. "I heard you telling them how you were going to dump me for that rich tramp."

"You, of all people, should've have understood," he shot back. "Hell, *you* don't even want to be here."

Sera threw back her head and laughed. "You give me too much credit. Your ass was not leaving me here. Better or worse, babe. And you haven't begun to see worse yet." Sera moved in, pushed Chase in the chest, and pounded at him when he didn't budge. "I signed on for life; not a few months—and so did you."

Chase yanked her arm to the side and watched as she stumbled a few feet. "Well, I guess you should've signed on with someone you'd known for longer than a weekend."

In the Midst of Fire

Sera walked up and tried to strike him again, "Well, I guess you should have found a dimwit to marry and not someone that knows the game a hell of a lot better than you do."

"Bitch."

Sera wheeled back and slapped him. "Bastard."

He blocked her next blow, grabbed her hair, and yanked her towards the bedroom. "I can't believe I married you."

Sera struggled to free herself. "You're such a punk ass. You should've taken my name. Chase Brooks has a nice ring to it."

Chase growled and whipped her around. The heat of his blood overwhelmed his senses until all he could hear and see was her. Didn't she realize that having access to money, meant she'd at least have something in the divorce. By the time Cathy realized that he was flat broke, she'd be too far in and give him anything he needed to be free—even paying off an ex-wife.

Reaching out, he looked at his shaking hands as if they belonged to another body. He shoved her out of the way and locked himself in the bathroom. With a roar, he yanked the shower rod straight out of the wall.

CHAPTER
12

Giselle Glen didn't know which was worse. Closing her eyes, the memory of leaving Hawk played in an endless looping video in her mind. She had left him shackled to Hades' throne while she had barely escaped.

Sera had set them up in a major way. Despite the promises the woman had made to their father (hell, the ones she made to them), she was putting them right in the line of danger and as far away from their dreams as possible.

Now, her train was pulling into the Philadelphia train station, taking her closer to a friend to hide out, with little more than the clothes on her back and a package of Chicago underwear they'd bought from the gift shop. She tried to keep a tight hold on the anger that beat in her head as hard as each blow delivered to Hawk hours earlier.

If it took every day of her life, every ounce of her intelligence, and every breath in her body, Giselle would make that bitch pay.

The train squealed to a stop. Anxious people gathered their luggage from the overhead racks. Giselle didn't have that problem. Everything, including the diamond earrings her mother had given her, was on her person.

Others dragged their weary bodies out of their seats. She was weighted down. Every inch of her screamed to go back to Chicago, to make Hawk listen to reason, to essentially break her promise to him, so that he could be safe, too.

That "promise" was as bogus as a politician guaranteeing clean government and a balanced budget. When Hawk was sitting there, bruised and battered, she couldn't fight him. Plus, her mind was frazzled from being thrown to the ground and attacked by a stranger, and she did want desperately to leave. But she should have been strong, like Hawk.

The conductor, a burly man with a well-trimmed goatee and a gentle smile, came towards her. She tried to hold back the tears, but they ran unchecked down her cheeks anyway. He reached into his navy blue jacket and pulled out a handkerchief.

"Thank you." Giselle inhaled the scent of a cologne that lingered on the white cloth and tried to think of anything else. But even this little act of kindness only made her want to cry some more.

He eased down into the seat across from hers. "So what are you running from?"

Giselle parted her lips to speak, but the lump in her throat blocked any sounds from escaping. She swallowed a few times, but to no avail. She blew out another breath.

The conductor leaned back, putting his focus on the emptying car. "You'd be surprised at how many people are escaping something on the train." He nodded toward a girl two rows over, almost cowering close to the window. "They always keep to themselves." Looking toward a man whose glare was more foreboding than the music played on every horror movie, the conductor warned, "They don't engage anyone." Then he nodded toward two women sitting across from each other. "They are always the last people to leave at their stop."

Giselle tore her gaze from the people he had mentioned, searching his eyes for anything other than the authentic sound of his gentle words. Passengers shuffled passed. He gently nodded to another group as they progressed towards the exit. He gestured her to lean in closer, which she did.

"I can tell you this. If you have the courage to get on the train, then you definitely have the courage to get off. Getting on is the most difficult step." He patted her arm again. "Are you alone?"

Giselle's words came out as a croak. The urge to tell this man everything that happened bubbled up in her throat, but those were a lot of words and a lot of emotion. And she didn't know if she could get through the story whole. Even now, she felt as if she was made of spun sugar. One wrong move, and she'd crack and crumble and disintegrate.

"Young lady, are you alone?" The conductor nudged, "Are you safe?"

Safe? *Oh, he thought maybe she'd been kidnapped or taken by some man who was on the train nearby, watching that she made all the right moves.* "No, my college roommate is waiting for me."

Only then did his shoulders relax. He leaned forward, blue eyes twinkling, with, "College is a great adventure, and family will always be there when you return."

Giselle ran her fingertips over the monogrammed letter on the corner of the handkerchief. That's the crux of the problem. He might not be. "Everything changed so fast," she admitted.

"And it will continue to change." Chuckling, the conductor leaned back.

He waved quickly at another serious-looking train conductor, who was followed by two security men, who quickly surrounded a middle-aged man, wearing a houndstooth jacket, sitting near the first young girl he had mentioned. They exchanged a few words before escorting him off the car.

The young girl stood and followed the second conductor, but she stopped long enough to whisper a "thank you" to the man sitting across from Giselle before moving away.

The conductor, whose nameplate said, Darnell, followed the exit progression, then put his focus back on Giselle "Life happens whether you're there to witness it or not. People grow and change. Your family . . . did they see you off?"

Giselle focused on the laces of her gym shoes, trying to forget the desperate look in Hawk's eyes as he watched her take the steps one by one. "Yes, well. My brother did."

"So he wants you here?" the conductor probed gently.

Giselle gazed out of the window at the 30th Street Station platform. The crowd that rushed off the train had disbursed. Another train pulled out. The sounds of the train and people were muffled through the thick window glass. "Yes, he does."

The conductor patted her knee. "Then you owe it to the both of you to meet that roommate and kick ass in college, don't you?"

Giselle locked eyes with him. "I guess. But—"

The conductor held up his hand. "Life isn't easy. And even though the people we love the most will try to shelter us from the really gory parts … truth is, we just have to live it."

"I want him here with me."

Smiling, the conductor leaned in as if he was telling her the location of the fountain of youth. "The great thing about life, there's always a tomorrow."

Giselle blinked. Tomorrow. Her tomorrow began . . . today. She jumped out of her seat and ran to the door. She froze at the threshold for a brief moment, then rushed back and engulfed the conductor in a hug. "Thank you, so much."

He gave her another pat on the arm before shooing her toward the door to get on with her new life.

She was dialing her cell phone before she had even cleared the stairs of the train. The diesel smell made her sneeze, but that didn't stop her.

When he answered, she gushed, "Hawk, I made it to Philly."

"Yeah."

Taken a bit aback by the flatness of his tone, she persisted, "So I know that you didn't want to come yesterday, but I'm going to keep trying until you say yes."

Again, Hawk merely responded with one syllable. "Hmm."

A passenger hurrying to the train almost bumped the phone out of Giselle's hand.

Giselle let out a loud, "Damn," at the lady, who had interrupted her attempt to figure out why Hawk seemed hesitant to say more than one syllable.

The passenger waved in a dismissive manner as Giselle glared at her.

In the background, a deep voice, "Is that Little Sis? Where did she disappear to?"

"Hold on."

"Hawk, listen. Maybe Lizzie can come, too. Then we'd all be together." Why didn't she think of this before? Of course, he wouldn't leave Lizzie. But if they were all together that made sense.

"Giselle." Hawk finally sounded a bit like his old self. Thank goodness.

She laughed. "I don't know why we didn't think of this yesterday. We can all live in Philly. You can get a job. It'll be great."

"Giselle, hold up." The stress in his voice caused her to pause.

"What's the problem?" she asked, slowing to a point near the exit. "This is the perfect solution."

"People are already asking where you are," he replied, causing her to frown. "Right now is not the time for me to disappear, too."

"But Hawk, I—"

"And I don't think you should be calling me on this number."

"What the hell?" Giselle screeched. "Smoke signals won't make it all the way to Chicago. What number should I use?"

"No number. Listen, I have people ear hustling all the time," he said. "Once I figure out what we're going to do, I'll get notice to you somehow. But don't call me," he warned. "I don't know what else Sera has planned, but we have to make sure you are not part of it."

Sera again. What is wrong with this woman? She needs to get some business, preferably some business that didn't include the Glens. But if Sera had plans, did that mean Hawk was in danger?

"Be safe. I . . . ." He paused as if he wanted to say more but settled with, "Well, just be patient and let me figure a few things out."

"But Hawk."

"I have to go. I love you, Giselle. Don't ever forget that."

"Hawk, don't hang up on me. Don't—"

Despite her plea, he disconnected the call. Giselle tamped down on the feelings of abandonment that threatened to overtake her resolve. Squaring her shoulders, she iterated in her mind, there was always tomorrow.

CHAPTER 13

After putting Giselle on that train, Hawk didn't speak to his dad for nearly a month. And when he did, he learned his father's grand scheme had fallen apart. Shocked, Hawk merely slumped into the couch and stared at the blank television screen.

Over the years, Hawk and Giselle had begged their father to stop marrying women for money. They pleaded for him to get a real job—something, anything. But he kept going back to the bullshit promise he'd made to his grandmother.

Chase kept saying, "If I move you out of this house that means I failed you, and her. I can't. Don't ask me to."

Hawk and Giselle stayed out of his way. They stayed together. Now they were out of said house, and thanks to his father's grossly inaccurate interpretation of his grandmother's wish, he was stuck with this crazy bitch. Hawk was sure that his great-grandma was doing donuts in her grave over this one.

Sera ran her tongue over her teeth, "Bad day?"

"No, I'm just . . . trying to figure out my next steps." He rubbed his hands against his jean-clad thighs. Maybe, he could get Lizzie to move to Philly with Giselle.

Getting her to leave her mother behind was going to be the issue. "You newlyweds need your own space."

Sera's jaw clenched so tightly that he thought she might chip a tooth. "No."

Hawk opened his mouth, then closed it. "No?"

"That's right. No." Sera smirked as she leaned back against the couch.

"What the . . ." Flattening his lips to keep some choice curse words from escaping, Hawk inquired, "Why?"

Sera looked at the ceiling for a minute as though trying to retrieve an answer from the taupe paint. "You got your sister out. That means you stay."

Hawk's anger spiked. "What do you need me for? Why keep me in this place?"

"Because I can," giving a smirk that made Hawk want to shake her. "And there's nothing you can do about it." Sera picked up the remote control and turned on the television show, *Criminal Minds*.

Laughing, Hawk answered, "Yeah, right."

Sera didn't even bother to look at him. She flipped through channels and said, "You know how many hypes live in the projects? Do have any clue how many of them are HIV-positive?"

"And?" he shot back, shifting so that he put a few more inches of space between them. "Who cares about hypes?"

Sera leaned over to the end table and pulled out a needle from the console drawer. "See, if you dare leave this house for 'greener pastures,' I'll poke your father with every needle from every infected person I can find until he's HIV-positive, too."

Sera's gaze sharpened. Her expression dared him to doubt a word falling out of her mouth. Hawk's stomach bubbled. "But then you'll—"

"Then I'll let him go."

Hawk scoffed, "You love the old man. You wouldn't do that."

"Love is for people who can afford that luxury," she countered. "You rich people have that luxury. People from the projects don't." Inspecting her new manicure, she added, "You spend more than twenty-four hours away from here, and I promise you that your dad starts his home-going early."

Disbelief caused Hawk's body to shake. Who was this woman? How

In the Midst of Fire

could his father have married her? But he did. Hawk had not. And with what happened to him and what almost happened to his sister, he couldn't believe that she would think he cared two drops about her injuring his father. Not that he wanted him to die; he just didn't believe Sera would kill him.

Hawk remembered when Sera had come to his house that first time. His father was grinning from ear to ear as though someone handed him a winning lottery ticket. Sera dressed in a Kenneth Cole jumpsuit that he'd seen his Lizzie wearing once, which signaled that she had at least two nickels to rub together. Her eyes bugged in amazement.

As he walked down the staircase and bumped into the back of Giselle, who stopped suddenly, he looked up to see why she had stopped. And he knew, the minute he saw the woman on the couch, without needing to see the suitcase by the door or the sparkling ring to confirm, that his father had brought home wife number five.

Hawk didn't need to share a speaking glance with his twin to know that she was as exhausted by the endless stream of women as he was. He just wanted stability. He wanted his dad to get a damn job and *earn* his money the honest way and not through some new get-rich scheme that involved ripping through a woman's bank account, then leaving her with nothing more than battered dreams and tattered trust. It's not like they were trying to hold on to a lifestyle. The government had already laid claim to that.

His dad wasn't trying to hold on to them either. He and Giselle had been their own parents since their mother died ten years prior.

The marriage wouldn't last. His marriages never did. So it was best to deal with the new development, keep their head down and out of the way of the nuclear fallout that proceeded every divorce.

Sera glanced their way and smiled, but her eyes weren't really on them. She was looking at every single couch, knickknack and piece of silver in the place. Even then, a sliver of suspicion crept up his spine. Normally, the other stepmothers glimpsed at their surroundings and concentrated on their father; sometimes the two children, depending on the level of maternal instinct.

While Sera held tight to their dad's hand, she also studied her surroundings as if she was amazed to be there. That should have been the first clue to Chase that she was not what she appeared to be.

His dad was different—in every touch, the way his father focused on Sera, the way he rubbed her arm, the way he ducked to whisper in her ear. Whether or not Sera was what he needed wasn't the issue; she was definitely what he wanted. Chase Glen had brought home women (well, wives) before, and he was usually puffed up like a peacock over whatever coup had taken place to keep him out of a real job.

Had his eyes sparkled when he looked at their mother that same way? Had he leaned into their mother like that? Had he touched her with that softness? Hawk and Giselle had exchanged another confused glance. Was this what their father looked like when he was in love?

Now, the woman, whom his dad wanted so badly that keeping her forced them into this den of despair, was threatening to kill him. The irony was not lost on him.

Hawk sighed with a weariness that weighed him down to the bone. He was so tired of living with his father's mistakes. Now, four months since that first meeting, sitting across the couch from the devil herself, he offered up, "You could just slice him. Rumor has it you're good with a knife."

She snatched her gaze from the psychological thriller and focused on Hawk. "No. I want you to watch him suffer—and die—and realize every day the role you played in his situation."

Hawk rubbed at his tightening shoulder. "My father hasn't been more than a figurehead to keep DCFS at bay for years. He's too busy running after one wife after another. You were his choice, not mine. So, whatever." Hawk pushed himself onto his feet, preparing to walk out the door and make some headway on plans to get himself and Lizzie out of Chicago.

"What about that fancy sister of yours?" Sera continued, tilting her head to the left, her eyes took on a more evil slant, if that was possible. "At some point, I'm sure she's going to show up at that fancy university."

Ice slid into his veins. Even if he risked his dad's life, no way would he put Giselle in danger. And if Hawk tried to take Sera out, which was a fleeting thought when she pursed her lips to threaten Giselle, he'd have to deal with Ninja. He'd seen Ninja and his crew in action.

Ninja alone was one of the smartest men Hawk had ever met in his life. All those children at the private schools he attended over the years had nothing on Ninja. The man had computer skills like Hawk had never seen—calculated intelligence. Shit. He wished he would have met him in high school when he needed a grade changed.

In the short time they'd been acquainted, Hawk had witnessed the methodical precision Ninja used to hack through firewalls and track down information he was sure the FBI or CIA couldn't even find. As the keeper of the secrets, Ninja's value to Sera was that he could get anything on anyone.

And when Ninja killed someone, they disappeared. No witnesses. No trail. No … body. Nothing. Killing Sera would put Hawk in Ninja's crosshairs. And if he didn't die, he'd absolutely go to jail.

It might even put Giselle on Ninja's radar. Sera wasn't worth Hawk's life and absolutely was not worth Giselle's—no matter how much the current situation sucked.

For some reason, it seemed that his father was going to stick it out in this place, with this woman. She might have Hawk on lock for now, but Hawk would watch and wait for his chance to escape.

Maybe someone would run over Sera with a Mack truck. Somehow, he didn't think his luck would extend that far. He had four years until Giselle graduated. In those four years, maybe he could get close enough to Ninja to enlist his help. He had saved her from NuNu, and that had to mean something.

Short of killing Sera, Hawk only saw two options. Perhaps, he could get close enough to Ninja to get him to at least look the other way, while he tried to get himself, Lizzie, and Giselle to safety. Or maybe if Hawk could stick it out until Giselle graduated, then he'd be free.

CHAPTER 14

"Look at Hawk's little sister," a raspy voice taunted from behind her, "all collegiate and shit."

Giselle froze on the quad of Lexington University. The action was so sudden that another student bumped into her back.

They both mumbled a quick apology. All the while, Giselle's heart was racing.

Closing her eyes, she recalled where she'd heard that voice before. She clutched her

T-shirt to her body, feeling suddenly exposed, more vulnerable than she'd been in a long time.

Anger warred with gratitude. "The Alpha," or Ninja as he was called in the streets, saved her life and her virtue; but he let them beat Hawk—bad.

She wanted to slap him and embrace him at the same time. Instead, she turned slowly towards the voice. The shadow leaning against the tree that had previously been a mere blip in her periphery suddenly became a fully formed body.

As he drew closer, she rubbed her clammy hands on her thighs. Giselle quickly glanced around the quad. Enough people were scattered about to provide some sense of security. A few shot curious glances in her direction.

In the Midst of Fire

This time was different. She wasn't on his turf, in his hood. This time she could scream. This time someone would help.

Giselle opened her mouth and closed it again. She wasn't afraid. During the time she'd stayed with Kim, she'd learned a few skills of her own. She would never be vulnerable again.

Ninja continued to stare her down, as he sauntered in measured steps that seemed frustratingly slow.

"Not running, Hawk's little sister?" Ninja pondered for a few seconds. "Impressive."

Giselle continued to take in the gaze emanating from his dark brown eyes. His height forced her to look upward to keep eye contact. As he drew closer, his exquisitely sculpted face had that clear chocolate skin over cheekbones that she tried to emulate with makeup on a daily basis; Asian-inspired eyes stared back at her.

"What are you doing here?" Giselle croaked out, pausing in her efforts to inch back, when a single thought popped up and she stopped. "Hawk? Did something happen to Hawk?"

Ninja's gaze travelled from her sneaker-clad feet all the way to her eyes. "Naw. Your brother's fine."

She blew out a breath and gave him the same type of perusal he had given her, taking in his fresh white gym shoes, jeans that, while stylish, actually fit around his waist and not on his hips. He wore a black knit shirt with a Polo emblem on it. He looked … almost like a nerd. If he had a backpack, he'd be any other guy on the quad; unlike Burnham Park where everyone clearly looked like they'd been made, molded, and dressed by the project itself, in jeans that wrapped around their thighs instead of their waist, threatening to hit their ankles with every stride.

A flash of memory brought a vision of her brother lying on the ground, writhing in pain. "What are you doing here?" she demanded, unable to keep her voice from trembling.

Ninja leaned in and whispered, "Maybe, I'm here to finish my degree. You know. Get all collegiate like you."

"Finish," Giselle swallowed hard. It had to be anger making her voice tremble. It couldn't be the smell of his cologne. It also couldn't be attraction.

"Start is more like it."

The weight of his eyes and the increase in the tension in his stance gave away his anger, even though he hadn't moved a muscle. "No. I started— network security major."

Those words brought her up short. "Why didn't you finish?" she asked.

"Life happened." He squinted, affecting an amused look. "Your brother's very familiar with how . . . life can happen."

Giselle nodded. "Listen, the only reason I haven't screamed bloody murder is because you're the one that saved me from that guy."

"NuNu," he supplied, folding his arms across his chest, emphasizing the sculpture of his pecs.

"Yeah, I guess."

"It was NuNu's creepy ass," he replied with a shrug, yet his body stiffened and jaw clenched as a group of students walked by. The tension in his muscles lessened as they got further away. "NuNu uses whatever means to get women to sleep with him, including force."

She bit her lip, looking around to make sure this NuNu didn't jump out from behind a different tree.

As though sensing her fear, he confessed, "He's not here."

"So . . . what are you doing here?"

"Sera sent me."

Shit. She had hoped that Sera had decided to leave her alone. Apparently, that wasn't the case.

"You are not going to jump me into a gang on the quad."

Ninja roared out a laugh. "No, her idea was just to let you know she could . . . get to you."

Giselle bit the inside of her cheek, trying to rein in her fear. "And you always do what she says."

Ninja reached out and pulled at one of the twists in her hair. "Sure."

Instinctively, Giselle jumped at the shock of him touching her. Then she felt the way her body was still wired, even after his hand had fallen back down to his side. Hitching her head towards him, she asked, "Why you?"

Ninja shifted his weight from right to left before answering, "She trusts me."

In the Midst of Fire

"Why?"

Ninja scanned the area. With a brisk nod, he encouraged two onlookers to keep moving. They complied, but one of them gave Giselle a lingering look over her shoulders.

"I've never given her reason not to."

Giselle narrowed her gaze on him. "That day did she really say that I wasn't to be touched?"

He tilted his head and took his time before replying, "No."

Giselle shuddered at the answer.

"But Sera had enough men in the hood trying that shit with her, that it's not a hard stretch to say she wouldn't order something like that."

Giselle closed her eyes as she took in his meaning. "But would she look the other way . . . if it actually happened?"

Ninja looked up at the one of the red brick buildings lining the walkway. "Nice campus you got here, Hawk's little sister."

"You know my name," Giselle snapped, for some reason irritated that she had yet to hear that familiar sound enhanced by the timber of his voice—not one time. "Use it."

Ninja's eyes twinkled with mirth. "That I can't do, Hawk's little sister. It's best if I'm reminded."

Giselle stepped back. She kept forgetting that she should hate this man. She shouldn't be carrying on a conversation. But here she stood, wanting desperately for him to touch her hair one more time.

She moved closer to Ninja and noticed the keen intelligence reflecting in his eyes; felt the strength he embodied in the subtle shifts he made. With his gaze fixated on her, a spark of energy shot through her body. *Remember. Remember that day*, she reminded herself.

"You had those men beat up my brother."

"Yeah."

Giselle shifted her eyes to look down at the concrete.

"And it's all good. He's packing now; at any point in time he could end me."

Giselle's head whipped to him. Shock zinged through her body, almost powerful enough to push her eyeballs right out of their socket. She was still having a hard time reconciling Hawk to his current condition. Apparently, those conditions now included a gun.

"Did he run out of bullets?" Giselle inquired.

Ninja stroked his chin. "Nope. So far, he's decided not to."

Giselle hesitated, not sure how to proceed. "Is that a good decision?"

Ninja leaned in until Giselle could feel his breath on her cheeks. "I don't know. Is it?"

Giselle wanted to respond, but all she could think was, if she shifted her head to the side her lips would brush his cheek. *Damn.*

CHAPTER 15

A week later, Hawk covered his mouth to keep the rest of tonight's dinner from making a comeback. His right hand was shaking to the point that he didn't feel comfortable gripping the gun any longer.

He scanned the warehouse, which was lit by sparsely placed metal garbage barrels, with blazing fire and holes in the roof allowing meager amounts of light to seep in. Sera's people handled their more illegal ventures here. Murder. Murder definitely counted as not legal.

One month in the projects, and he was already an accessory to murder. His mind was replaying the last 30 seconds, as if it was trying to come to terms with watching Ninja put a bullet in Tate, a low-level snitch who served no other purpose than to run his mouth when it should be shut.

After the man's lifeless body hit the concrete, Ninja had walked out of the door as though going for a Sunday stroll after church. Hawk's feet refused to budge. His mind still couldn't process what just happened.

No matter that Tate had every intention of getting Ninja to shoot Hawk. Did that count as self-defense? Could accessories plead self-defense? Should he go to the police?

However, a black man in a police station might be more dangerous than pitching a tent next to a dead body with a gun in his hand.

Ninja strode back into the warehouse with his arms full. Hawk jumped at his unexpected return, putting his hand over his pounding heart. Watching Ninja slip on a pair of gloves and lay a large black garbage bag on the concrete right next to several tin cans of chemicals, he didn't know whether to help, run, or to pray to every known deity for help.

Ninja turned to him—eyes glittering with such intensity, it forced Hawk to take two steps back.

Ninja turned back to the task at hand. "Get out of here."

Hawk inched towards the door, cracked it open, and peered out onto Kingsbury Street. He stood perfectly still, watching the dark and shadows for any unusual movement. Think. Think. He had to leave before the police found him.

When he felt sure that he wouldn't be discovered, he rushed out of the warehouse and hurried down the street.

The heat of the late-day sun was still hot enough that it caused beads of sweat to stream down his back. Or maybe it was the fact that he had seen a life end firsthand. A man's future, such as it was—gone. Though his heart was still racing, Hawk couldn't stop; he had to keep moving.

He needed to talk with Giselle. She would know what to say, what to do. When they were together, her mind helped them navigate through all sorts of ills. She'd been the one to provide a softer presence in the absence of a mother, the emotion with the logic. Now he was alone, trying to figure out how to keep from losing it—and failing miserably. He couldn't hold back the tears that pushed themselves out of his eyes.

A police car slowed down as it aimed in his direction. With his heart pummeling against his chest, he wiped his nose with the back of a shaky hand, then watched the cruiser out of the corner of his eye.

The pudgy white officer he'd seen on the block from time to time leaned out. "You alright there, son?"

Hawk simply nodded, trying to slow his pace to something close to normal. He couldn't imagine what the officer was thinking, seeing a grown man blubbering on the way down the street. "Yeah, I'm just walking . . . my mom died and . . . ."

The officer slowed a little as he nodded. "It'll be okay, son."

In the Midst of Fire

As the police pulled off, his thoughts spanned to a place he could settle into. He couldn't roam the street all night. He wasn't welcomed at Lizzie's, but that was the only place he could think that would be anything close to "safe."

The more he walked, the more sanity returned. But his mind couldn't erase Tate's face when Ninja snuffed out what little life the man had.

The shocked expression when Ninja and Hawk turned their guns toward him was etched in his eyeball. The indecision before Tate turned his gun to Ninja, Tate fumbling with the safety of his gun, those split seconds cost Tate everything. Ninja wasn't forgiving someone trying to shoot him.

The shot rang out. Tate's boneless body fell with a thunk.

Hawk forced those last images from his mind, passing the front of Lizzie's three-story house without breaking a stride. Walking around the back, he kept to the shadows as he dodged the security cameras until he reached the back gate. Taking out the key Lizzie had given him six years ago, he opened the steel gate.

Seeing Lizzie in the kitchen speaking with her mother, his heart quickened. She looked fuller, more . . . lush. Evidently, her mother hadn't realized what the weight change meant yet.

They wanted to keep it a secret as long as possible, at least until he came up with a viable plan to ensure he could take care of them both.

Hawk crawled along the back bushes until he made his way to the side door. Lizzie's mother never set the alarm until they went to bed. He let himself in and hurried up the back way.

Things weren't always this way. In fact, Lizzie and Giselle started out as best friends freshman year in high school. Growing up, Giselle always had her own friends; however, no one was considered a best friend, until Lizzie.

She loved to laugh. That was probably the thing that drew Hawk in first—her sense of humor.

He would hear the side-splitting laughs she shared with his twin. He'd be in his room with his friends trying to be cool. They sounded happy, he wanted to be a part of that.

Bar none, Lizzie was the nicest person he'd ever met. At times, even Giselle could be calculating and demanding, as the only female in the house. The two unlikely friends balanced each other well. Giselle would fight battles that Lizzie would walk away from. Lizzie was Giselle's barometer on what battles were worth fighting.

Lizzie had a very distinct understanding of right and wrong and went out of her way to do right. But she wasn't preachy or boring with it. After his dad starting picking wives like some people picked up flowers, Hawk's own moral barometer became a bit skewed.

Lizzie helped him stay true to himself. She helped him realize the value of friendships; the value of relationships. As crazy as that sounded for a teenage boy, he preferred being his mother's son more than his dad's clone. That alone was a gift which Lizzie gave him that few people understood.

Lots of time was spent at the Warner house. The Glens constantly struggled with finances, but money was no issue at the Warner house. Lizzie's father had a heart attack when she was five.

His legacy of loving his daughter and loving to make money ensured Lizzie never had to work a day in her life. Whatever Lizzie got, Giselle and Hawk were blessed with, too.

One ordinary day, he saw who Lizzie truly was. He had set his eyes on her often; but this day, the beauty in her heart radiated from her eyes, causing him to hunger for her conversation, her spirit, and, eventually, her body.

Hence, she is now pregnant; unplanned, and a shared secret between them.

Hawk stealthily eased up the back staircase, keeping close to the wood paneling. The carpet muffled his footsteps; but as he reached the top, he paused, making sure that the help weren't there. Usually, Mrs. Warner dismissed the house manager and maid by 3 p.m.; at which time, they went to their home.

Hearing nothing, he quietly slid into her room and collapsed in a chair.

An hour later, as Lizzie came into the room, she started but quickly recovered. Closing and locking the door, she rushed into his arms.

"What are you doing here?" Lizzie whispered.

Hawk pulled her close and put his forehead against the gentle curve of their unborn baby. He couldn't believe with all the obstacles they had to being together: her mother; his family; his neighborhood; his financial status; and her pregnancy, especially when her mother found out. Now he would likely end up in jail because of Tate's death.

In the Midst of Fire

"Hawk?" she whispered, placing a hand on the top of his head, gently rubbing his close fade.

He pulled her tighter. She walked Hawk to the attached bathroom and locked the door. She turned on the shower's spray, then stepped into the Jacuzzi and let the water run. As she began removing his clothes, she frowned at the dark spots on his skin.

Lizzie pushed him into the shower and let tiny rivers of red-pink wash off of him. She pulled him out, let him sink into the tub and turned on the jets.

"Hawk, you're scaring me."

He stared at the water, not daring to meet her eyes. "You see it in the movies all the time. You know. Someone just pulls the trigger and runs."

Lizzie's eyes widened to the size of watermelons.

"It's that easy," he croaked, barely managing around the frog in his throat. "Shoot and run. But baby, it's not that easy."

Exhaling a deep breath, Lizzie inquired. "You killed someone."

Turning to look at her, chilled by the fear he saw in her eyes, he replied, "No. Ninja did. He shot him and then started cleaning up the mess. And I stood there. But I stood there."

He pulled his focus from her hazel eyes and onto the clear water. "I'm an accessory. Tate was going to kill someone, but he's dead now."

Lizzie slipped into the tub without removing her clothes, put her arms around him, and laid his head on her breasts.

They stayed that way for a long while before he whispered, "I can't get his face out of my mind."

Lizzie's voice cracked as she replied, "I know, honey. I know."

Hawk tightened his arms about her. "I could go to jail for this you, know. I might never meet our child. He won't know me."

That admission was met with silence and the drip of her tears falling onto his face.

"Why is this happening?" he begged for clarity, but wasn't expecting an answer.

They remained in the tub until his fingers wrinkled, but at least his breathing and heart rate had returned to a normal pace.

Lizzie took a thick, thirsty towel and brushed it across his skin, then gave him a pair of jogging-suit bottoms that she had stashed for him in the bottom of the closet, and then tucked him into her bed. She changed into a pair of silk peach pajama bottoms with a matching tank and crawled in next to him.

As she lay in his arms and the world around him felt small and fleeting, she said the words that eased his soul: "The things we do don't define who we are. You are the man who will do anything to protect his family."

The wonder in her voice and the beauty of her touch soothed him. "You are the strongest man I know. You stay in that house with Sera to make sure she doesn't hurt Giselle," Lizzie whispered. "Even with everything that woman's putting you through, you're working toward your degree."

Snorting, Hawk added, "Yeah, but at the pace I'm going, most people will be getting a master's before I even see an associate's."

The computer was a powerful tool and, besides clothes, one of the few things he kept from his old life. He used it to make his legitimate money.

Although he wasn't a graphic designer, he had learned enough about website content management tools and the application of graphics to make some pocket change. Now he was able to send some to Giselle and put a bit to the side for the baby.

Lizzie ground out, "Don't talk like that. You have to hide the fact that you're making your own money; working and taking classes online at night so Sera doesn't catch on that you're not really into the 'family' business. That's amazing by anyone's standards."

"But Lizzie—" Lizzie touched his lips to keep him quiet.

"You could have left us," she insisted. "People with far fewer reasons than you,

leave every day. People think it takes strength to act. It takes even greater strength to endure."

Hawk pursed his lips to kiss the pad of her fingertips. "Don't build a statue on the Washington Mall just yet. I witnessed a murder. This wasn't about my family," he said, "Tonight was about saving my own ass."

Lizzie kissed his back. "Was it an innocent man?"

"No," Hawk confessed, thinking of Tate's machinations and the people he worked for. "He was trying to get Ninja to shoot me."

Lizzie's jaw clenched against his back. "Sweetie, I don't know what I'd do if it was you who died tonight."

Those words provided a sense of comfort.

"We'll work everything else out," she declared. "You know I'll get my inheritance when I turn twenty-five. Once that comes through we'll be free from all of this."

"I may not survive until then," he admitted, rubbing the pad of his thumb along her cheek. "It's been what two and half months and I've done things that I don't even want to talk about," Hawk sighed, "things I can't tell you about."

Lizzie placed her hands on his shoulders, forcing him to turn and face her. "You also saved your sister and yourself. You will survive this. *We* will survive this."

They stayed facing each other, exchanging air and whispering into the night. Her strength ebbed into him. Her words calmed his psyche. Her nearness eased the ache in his heart. Her arms were home. Nothing could hurt him when he was nestled at home.

All was still as he listened to the soft beat of her heart, then . . .

Suddenly, the doorknobs rattled and the lock clicked. They both shot up from their place in bed, only to be confronted with the angry face of Lizzie's mother.

CHAPTER 16

Hawk couldn't believe this was happening. Of course, Lizzie's mom would catch him tonight of all nights.

Mrs. Warner's hazel eyes glared. She mirrored Lizzie's 5-feet 9-inch height, cinnamon complexion, and hazel eyes. Years of workouts kept her lean. However, the softness in Lizzie was missing in Lizzie's mother.

Mrs. Warner's eyes were fierce and calculating, especially when she thought no one was looking. Though they both had lean frames, Mrs. Warner's breasts were well-endowed, highlighted by the angry heaving of her chest.

"What?" she roared. "You thought that I never check the security tapes?"

Hawk's pulse raced. *What do you say when you're caught red-handed in a woman's daughter's room?*

He jumped out of the bed and held his hands up. "Mrs. Warner. Please wait. There was nothing going on. I just came over because I had a bad day."

He took a deep breath and ventured ahead with, "Ma'am, you know I love and respect your daughter."

Mrs. Warner's body tensed with anger. Hawk's heart pounded against his chest. "I . . . ."

What else could he really say? Nothing. He was wrong for being here.

He didn't want Lizzie to suffer. He had to leave. Hawk grabbed his clothes from the chair where Lizzie had placed them.

He inched by Mrs. Warner, aiming to make it out of the house in the opposite way that he had come in.

Suddenly, with a roar, her hands went around his neck. Hawk dropped his clothes and struggled to free himself, all while reminding himself not to punch the woman.

Lizzie jumped out of bed. "Mom, no!" Rushing to their side, she maneuvered herself in between the two.

Suddenly, he was breathing freely again as Mrs. Warner pushed Lizzie out of the way. As Lizzie tumbled to the floor, the irate woman turned to reach out only to snatch her hand back. Her eyes bulged, taking in the subtle rounding of Lizzie's belly.

"Lizzie?" The anger left Lizzie's mother's as she crumpled to the ground in defeat. "You're pregnant?"

The bump protruded proudly beneath the pajama tank that Lizzie wore. How she had managed to keep it hidden all this time was damn near a miracle.

Mrs. Warner glared at Hawk. "My God, what did you do? Get the hell out of my house."

Hawk held his hand out to Lizzie. He couldn't leave her and his baby, not tonight. Regardless of what it cost them, money didn't matter. However, Lizzie didn't get up. She didn't take his hand. She didn't move.

"Get the hell out of my house!" Mrs. Warner shrieked. "Fucking Glens ruin everything,"

Lizzie closed her eyes and shifted her focus to Hawk. "I need to talk to mom. I can't just leave."

Nodding, Hawk picked his clothes up from the floor. "I do love her, so much."

Mrs. Warner growled deep in the back of her throat.

He straightened his shoulders.

"Everything is ruined—everything," Mrs. Warner said in a strangled whisper.

He locked gazes with Lizzie. She turned away from him and put her eyes on her mother, sobbing like someone had died; it cracked something inside of him. His soul split as he walked away from his family. It was another casualty of Sera's machinations, another example of his inability to protect and care for his family.

Something he'd do everything in his power to make right—soon.

CHAPTER 17

Sera sat in the living room, tapping her finger against the arm of the couch. She focused on Ninja. "Say that again?"

"He's dead."

Sera stiffened with anger.

Ninja stood at ease, not moving a single one of those well-defined muscles.

"Who did what?"

"I shot him."

Sera focused on Ninja, taking in the furrow in his brow, the tension in his shoulders, all the way down to the spatter of something on his white shoe. She waited for a rare smile, an eye twinkle, something, any signs to indicate he was joking. "How the hell did that happen?"

Ninja smiled then. But it wasn't filled with any type of joy, it was more like a growl without sound. "So we're standing there, right? I'm pointing my gun at Hawk, and then he's pointing at me." Ninja shifted slightly, as if mentally playing back the events that occurred earlier in the evening. "Yeah, you could have told me you gave him a gun."

Sera laughed. "Well, it made it more interesting, didn't it?"

"Damn, you're crazy," Ninja muttered. "Anyway, I know I'm a quick shot, but I'm looking at Hawk, right. I could see his mind racing—ideas coming and ideas going."

"You should've just shot Hawk." Sera raised her left eyebrow. "Obviously, you're not that quick."

"Shit, he was still talking. When they're still talking, they're trying to figure a way to get out of it." Ninja shrugged. "If he wanted to shoot me, he knew he should've done it when he whipped out the gun."

Sera's eyes narrowed as she took in the logic behind those words. "So now you can read minds?"

Ninja tilted his head. "I managed to stay alive this long."

Well, he did have a point. That's how Ninja got his name. He moved in the shadows and combined brilliance with an uncanny instinct that kept him ten steps ahead of anyone who even entertained the notion of coming for him. Cursing from the sidewalk crept up the building and into open window, adding another layer of tension so thick it could have smothered fire.

After she broke eye contact, he continued, "So then he turned his gun on Tate, making him confess that he was the one that stole money from me—not Hawk." Ninja's eyes were unfocused as he continued, "Then Tate whipped out his own gun. He shifted it between me and Hawk. I know Tate. He's not like Hawk. The first time a man shoots, he's a bit slow . . . like Hawk. Tate knew he was going to have to shoot his way out of there. So when he turned his gun on me again, I saved him the trouble of making a decision."

Sera leaned in. There was a beauty and power in watching someone's life ease out of their body. She wished she had been there. "Kill shot."

"Kill shot," Ninja confirmed.

"And where is Hawk now?" Sera inquired.

Ninja assessed Sera with a lingering, curious gaze, "He's your son, isn't he?"

Sera's temperature rose a bit; the glare she gave him normally made a lesser man take two steps back. Ninja had never been anyone's lesser man.

"I pried the bullet out of the wall, got that shell casing, wiped down anything we could've possibly touched, and got the hell out of there."

Sera shifted on the sofa, pulling one of the pillows to her breasts. "Can you roll with him?"

Ninja lowered his gaze, shielding his reaction. "Yeah, but what makes you think that he'll roll with us like that?"

Ninja got a bit more leeway with his tongue because he was so valuable. Sometimes, though, she wondered if maybe he had too much power. How dare he doubt her control?

"What makes you think he'll roll with us," she parroted. Her hand itched for a knife to make him pay for doubting Hawk's allegiance. "Well for one, he'd hate for something to happen to his dad or little Miss Priss; and two, because as you said, he's my son."

Ninja merely gave a short, mocking bow and walked out of the apartment.

Sera let this new information ping-pong in her mind. Tate was scum. Before tonight, he was useful scum because he could be bought. She thought having him drive a wedge between Hawk and Ninja would be entertaining. She rolled the dice and Tate was the man down. No one but his family would miss him. His life choices hadn't led to a long, productive life. They probably already assumed he'd end up on a slab at some point.

At least Ninja and Hawk's little adventure tonight answered one question. The Knights may have full faith in Ninja, but he was too good. Too clean. Too efficient. The fact that no one had actually seen him kill anyone made Sera suspicious. Tonight had been a test for him as much as everyone else. Lucky for Ninja, he proved to be as good as his reputation.

Sera tapped her finger on her bottom lip. Hawk would be useful; even more so, now that he truly understood how precarious life in the hood was.

The first time witnessing a murder changed someone. Forever, humans are preprogrammed with the fight or flight mentality. Before he got either idea in his pretty little head, Hawk Glen had to know they were playing *her* game.

Sera crept into her bedroom, stood at the threshold, and let her gaze fall on Chase. His chest rose and fell, set to the rhythm of this precarious life. Her Chase.

Thinking back to the weekend she first saw him at Aria in Vegas, the way Chase gently grazed his hand over her shoulder at the blackjack table and nodded, acknowledging her presence as he lowered himself into the empty seat at her left. Handsome. Smooth. It had been six months since she had even thought about sex, but that one touch created a heat path down her body and shocking her V-ness back to life.

This man could be what I need to work the cobwebs out. He glanced down at her breasts, enhanced by a great push-up bra and the second skin of the Versace dress she had found at a high-end resale shop. She crossed her legs towards him, her posture emphasizing her hourglass figure—an unconscious move before she remembered her rules: She would not be a one-night stand. No one would use her for sex again.

She turned to see eyes on her. Apparently, the dealer was waiting for her to do something. Looking at her hand, she requested another card and hoped for the best. The others around the table groaned in unison. Black Jack should be as easy as counting to 21. However, in Vegas, there seemed to be some unwritten rules at play that made her the most hated person at the table.

Chase leaned over. "Distracted?"

Inhaling his spicy cologne, she wondered if her rules would be null and void if she used him for sex instead of the other way around.

"I'm fine," she muttered, vowing to pay closer attention to the cards before she caused a full-scale riot. She tried to drown out the dinging slot machines and the enticing man on her right to focus on the cards.

After trying another hit and going over 21, Sera surrendered to the fact that Black Jack wasn't her game of choice. Chase did too. Their seats were immediately filled. One woman bumped her out of the way.

As she turned to give the woman the business, that fine man leaned in and stated, "I guess you don't play often."

The lady was quickly forgotten as she batted her eyelashes. One side of her brain said to go for it, and the other side warned that she should pump the brakes.

Sera gazed into his eyes. It wouldn't hurt to be polite. "No, not really."

She took inventory of his suit, which was cut so well that he might have a tailor locked in his room. And it didn't escape her notice that he had been playing with $1,000 chips.

Suddenly, amid the normal cheers and groans, a consistent bell followed by a high-pitched squeal could mean someone had won a jackpot. With this man in front of her, Sera was convinced it was she.

In the Midst of Fire

He inquired, "Your date didn't show you how to play."

Sera chuckled, "Wow, are we still doing that? You could just ask if I was here with someone."

Chase's voice lowered an octave, "Well?"

One word, just one, and her nipple tightened. Tucking her hair behind her ear, she responded, "No, I'm here by myself."

"Let's solve that little issue," taking her hand and tucking it in his elbow, he introduced himself, "Chase."

Sera hesitated. This wasn't Michael. He didn't look like Michael. He didn't have that cruel hard look in his eyes. Licking her lips, her eyes roamed Chase's body. He was tall and athletic with "big dick" swag.

He laughed, and the sound was open and carefree. Tilting her head, she assessed him. What was that like? In what kind of world did he get to be free, to not worry about who was around the corner? Where did he come from, where he didn't have to worry about the next man? What was that like?

She replied, "Seraphina. Well, Sera."

Where she was from, emotions were dangerous things; even when people laughed, there was no freedom in it. That freedom she experienced through Chase, as they ventured outside of Aria and onto the Vegas strip, was like that first drop of a victim's blood on a blade.. She wanted more.

"All these casinos and you want to go to Rio?" he inquired.

Sera beamed up at him. "Yes, I love it when they throw beads down from the ceiling. It's like Carnaval."

Chase's timbre reverberated through her spine. "And what do you know about Carnaval?"

Laughing, Sera inched back, giving him a saucy little dip and a wink. "I know what happens there stays there."

Chase threw back his head and laughed. "I thought that was here in Vegas."

"If I like what happens in Vegas, I may take it back home."

Rubbing his knuckles along her arm, he added, "Maybe we'll both be so lucky."

Chase's laughter crept up each vertebra, breaking through every level of stress that bound her spine. She wanted to laugh like that—free, without a niggling worry floating through her mind. She wanted that so desperately.

Actually, that freedom was a mirage, even then. He must have known how close he was to financial ruin, but he talked and acted as if he owned the world.

Now it was seven months since she had left the dreams forged in Vegas behind. Now she concentrated on keeping this family, here, with her.

Sera stood watching Chase sleep. Freedom meant no one was watching the shop. She kept her eyes out for everything dealing with her family. Even now, staring at the clock and realizing that it was late and Hawk may not come back, she had to take action. She'd know how the first experience with death could make or break a Knight. She needed it to make Hawk.

She walked to her dresser drawer and pulled out a bag that contained a needle. Walking towards the bed, she smiled when his breathing caught up in a snore. She eased on the bed by his leg and drew the covers back. She rubbed his muscular calf, letting the soft hair tickle her finger.

Her finger traced the outline of his muscle and up to the knee bone that was connected to the thigh bone. Spreading her hand, she felt the difference in the hair here—thinner, finer. Chase stirred a little in response to her touch.

Closing her eyes, she took a deep breath. Her heart skipped. She plunged the needle into Chase's thigh.

He jerked upright, snatching his body inward. "What the fuck?"

Sera reached up and rubbed his thigh. "Sorry, babe."

As she walked towards the door, Chase's confused, sleep-muddled voice made her pause. "No, Sera. Really. What the hell did you just do?"

Opening the door, she paused. "It was just a little stick, babe; barely made a scratch."

"Why the hell are you pricking me while I'm sleep?" Fury replaced shock. "It's not like I have sugar."

She felt fire pulsing from his eyes as if he'd become Superman or the Cyclops.

"It's just . . . it's nothing. Go back to sleep."

Sera pulled out her phone and sent one text: "*It's after midnight. Ask your father about the needle in his leg. And then ask yourself if you know where your sister is. I do. See you soon.*

As she leaned against the wall and slid to the floor, her hands covered her face. Her breathing was ragged, and she forced herself to remain calm. She had promised Hawk what would happen if he tried to disappear. He had to know she was serious.

Some games she refused to lose. Keeping her family together was one of them.

CHAPTER 18

Giselle walked into her dorm room and quickly locked the door. This made her roommate, Kim, shriek when she came home and had to use a key, especially when Giselle was sitting right there in the room.

Kim didn't know anything about the ghosts Giselle was battling. While it was unnerving that Ninja appeared on the quad, Giselle never felt malice from him. Funny, his people stomped the shit out of her brother; but other than that, Ninja had just been himself. He even called every now and again.

Giselle was more worried about Sera sending someone else to check on her, someone like NuNu, who would want to do more than grab at her crotch and wouldn't take no for an answer.

Ninja laughed when she asked him about that. He assured her that Sera would never trust NuNu to carry out any important missions or instructions.

Still, the locked door made her feel safer. Giselle wondered how they expected two people to live comfortably in this tiny space. Granted, it had two closets, two desks, and two chairs. And as long as no one was a pack rat, or a clothes horse, or basically anything that required extra stuff, it was okay.

To say her first year at school has been difficult would have been a monumental understatement. The strain of not having Hawk by her side made her reach out for the first male that appeared before her eyes.

She was more discerning now, smarter. Now she concentrated on how to get her degree as quickly as possible. She didn't live a life in which one door closed and a window magically materialized. She needed to fight for her place in this world. And she was up for that.

Giselle's cell buzzed. Only two people from Chicago had that number—Lizzie and Ninja. He had insisted on getting her a new phone after Sera had him track her. Ninja said he felt more comfortable if Sera had to come through him for information. He didn't want Sera to use the cell against her. Hacking was one of Ninja's many valuable roles in the Knights' organization.

"Hey, Hawk's little sister."

Giselle smiled, hearing the deep voice on the other end.

"Hey, Ninja." Then a thought made her heart stop. Ninja normally called in the evening, as he understood her economics studies required focus. "Wait, Hawk. Is Hawk okay?"

"He's maintaining." Ninja chuckled deep in his throat, "You do know that one day you're going to ask about me first."

Giselle grinned at the confidence in his voice. "If you say so."

"Oh, I'm sure of it," he countered. "One day you're going to be daydreaming and my fine ass will pop into your head."

"I thought you called me Hawk's little sister to remind you," she taunted. "Isn't this talk against your moral code?"

If possible, Ninja's voice got even deeper. "Little Sis, I never said what you'll be thinking about in that daydream. So what would you be dreaming about that would be against my moral code?"

Caught. Giselle hit her hand against her head to try to clear out the cobwebs. "Well, I'm fine and school is good. So, all is well."

Ninja was silent for a few moments, then, "Don't you want to know about your father?"

Giselle thought for a minute. Her first instinct was to say hell no. He let that witch run her out of town. But something in her paused, probably her mother's influence.

Someone must have taught her manners. She didn't think anything besides marrying women with money was high on Chase's list of things to do.

Her mother had been the hands-on parent; the one who kissed the boo-boos. Giselle remembered Saturday mornings. Her mother was always an early riser. She would sit in her favorite chair in the living room with a newspaper and a cup of chamomile tea on the end table. The chair was a huge, comfy rocking recliner. Giselle would climb in her mother's lap. They'd sit there gently rocking, enjoying each other's presence before the rest of the house even stirred.

"We all have to make decisions that we feel are best at the time," her mother said, breaking the calm and silence that enveloped them. "You have to live with the decision you make. And if you realize later that it's wrong, it's okay. You grow and learn. Don't ever put your destiny in the hands of anyone else. Don't relinquish control of your future. If you make a decision based on what's right for you at the time, you don't have to apologize to anyone, including yourself."

That was the thought process that kept her at school, pulling the kind of grades that kept her scholarship intact. Hawk was right about one thing: after he'd been beaten like he'd walked naked into a KKK rally, leaving was the right decision at the time.

His decision not to join her was so very wrong. But his mind was as one-tracked as a dog sniffing around a bitch in heat. In that way, Hawk and her dad were exactly the same. When Chase had a woman in his crosshairs, his focus was as sharp as a razor.

When Giselle arrived at Lexington, she gave her father a call. She didn't want him to worry, and maybe he could get Hawk to join her away from the madness.

"Um, Dad?" Giselle tentatively stuttered.

"Oh, thank God, Giselle," her father exclaimed. "What were you thinking disappearing like that?"

Before she could get a good thought past her lips, the witch in the background crooned, "Is that Giselle? Where is she? Let me talk to her!"

Giselle disconnected immediately. There was no way she was talking to Sera: not after the stomping that Hawk experienced; not after one of her thugs nearly raped Giselle, and Ninja had to stopped him. Sera and her father were now a package deal, and Giselle would be better off alone.

In the Midst of Fire

She placed a few calls to Lizzie, trying to convince her best friend to make Hawk come down to Lexington. Lizzie staunchly refused to get in the middle, by deflecting, "You need to talk to Hawk."

Giselle wanted to wring Lizzie's neck through the phone. "I would if he ever called me back."

"Maybe if you didn't harass him about moving every time he called," Lizzie advised, her tone disapproving. "You might have more success."

"Next year will be perfect. I get to live off campus. We can live off campus. He listens to you." Lizzie paused, and Giselle could envision her plucking away at whatever jeans she was wearing. "That's not fair, Giselle."

This was definitely a touchy subject, but she was fighting for her brother's life. "But it's true."

Lizzie took fewer calls from Giselle after that. So now, those updates on what was happening in Chicago were few and far between. She might as well get an update from Ninja, since he was offering.

"How is Sera's husband doing?" Giselle picked up paddleball, which she was trying to perfect, along with her roommate. Funny how something as simple as a paddleball contest can bring out a serious competitive spirit. Giselle walked the tiny bedroom hitting the ball, hoping it would distract from the seriousness of the moment.

"Funny thing. Your dad let it slip one day that Sera stabbed him with a needle. It's odd. That's not her style. When I mentioned it to Hawk, he got this weird look on his face, said it must be domestic issues. But I think it's way more than that."

Giselle plopped down on her bed. "Needle? What kind of needle? What was in the needle? Was she trying to kill my dad?" Giselle started paddling the ball even faster; fear making her hand move on its own accord.

CHAPTER 19

Chase couldn't be encased in the apartment walls one more day. The air smelled casket-stale. Hawk and Sera left hours ago. If they stayed true to schedule, they wouldn't be back for hours. Perusing his closet, he realized the closet was stuffed with slacks and dress shirts. He'd worked hard on his image and his ability to fit into the Lincoln Park lifestyle. Even when others showed up to a meeting in designer jeans and blazers, he insisted on wearing slacks.

Pushing one pair of slacks after another aside, he found the designer jeans Giselle and Hawk gave him for his birthday a few years ago. The tags were still on. He pulled them out of the closet and pulled a polo shirt out of the dresser. He had an outfit for every occasion, except walking through the hood.

He exited the building intent on making it to the Walgreens on North and Wells; however, his steps paused on their own accord when he saw the black Hulk Hogan, also known as Vincent, talking to some Knights in the courtyard.

Chase considered going back into the building, but instead he forced his feet to keep walking.

Vincent's gaze fell on Chase. Whatever he murmured to his crew caused them to scatter. Crap. The last thing Chase wanted was a run-in with Vincent.

As Chase arrived to where Vincent was standing, he realized his bad luck; because if Vincent jumped him, he would need to beat him with something and the courtyard was empty.

"Vincent, "Chase acknowledged.

"Chase."

As Chase tried to go around, Vincent cleared his throat. "Chase, why are you here? For real, this isn't your scene.

Four smart-ass responses ran through his head, but Vincent was a big man. He might out-run him, but he'd just have to deal with it on the way home.

"I don't want any problems with you, Vincent."

Vincent laughed, "No shit."

Chase felt the electricity from a thousand pairs of eyes. As he looked around, people were popping up in their apartment windows watching him and Vincent. Didn't anyone work around here?

Vincent's posture relaxed as he waited patiently.

Chase focused on Vincent's eyes, but he couldn't read them. "My wife lives here." Chase continued walking, but Vincent shifted. It didn't completely block Chase's path, but clearly Vincent wasn't done talking. Chase stepped back and folded his arms.

"What?"

"Half this yard knows that you were going to leave her anyway. How much you need to make that a reality?"

Was it that easy? Really?

Before Chase responded, he needed to know. "Why do you care? She made her decision. She chose me. Why are you still here?"

Vincent smirked, "I have a job to do old man. You make it hard."

A group of boys were about to walk up on them. Vincent merely shook his head, and they took a different direction.

Vincent continued, "You are weak. And you make her weak by association. I have to work twice as hard to ensure she keeps her cred with you around. With you gone, we can get back to business."

"So," Chase inquired, "the Knights are willing to front me millions of dollars for me to leave. That's what it would take—not hundreds, not thousands, but millions."

Vincent's chest swelled. "If I had the money, I'd be gone. But your girl ensured that I couldn't. My whole social circle now knows that I'm married. There are no rich widows or divorcees. I'm stuck. Just like everyone else here."

"That's the problem with you. There is no amount of money that would make me leave Sera. No number is big enough. That's what she thought she had with you."

"Yeah." This time he continued walking past Vincent, "Well, we all thought wrong."

CHAPTER 20

Hawk closed his eyes against the blazing Chicago sun. In the three months since they moved, Sera's apartment had become a box with walls that seemed an inch tighter each day. Freedom was sitting at the park with Lizzie's head lying on his thigh.

Hawk envisioned his son or daughter running along then playing with the other children on the swings. He imagined their shrieks to high-pitched squeals mixed in with laughter.

He reached up, toying with a few strands of Lizzie's brown hair. "What's the matter baby?"

Lizzie moved away and the wisps slipped through his hands and landed back on her shoulders. "My mom wants me to get married."

"We'll do that," he replied, relieved that was all that was causing the furrow in her brow. "It's just my life is complicated right now, but I'm working to get it straightened out."

Lizzie blew at her bangs, rifling the whisper-thin strands resting on her forehead, "I'm six months pregnant. You're not working fast enough."

Hawk's eyes narrowed. "Refuse."

"Like it's that easy," Lizzie scoffed. "I'm pregnant. I don't have a job. I don't have skills. All that I have going for me is that I'm pretty and rich."

Hawk reached for her, but Lizzie held up a hand to halt his protest. "I mean, my father was rich, which is what my mother reminded me of when she told me to marry this guy."

Hawk pleaded. "But we—"

"I have to take care of myself and my baby. You can't do that, Hawk, not today." Lizzie blew out a breath; the sound was like a gunshot to him, compared to the background bustle of activity around them. "Let's not pretend that you can."

He closed his eyes, processing the words slicing at his soul. "Who is it?"

Lizzie shook her head. "It doesn't matter."

Hawk closed his eyes and tried to do the same with his ears. Unfortunately, his mind couldn't be shut down. He envisioned that same child in his mind's eye that had been playing on the swing, now running up and calling someone else "Dad."

First, he had to watch Giselle escape after the attack, and now he was supposed to watch Lizzie and his child do the same. His temperature rose at least five degrees with the unexpressed anger rolling through his system.

He couldn't control the primal scream that finally escaped from his lips any more than Benjamin Banneker could avoid becoming the Hulk.

And when he finally opened his eyes, everyone in the park was staring at him as if he had actually made the transition to the Hulk himself. Even the pigeons stood still, as if they were wondering what the hell they were supposed to do.

Hawk held up his hand in apology, and seconds later the normal buzz of the park continued. It was a little heightened after his display, with a few over the shoulder glances, but he hadn't expected anything less.

So this was his life—shit piled on shit, with extra shit on the side. And he was supposed to, what? Just say, *Congratulations*.

Hawk looked at her—really looked this time. The slump of her shoulders, the bags under her eyes that ended at the cheeks, she didn't radiate youth and happiness as she had since the day he first laid eyes on her in grammar school. The sun no longer shone out of her pores.

"Did she take away the inheritance?"

Lizzie whipped her hair around and focused on him. Hawk gasped at the pain in her eyes. "There isn't any inheritance, not anymore. There's a stipulation. If I have a baby out of wedlock, then I won't see a cent until I'm 35 years old. And then it'll only be a fraction of the value of the estate."

"We could get married, now," Hawk pled. "We were going to anyway."

Lizzie's lips curled in the saddest smile. "My support stops once the baby is born. Any baby before the age of twenty-five is an issue. Hell, had my mom told me about that little stipulation I might've made better choices"—then she turned back to stare at the children running around—"at least different choices."

"Don't regret this. Don't regret us. Come on, Lizzie." Hawk drew closer to her, taking those soft, familiar hands in his. "What about your mom? She won't kick you out."

"My mom gets a stipend for raising me. My 'situation' negates her money, too," she replied. "Basically, we're broke."

Hawk pulled eye level with her. "We'll get jobs. We can make it."

Lizzie shook her head. Even though Hawk could see her hands in his, they felt weightless, as if she were a ghost.

"Or I can marry Tory Carlson."

Her words pushed Hawk's torso back. "But—"

Tory Carlson was a thirty-year-old black financial whiz kid. He was actually Hawk's cousin somewhere down the line. His father was a popular Chicago pastor, with a little money that made them a well-known, philanthropic presence in the community. But Tory didn't need his family's money. He bought and sold stock like he'd earned an intrauterine Ph.D. in economics. The man would give Lizzie the life she'd been born into, the life she would still have if they hadn't ….

Hawk grabbed her fingers. She winced, but he couldn't help himself. "Don't leave me. Please don't leave me."

"He's rich," she explained, her tone resigned and eyes pleading for understanding, even as her shoulders were resolute. "He's willing to support me, my mother, and my baby."

Hawk stood still, then his mind went into overdrive. He came up with one plan after another after another and then shot each one down with reasons why none of them would work. Lizzie would struggle with him. She would. There was no way around it. He didn't know how he'd take care of Lizzie and a baby, let alone a woman who hated him.

He rose. "Tory is a stand-up guy."

Breaking eye contact with Lizzie allowed him to notice how the children still played as if life hadn't changed. Parents, however, were stealing glances every now and again. He hoped they enjoyed the show because this was it—the end of him and Lizzie.

Lizzie snorted as she stood up, her laughter startled Hawk as she spat, "Tory is gay."

Even that announcement did nothing to ease the pain in Hawk's chest. Did they have Novocain for the heart? Every beat hurt. "But you're going to marry him anyway, have half a marriage and a life that's nothing but a lie."

"Tory is going to live his lie for Pastor Carlson," she replied softly. "We are both getting something out of the deal."

"Why would he do that?"

"Does it matter?" she shot back. "It works."

Hawk heard her words, but was still having problems accepting that Lizzie was leaving him. "How did all of this come about? Two weeks ago you were mine, all mine. When did you hook up with Tory?"

Lizzie absently rubbed her stomach. "Hooked up may not be the correct phrase in this case; seems my mother knows some people who know some things."

Hawk turned his back to her, still trying to process, still trying to find another solution that wouldn't end with him walking away from the only family he had left who mattered.

"It's just until I'm twenty-five. That's all," she begged, "Wait for me, Hawk."

It should've been him. She should've been married to him, but no. Every night she'd crawl into bed and snuggle against his cousin—distant, but still.

He'd have to become a bystander in what should've been his life. He wanted to wrap his hands around someone's throat—preferably Sera's. That would be a beautiful death.

Hawk couldn't stay. He couldn't look at her for one more second. As he turned to walk away, Lizzie called out, "I don't have a choice."

CHAPTER 21

Sera attacked her father? That didn't even make sense, and Ninja hadn't added any details.

"Well?" she snapped, frustrated with his attitude and the fact that she missed the ball.

Giselle couldn't believe that Sera was a threat to their father in any way. The woman, for some reason, seemed to love him. Unlike the others who let him ride off into the sunset when things went downhill, this one wanted to keep him.

Giselle liked to pretend that she didn't care about him, but she was the daughter and he was her knight in shining armor. That was before mom died. Back then, she considered boys stupid. Hawk, as the typical boy, proved her right so many times.

Like the day he swapped all of her dolls for his green army men and refused to give them back, unless she promised to sacrifice one of her dolls to his makeshift altar.

his had been done in retaliation for Giselle forcing his "action figures" to marry her dolls. Didn't he believe in true love?

Hawk always took matters into his own hands. She, of course, went running to her dad, who made Hawk give back her dolls.

In the Midst of Fire

More than that, her dad scooped her up in his arms and said, "No one messes with my baby girl, not even her brother."

Beaming, Giselle stuck her tongue out at Hawk over her father's shoulder. Granted, one of her dolls didn't quite make it back in one piece. Apparently, in Hawk's custody, the doll needed to go to the barber for a Mohawk haircut.

Giselle didn't remember the exact age the incident occurred, but it was definitely before her mother died. Everything good in their family happened before Rose's life was slammed short when a drunk driver ran into their car. Afterwards, well, they were still living in the afterwards.

The dynamic chatter from students trying to outdo one another as they headed down the hallway snapped her back to attention. A quick glance at the watch Hawk had given her for her thirteenth birthday meant dinnertime was already underway. At the rate Ninja was going, she'd miss the whole meal just to get a sentence out of Ninja. "Well," she grumbled into the phone.

"Hmmmmm," he drawled, "such impatience from someone who didn't even ask about him."

"I will cut you through this phone, Ninja. Doubt me if you want to," Giselle growled.

"Oh, I don't underestimate anything about you," he continued, his voice still holding mellow tones as though talking about the weather. "But that's the thing, Sera is more of a stabbing sort of girl. She doesn't mess around with needles."

Giselle's thoughts raced from one side of her mind to the other, trying to figure out what that meant. "I don't understand why she'd do that."

"I don't think you're supposed to," he continued, "but something in his expression told me that Hawk does."

Giselle went to the window facing the expansive park-like quad surrounding the majority of buildings. People scurried to and from class, laughing with their friends, enjoying the college experience while she held the phone to her ear, trying to figure out if her stepmom was trying to kill her father.

Then it finally clicked, why Hawk refused to come to Lexington and why Hawk didn't try to get Lizzie away from her 'husband' (as if Tory could be called that, given the fact that his preference was something that was swinging the same genitals as he was). Every time she set something up, Hawk shut her down. To add insult to injury, he sent Giselle money on a monthly basis. Wouldn't talk to her, but he sent checks. Now, Sera had stabbed her father with a needle.

"Do you think that's why Hawk stayed?" she asked, even as she closed her eyes praying Ninja would tell her she was wrong. "Do you think he stayed because she threatened my father in some way?"

Ninja paused, as if to reflect; or it could be one of his normal mind-wracking pauses. The silence that stretched between them was unnerving, and she almost disconnected the phone rather than ask again. But then Ninja said, "I think there are few people that Hawk loves enough to give up his life for—and your dad doesn't fit the requirements."

Giselle inhaled sharply. "That's why she used you to check up on me. It's me. She's using me."

"Perhaps. One or the other, or a combo of the two," Ninja said in a nonchalant tone that made her bristle. "Either way, Hawk's here and it doesn't look like he's leaving anytime soon. Leave well enough alone, Giselle. He's a grown man. He's got this."

Giselle didn't respond because the response that would work for Ninja would be a lie. No one was going to use her to control Hawk. No one was going to use their bond to shackle her brother that way. And absolutely no one was going to control her from a distance.

She had made Hawk a promise. She'd finish school. He had insisted. As long as Sera's craziness was focused on Chase, she'd finish. Plus, the couple of fighting lessons that Kim had taught her weren't enough to take on that knife-wielding bitch—not yet.

CHAPTER 22

Giselle stood at the top steps of the Lexington University Administration Office. Although she could see students walking on the sidewalk in front of her, she couldn't hear a thing. Her heart was beating like Holly Holmes on Rhonda Rousey in that first fight.

With a shaking hand, she held on to the handrail and made her way down the stairs. Even with that, she missed the last step and stumbled into a pair of solid male arms.

As she raised her head to apologize, she found herself face to face with Ninja. On campus, again, his ass needed a cowbell. The last thing she needed was a second unannounced visit from Ninja. As she tried to bring together the shattered remains of her dignity, he righted her, inquiring, "Are you okay?"

Jerking back, she responded in the only way she could, "Fine. Great. Stupendous." When in actuality, she felt as fragile as a vanilla wafer. "Don't you have some drugs to sell or Sera to suck up to? Or is that why you're here? Another message from the dear Seraphina?"

Feeling Ninja's eyes rake over her body, she studied the ground. If she looked in his eyes, she would be lost; and she couldn't afford to be lost.

Ninja leaned close enough that she could smell his Burberry cologne. Damn, she wanted to lick him. So now, when she should have been scurrying across the quad to her dorm, she was immobilized by a Ninja's deep voice, manly smell, and flashing eyes.

His eyes continued to search for hers as he asked, "Why didn't you tell me?"

Finally, she met his gaze, "Just because we talk once in a while doesn't mean I have to tell you every single thing going on in my life. And how did you know there was something to know. How . . . why are you here?"

Giselle felt a tingle on the back of her neck. Shit. She stayed too long.

Ninja planted his feet hip-width apart and used his arm to move Giselle behind him. As she turned, she saw her nemesis, Raymond Scott, coming out of the administration building. The palpable anger emitting from Ray's eyes seared onto Giselle's forehead like a tattoo.

This was the man whom she decided to date. This was the man who decided that one girlfriend wasn't enough. How could it have been? He needed one doing his homework in each subject, didn't he? Stupid Giselle only smartened up when she saw him kissing another girl on the quad.

Revenge meant turning herself and the other silly girls in to the dean. She got probation. Ray got kicked off the basketball team and out of school. Colleges were too skittish about NCAA violations to risk it all on a bench player, sixth-man award-worthy or not.

Ray's loose gait contrasted the way his eyes stalked her. Maybe she should have just broken up with him, but no. She had to make a statement. She had to be the shero. She had to not feel victimized. Wasn't a victim better than a corpse?

Although Ninja barely touched her, she felt the tension bunching up his muscles. Even though Ray was taller and more muscular, something deep in her said he'd get his feelings hurt messing around with Ninja.

Keeping eye contact with Giselle, Ray reached the bottom of the stairs. "Hey, dude, do you mind if I talk to Giselle?"

Ninja relaxed his stand. "Yes, dude, I do. Keep moving."

Ray reached his arm out to grab Giselle. Ninja grabbed Ray's wrist, twisted it, kicked the back of his knee, and had him down on the ground before Giselle could inhale. He leaned over and whispered, "Listen, you punk bitch-ass bench rider, I'm that nigga from the shadows of your nightmares."

Students began to gather in clusters and stare. Giselle hit Ninja to try to get him to let Ray go. She was certain that getting into a fight on the quad went against the probation she just received.

Ninja didn't budge, no matter how she swatted, pinched, or prodded. He just kept talking. "You fuck with her, and you fuck with me. And I'm not one to be fucked with. I'm straight from the streets of the Chi, and the reports are true. We kill motherfuckers for less than you've done to her already. Give me a reason to use your ass for target practice—just one."

Giselle noticed campus security hustling towards them as Ninja drew Ray to his feet. By the time security reached them, Giselle was praying for a crater to open up to the earth's magma so that she could jump in.

Next thing she knew, Ninja was dusting off Ray's pants, asking, "You okay, dude. That could have been a nasty spill."

Big bad Ray, who one second before looked like he was going to slice Giselle into tiny pieces and make a necklace, actually thanked Ninja. Thanked him. WTF. Campus security turned to Giselle. "Ma'am, did this gentleman start a fight with Ray?"

Of course the police knew Ray. Damn small school and basketball player worship. They probably had Ray's number tattooed on their ass. Giselle lifted her eyebrows in what she hoped was a look of pure-as-the-driven-snow innocence.

"You know, officer, he just caught me when I missed the bottom step, too. I don't know why the stairs are so dangerous today."

The two officers looked at each other. One's eyes narrowed so tightly with suspicion, that there was no guarantee he could still see out of them. The other officer just shrugged. They moved on.

Ninja patted Ray on the back. "That's probably the best choice you made all semester. Plus, you have bigger fish to fry. Your father just declared bankruptcy. Now that you have to do your own homework, good luck getting into school."

Ray turned, "How the hell do you know that?"

Grabbing Giselle by the hand, Ninja responded as he drug her away, "There's nothing I don't know. Remember that."

Giselle trotted to keep up with him. "How did you find out? I never told anyone about Ray. I just turned him in last week." Ninja didn't break stride. Giselle yanked him to a stop. "Ninja?"

Ninja assessed her, "Ninja!"

"I may have written a small program to look for your name under defined parameters, which might have flagged me that you were having a meeting with the dean this morning."

Turning to make sure no one was listening, Giselle shrieked, "Fuckin' network security degree. If the school finds the hack, they'll kick me out."

Ninja's eyes gleamed as a smile transformed his normally blank expression. His shoulders shook. Laughter. He was laughing. "Your school will never find my hack."

"Okay. How about this? Why? Did Hawk tell you to?"

Ninja's expression closed once again. Even so, she read the energy radiating from his body. Without laying a hand on his skin, she felt his warmth. This man wanted every inch of her. And damn if she didn't want to answer his body's call.

Maybe if she had just a taste, a small nibble. Reaching up to caress his face and bring it closer to her, she noticed the question in his eyes, her answer was yes. He whispered, "Giselle," before their lips met. Ninja forced her mouth open and devoured her.

Damn, this man knows how to use some lips. She relaxed into the kiss, letting her mind wander until it landed on that day with Hawk on the ground.

Wrenching her lips away, Giselle gasped for air. What the hell was she doing? She couldn't: not with Ninja; not with Hawk still trapped in Chicago; not with the man that got Hawk beaten up—the man who worked for Seraphina, the man who lived in Chicago while she lived in Philadelphia.

"Are you willing to leave Seraphina? Are you willing to grab Hawk, willing or not, and move here? Are you willing to give up your rent-a-thug life?"

Amused, Ninja answered, "I'm not a rent-a-thug."

"Oh, I'm sorry." Giselle held up her hands. "What do you call it?"

"I prefer the term consultant," he replied, crossing his arms over his chest.

In the Midst of Fire

Waving him off, Giselle tried to keep her eyes from rolling. "Whatever you call it, are you willing to give it up?"

Ninja opened his mouth as if to say something. Then he shut it tightly, Giselle could see the muscles underneath ripple. "I can't. It's not that easy."

Snorting, Giselle realized another Sera conquest. "You're just like my father. Are you sliding her dick, too?"

"Not even close. I wish I could explain, but . . . ."

Giselle held up her hand and wrapped her courage around her like a cloak, "I can't either. Go home to Sera. And don't come back. I will fight all my own battles in the future."

Ninja stared at her for twenty seconds. Giselle watched some kind of struggle going on internally and counted. "One day. We will get back to this. Believe that." He leaned over and gently pressed his lips against her cheek before turning to walk back across the quad.

Book Two

In the Midst of Fire

CHAPTER 23

June 2013

At the time when the newspapers were tracking homicides in Chicago every weekend, Hawk lounged against the hood of his electric blue I-Roc Z Camaro, languishing in a state of boredom—a constant thing in his life nowadays.

He kept his emotions buried, deeply, especially when he realized how they could be leveraged and used against him. Hell, over the years, he had made more than one person bend to his will by using what he loved most against him.

Take Lil Tev, the Knight who started harassing the white people who lived in those condos directly across from Burnham Park Apartments. Without the consent of the organization, he was breaking into cars and houses, making off with anything he could carry, including jewelry and money, which he kept all for himself.

His action brought the police out in full force; scouring their block in Old Town, like they were searching for lice in the heads of blond children. Black-on-black crime was one thing. Messing with the good tax-paying white folks was an entirely different thing.

The Knights didn't need the police crawling around the neighborhood asking a whole bunch of questions; prying into business that ran in secrecy, away from the eyes and wallets of Uncle Sam, and brought in the kind of dough that kept them quietly in comfort.

So they gave Tevin up to the cops. It was Hawk's job to visit him in Cook County Jail and show him a photo of his grandmother, who still lived in Burnham Park, to ensure Tevin kept quiet about Knight business—very quiet.

Hawk didn't know what would've have happened if Tevin decided to talk out of turn. Thankfully, Tevin kept his mouth shut, pled to the charges for the shit he did on his own, and was now serving a dime bid.

Trips like that made Hawk's stomach turn. However, it was infinitely better than some of the things that Ninja had to do. He didn't have a clue how Ninja could stand cleaning up dead bodies. He would share a warning photo any day over mopping up someone else's blood.

Sera has already pricked his father with a needle, just like she promised. It was a clean needle, but he hadn't believed she was capable of doing that, not against his father.

He should have known better. Although Tev's silence saved his grandmother, Sera still visited Tev's twin brother, Kevin. His face still bore the scars. He wasn't the only one traumatized. Kevin's neighbor told horror stories about the screaming coming from the apartment while Sera worked.

That's why Hawk didn't even talk to Giselle anymore. It was better if Sera felt they weren't as close as they had been. It was better if she didn't suspect that he wasn't going to stay in the apartment for one second after Giselle graduated.

He kept his eye on the street, which was his job, his life. Sera controlled the security in Burnham Park officially and unofficially, keeping just under the police's radar. Her "staff" watched what was coming and going and dealt with those who didn't play by the Knight's rules.

Today, all that was going down was the usual exchange of money and drugs. There were no unusual activities—or even worse—unusual people. People scattered like ants running from a direct spray of Raid® when Five-O rolled around. The police had a job to do, too. Just as watching the hustle was his.

In the Midst of Fire

A small burst of pain exploded as someone slapped his left shoulder. He shifted to focus on Ninja, who stood a few inches behind him. Dark, quiet, and deadly, Ninja received his name by being light years better than anyone else in the game. He moved in stealth. He disappeared for days at a time and reappeared. However, he also knew everything that happened while he was gone. Rumor had it he was always watching, everyone and everything.

Their partnership had been forged in battle, when Tate pitted them against each other. It ended with Tate, Hawk, and Ninja in a warehouse—two guns, three people, and one huge lie between them.

Hawk's piece was pointed at Ninja's heart. "I don't want to shoot you."

Ninja laughed, his Glock was pointed at Hawk's head. "Your aim better be dead on. I'm gonna make you pay for pulling a gun on me. If I have one breath in my body, I'll use it to pull this trigger."

"I wouldn't steal from you, Ninja," Hawk shot back.

"Tate. Tate," Ninja called out. "What did Hawk here say about me?"

Tate shuffled out from the back of the room and whispered, "He said you'd never suspect him, being Sera's son and all."

Hawk's nose flared as he retorted, "Never. Happened." *Shit, I'm about to be shot on a lie. Not good.* Hawk shifted his gun from Ninja to Tate. His life wouldn't be worth shit if he killed Ninja anyway. Tate was a different story. "Tell him the truth, Tate."

Tate's eyes popped wider, as his eyelashes did their best to meet up with his eyebrows. "I didn't."

"Tate."

"I was told that you said that . . ."

Hawk took two steps towards the man who was now sweating, either because of the heat from the barrels that provided supplemental light or because of fear. "Did you hear me say that shit about Ninja?"

"Well, I . . ."

Two more steps nearly closed the distance. Ninja's gun continued following Hawk. "Did you . . . hear me . . . say that shit . . . about Ninja?"

Tate visibly swallowed as he looked between the two men. "I don't. Well. Umm. But I heard . . ."

Hawk advanced until the barrel of his gun was against Tate's heart. "So the answer is no. You didn't hear a thing."

Tate's breathing labored. "No. I didn't hear."

Hawk put his arms down and turned to look at Ninja. "If I have something to say to you, I'll tell you face to face. *That's* my style."

Tate whipped out his gun and aimed it at Hawk. Hawk didn't react fast enough. In a flash, Ninja shifted his gun from Hawk to Tate. Hawk took a deep breath, ready to meet his maker.

But then Tate trained his gun to Ninja. That was his mistake, as a single shot from Ninja's gun slammed the man's soul into the afterlife.

The moment the body dropped to the concrete, Ninja stepped over it and stated, "You know both of us weren't supposed to walk out of here."

Hawk continued to stare at the body, but responded. "Doesn't matter." Then, he slid a gaze at his frenemy. "Do we have a problem?"

Slowly, Ninja assessed Hawk with a piercing gaze. "We're cool, man."

A lot of people still underestimated what drove Ninja. They'd do stupid shit like pocketing drugs and money. It was like they thought the stories about the man were fables, like Ninja wouldn't just end their lives.

Lying was high on Ninja's list as well. People had a better chance of winning the lottery than surviving lying to Ninja. They learned the truth soon enough.

There were plenty of stupid reasons to die. The streets had plenty of drugs and money; no need to skim off the top. Ninja took every infraction like a personal assault.

Once, when he found out that his cousin had lied about how much money he collected in a day; he slit his own cousin's wrists; then called the ambulance and told him that if the ambulance arrived and saved his life, he'd get another shot at redemption. It was a sad funeral.

In this life, people died or went to jail. A few died while behind bars, which was craziness, if he'd ever heard it. What's the point of snitching, if you're still going to jail? And when the Knights found out about the snitching, they killed the culprit anyway. Hawk would prefer if his last breath was a free one.

Hawk had never underestimated Ninja. That mutual respect kept them on more friendly terms than most. They each knew, though, that they'd take the other out if the situation demanded; or more importantly, if Sera demanded. They kept secrets from one another, but never lies.

Lies undermined trust. To a point, they had a sort of tentative trust—the kind that allowed for partnerships that could save Hawk or Ninja.

Today, years later, Hawk and Ninja were as close as two people—who couldn't talk about anything that really mattered—could get. So they were slightly better than passing acquaintances.

"I came up behind you and you didn't even jump. Dude, don't you have a reflex?"

Hawk studied Ninja for a moment. This wasn't small talk, not even close. For years, Ninja had peppered normal conversation with questions meant to draw more personal information.

Ninja wanted in Hawk's head, to figure him out, what made him tick, what made him vulnerable. Too bad for him.

"If you're going to shoot me, you're going to shoot me—whether I jump or not. So why give you the pleasure of reacting?"

Ninja laughed. "Okay. Okay, I gotcha."

Hawk could feel Ninja's eyes taking in every element of his attire. Hawk was dressed in Seven Jeans, a Ralph Lauren purple label polo shirt, and dress shoes.

He never put on a pair of gym shoes for any reason other than exercise. It made a difference to him to be different in little ways. It reminded him that this wasn't truly his life.

Ninja leaned on the I-Roc next to Hawk. "You dress like you should be steppin' out of a Porsche. Yet you keep this old I-Roc runnin'. I don't understand you, man."

"It's my car. I like it," Hawk smirked. "What's there to understand?"

Hawk continued to peer down the block, but he felt the intensity of Ninja's stare as he offered, "You do know that if you actually moved product, you could get that Porsche you've had your eye on."

Who didn't know that? Hawk could also get a significant amount of jail time. Hawk wasn't trading his current jail for a county one. This job with

Sera assured everyone he was part of the Burnham Park without having to sacrifice the rest of his life to it.

When Sera tried to move up in the Knights organization, she ended up in a fight that spilled blood on a supply of crack. Two things you can't fuck with— the money or the product. Sera cost them both with her temper. As long as she stayed with her current job, he could remain in his without issue.

Hawk turned towards Ninja. "Why aren't you selling? You could easily bring in the kind of money that lines your pockets with gold. I'm sure."

"Who has that kind of time?" Ninja chuckled, but his eyes sharpened. "Plus, my services come at a higher pay scale than yours."

Hawk eased up from his position. "It's been quiet, but it's all yours."

Ninja's lips flattened, "Where you off to?"

Walking backwards while answering Ninja, "I don't know. I'll be around."

Ninja's gaze probed Hawk's as he asked, "Without your car?"

"Don't need it."

Hawk saluted and walked off the block. He had a two-mile walk ahead of him and a lot of time to think about his current state. Life on the street was about one thing—survival. Part of his survival was all about his image.

When people saw him walking in his "good" shoes, they assumed he wasn't going too far. The Knights already questioned his whereabouts when he disappeared from time to time. Let them look for him locally.

They knew he was the kind that never gave a response unless he was asked a direct question. Hawk minded his own business and kept it to himself, unless someone was dumb enough to cross him.

Then Hawk was like a news reporter blasting whatever needed to be known. As he told the Knights that day after he "joined," important information wouldn't die with him. It would live on and come back to haunt people at the most inopportune times.

Hawk glanced upward at the late summer sun, and he went North on Wells until he came across a park and sat down on a bench close to the jungle gym. Dressed as he was, he fit right in with Lincoln Park mothers, fathers, and nannies.

Of course, there were more nannies than mothers. Nannies were charged with taking care of other people's children, good care of them; u unlike Sera, who harbored anger against her husband and her stepchildren, while at the same time making sure they didn't leave that godforsaken place.

Taking a handkerchief from his pocket, he wiped the sheen of sweat from his brow.

The soft steps signaled her presence, before a pair of hands covered his eyes. The lilac scent was all too familiar, as were the softness of the hands and the gentle giggle. His heartbeat sped up. He almost cried with relief. He was home.

"Lizzie."

He grabbed her hands from his eyes and pulled her around. Still holding onto the manicured digits, he drank in her light brown hair, hazel eyes, and the peach silk jumpsuit with a deep neckline draped over her medium frame. She was still the one person that could drive him crazy, just by being herself.

Hawk turned, trying to memorize every detail of how the sun bounced off her high cheekbones, how her eyes twinkled with excitement. If he touched her, he'd bury himself deep inside—again.

All he had to do was lean in, pull her towards him, and feel the caress of her lips against his.

A small, excited shout interrupted them, "Mr. Hawk."

Thank goodness. A few more seconds and he would have had Lizzie straddling his lap regardless of who was around. So he left the bench, walked over to the slide, lowered to his knees in time for Gregory to slip from the silver slide and straight into his arms.

"Hey, Gregory." The boy was a pint-sized dynamo with a great laugh. His hazel eyes twinkled like his mother's. Hawk hugged him hard before placing him down. Everything else about Gregory was the spitting image of his father, making Hawk proud and pained at the same time.

Lizzie joined them. Her giggle turned into a seductive laugh as she watched Hawk spin Gregory around. These precious moments with his family, who now belong to someone else, were like finding an Ice Mountain water factory in the middle of the Sahara Desert. His son thought Tory was his father. The woman he loved was someone else's wife—in name only.

"Hey there."

God, her voice. How the coral outfit hung softly off her narrow shoulders and caressed her breasts, which were barely contained by her bra cup.

That's how they ended up in the park's bathroom over a month ago with one of those same nannies watching Gregory. He and Lizzie had played around over the years.

Lizzie was the one who initiated each time, knowing that an ear nibble or a seemingly innocent brush against his penis was enough to make him crazy with need. Or even words—if anyone knew how to bring a man to life with just her words, it was Lizzie.

Ever since she was married, she always handed him a condom. At first, he would argue, but she had a valid point. He couldn't argue about the fact that the rhythm method hadn't worked for them. Their son was proof of that.

Gregory rushed to the slide as Hawk sat beside Lizzie on the bench. "Hawk," she whispered, lifting the corners of her lips. She settled into the space next to him.

His hands itched to pull her into his lap, but several people were watching. "You look so good."

He rubbed his head. "Well, you know how I do,"

Lizzie threw her head back and laughed. "Yeah, I do."

His gaze lingered on those beautiful, bouncing mounds and then focused on the fullness of her face. You have got to be kidding me. "Marriage seems to agree with you," he whispered. "Or is it the pregnancy? You are pregnant, right?"

Lizzie whipped her head around. "How do you—?"

Hawk hesitated. How could she do it? How could she force him to use a condom only to let her husband, who shouldn't even want to have sex with her, hit it raw?

Really?

CHAPTER 24

Giselle's pace matched the beat of the Jennifer Lopez song blasting through the earbuds, as she ran from her dorm to the off-campus gym. The run, which happened at least four times a week, totaled five miles.

Opening the door let in a bright flash of light, before swallowing the sun and replacing it with artificial lights cast from overhead. The gym smelled of day-old male sweat, and no amount of fans fixed on the ceiling and in the corners moved that stale air around enough to help.

This was the type of gym where people might nod as she walked by; but they never missed a rep count, and that's how Giselle liked it.

When she arrived on the Lexington University campus she'd been thin, but in poor shape.

Once she made the decision to go back and free Hawk, she had to know about more than horseback riding, skiing, archery, fencing, and all the fancy athletic dabbling afforded by her privileged upbringing.

Even she didn't know how bad things were until she started working out. Coming to college, she couldn't manage ten pushups, had no core strength, and the most she could do with her upper body was hold up her B cups.

The golden girls went to the campus gym: the ones who didn't sweat; were never out of breath; and probably didn't eat much more than a kale leaf for breakfast, lunch, and dinner. All of their clothes matched, along with a lot of hair flipping going on.

Giselle tried the spot for a week. But the threat of nausea, brought on by watching the golden girls giggle their way through each workout, made her yearn for a change.

That change came in the form of her martial arts instructor. Since Kim was in phenomenal shape, Giselle gave it a try. A year in, the white-haired instructor pulled her aside and demanded to know, "What are you doing here?"

Wasn't everyone in the dojo for the same reason? She pointed to the poster on the wall. "To learn various forms of martial arts?"

Lee reared his head back and laughed. "You come to class an hour before everyone else."

"I'm a good student."

"You barely work the folds out of one belt before graduating to the next," he commented. "You have a purpose. Tell me about it."

Giselle hadn't trusted anyone with her whole story; not even Kim, when she'd stepped off the train with little more than the clothes on her back and a pocket full of cash. She merely said she had a fight with her new stepmom and couldn't stay in Chicago any longer.

Kim didn't say much about the life Giselle left behind. Occasionally, when money came from Hawk or she talked to Lizzie, Kim's gaze followed Giselle's every move, even when Kim pretended to be studying.

Kim didn't ask. Giselle didn't offer. That was probably the best present that Kim could've given her. However, now that 5-feet 6-inch instructor was asking about her deepest secret.

The things Giselle had planned for when she walked out of Lexington University with an economics degree would make him an accessory to something. She wouldn't bring that on anyone, not even Hawk.

Giselle frowned when she thought of the brother she'd left behind. The yells from the other students fell into the background, as she pondered how much to tell this man. What to do. What to do.

She was sure she could trust him, but to bring him into this; that would make him a witness. If she learned anything from watching Snapped, Criminal Minds and The First 48, it was don't tell anyone your business.

In the Midst of Fire

"Before I left for college, we moved to a new neighborhood—a bad neighborhood, the kind where gunshots rang like church bells daily. I haven't been back and won't go back until after I graduate." Giselle focused on her trainer/sensei/master's eyes. "I have to be ready."

The short, concise nod indicated he understood. "This is different from what we do and what you need." He stalked towards his office, leaving Giselle standing in place with her mouth open.

"Come," he insisted, without breaking his stride.

Giselle scrambled to catch up, then matched his brisk pace as they went into the sparsely furnished office. Shutting the door, he gestured toward a seat. The closed door muffled the shouts and yelling from the other students.

As Giselle took a seat in one of the two grey tweed chairs facing the desk, all she wanted to do was join the rest of the students on the other side of the door. She didn't want to have to answer questions, face her cowardice or her desertion of her brother.

She lived with it; felt the kind of regret that some days felt so heavy she thought her legs would bow under the weight. She didn't want to explain her life to anyone, least of all the miniature man who insisted on getting in her business.

Sensei Lee folded his arms over his lean chest as he stared at Giselle. Not used to this type of appraisal, Giselle figured she had three options. She could squirm, run out the door, or commit to the process.

She'd promised herself that backing down on anything was no longer an option. After taking two deep breaths, she raised her eyes and inquired, "Yes?"

"You require street fighting instruction," he stated. "We don't provide that."

Giselle sat back in her chair, perplexed at the term. "Street fighting?"

Smiling, Sensei Lee leaned in. "When you're in a tournament, you know you have the option of tapping out. No one is intentionally trying to hurt you. They're fighting for points." Leaning back with his hands in a steeple, he continued, "On the street, they want to hurt you, kill you. That's a totally different fighting style."

Giselle wished the blinds over the glass that looked out on the workout area were open. Then she'd have a distraction. Now, she was sitting across from Sensei Lee with nothing else to do or anything to distract her. She just had to feel her way through.

"That's why I'm taking martial arts."

Sensei Lee got up from the chair and leaned his rear end on the front of the desk. "You need a street fighting class—down, dirty, and maybe deadly. You know, your first strike has to count."

Giselle nodded. "That's why I'm here."

"Well . . .," Lee reached behind him and pulled out a flyer, "you should be here."

Giselle took the document from his hands, which told about Bruce's Street Fighting Academy.

"There's a reason why you fight. You fight for a purpose. I'd be wrong not to give you all the resources to reach your destination."

Compared to the dojo, the place on the flyer looked like a dump; or at the very least like it was a staging area for another Rocky movie—*Rocky Twenty-Five, the Ghost of Apollo Creed.*

"This looks . . . hard."

Sensei Lee leaned closer. "Are you scared of hard work?"

Feeling trapped, Giselle stood. That way she had the height advantage working for her. Sensei Lee merely smirked. It was as though he read her mind and confidently retained his relaxed position.

That made Giselle even more nervous, because this street fighting academy looked real. Their flyer didn't have sharp blue mats or clean, even floors. This flyer showed bruised and bloody people grappling with each other. This place wasn't about "pretty" fighting.

Another yell came from outside the door. Tension continued to choke the air out of the office. This wasn't her talking about what she was going to do. This was real training to survive Burnham Park Apartments.

"Have you ever been punched by a raw fist to your face?" Sensei Lee asked in a deceptively soft voice.

Giselle felt like a fraud. All the training she'd done, bouncing around on the mat like a bad ass, using all the great technique she'd learned; and truthfully, even now, two years since she started working out, well into her junior year, she realizes she'd been half-assing it. "I . . . well

. . . no. I haven't."

Sensei Lee continued, "If you were working towards competition, I would have just recommended different classes. But you need more than I can give you."

Standing, he approached Giselle. "You have to capitalize on the fire inside. You have to do more than what you think will help and get the kind of instruction that will actually help."

Giselle took a deep breath, "I'll look into it."

At the beginning of her senior year, she walked through the doors of Bruce's Street Fighting Academy. Four months later, she could now say safely that she was in the best shape of her life; and to answer that question—yes, she had been punched in the face, more than once.

She learned about striking offensively, defense tactics, wrestling fundamentals, and how to stay on her feet; but more importantly—how to get back up after being knocked down.

It would take years to get to the place where she was a true expert, but right now she had an advantage. And that was all she needed to take Sera out.

At least, she hoped so.

CHAPTER 25

Hawk ground the pads of his hands into his eyes. He'd been battling to keep them open for the better part of the night. Midnight had come and passed and he was still in front of his computer working.

The open window allowed a breeze and peace to waft back in forth into the small room. At this time of night/morning, his neighborhood was quiet, resting like any other one. Even the rowdiest hypes had passed out or passed on.

His client needed a new website by the time he arrived in the morning. The problem with working this late was that everything took twice as long. He was constantly second-guessing his process.

The decision-making portion of his brain flipped him the bird around about thirty minutes before midnight. Now he was functioning solely on grit and sheer determination.

This client, a software start-up, was his largest one to date. Hawk had no illusions that he was a great graphic designer or even a web developer. He was good enough to get paid, good enough to be able to put money away, good enough to send money to Giselle.

He needed more. Every time he looked at another magazine cover with Tory Carlson's image displayed across the glossy page, it brought home the fact that the money he brought in would never be enough to support Lizzie. He kept plugging away, and playing the lottery, and praying for a miracle.

Taking a break, he went to his fake Facebook account, which he'd created using a photo from a guy on one of the brochures that Lexington University sent to Giselle. He was officially stalking his own sister. But he couldn't stay away completely. He had to know she was okay.

It had taken him a while to find her online. She hadn't used her given name; instead she used Rose, their mother's name. It made him smile every time he went online.

This time she was tagged in a photo with her roommate Kim, at some type of costume party. They were both dressed as clowns, with Kim holding a spray bottle and Giselle holding silly string.

He'd seen that particular look in her eyes. She was up to some mischief. He would spend a thousand lives with Sera and his dad, if it meant he could keep that look on her face. And he would do it without thought, without complaint.

His father had abdicated responsibility for them the minute the first handful of dirt sifted through Chase's hands onto their mother's coffin. He couldn't do both. He couldn't pretend that he was fine and raise his kids, too.

Hawk had seen the sadness, the depression behind Chase's too bright smile and endless procession of wealthy wives. Those quiet moments when Chase didn't know anyone was looking, when his mask was completely down, Hawk saw how lost his father was.

When Hawk was thirteen, he heard a fateful noise coming from his dad's bedroom. Lizzie and Giselle had gone shopping, so Hawk inched toward the open door. His dad's wall safe was open, and photos of Rose were strewn across the bed. Chase was sitting on the floor with their wedding photo in his hands, using his forefinger to rub at the picture.

"Dad?"

Chase's head snapped up. His mouth open and closed before turning to put his focus on the photos once again. Then his broad shoulders slumped, as though the weight of the boxes were on his back instead of on the bed.

Your mother was so beautiful," Chase whispered. "What the hell did she see in me?"

Hawk lowered himself onto the carpet. Alarmed by the dejected tone in his father's voice, he responded, "You made her happy."

Chase scoffed, "No, she made herself happy, and me and you and Giselle. I didn't deserve it." A pair of piercing dark brown eyes lasered through Hawk. "You're like her. You have her strength, her determination."

Hawk didn't know how to comfort his dad. The parent was supposed to be strong. He was supposed to know what to say and do. Dads didn't leave the knowing to the son. That's not how it was supposed to work.

"Why didn't I go with you?" Chase ran his hand over his shorn hair. "What was so damned important that I couldn't go to the circus with my family? Was it a football game? Laziness?"

By this time, tears were sliding down his father's slightly tanned cheek. "If I'd been driving, she would've been in the passenger's seat. The driver's side took the brunt of the hit."

Chase absently rubbed his face. "You need a parent. You should have two, but you need at least one. I'm so sorry. I can't. I don't know how. Oh my God. I'm such a failure."

At that moment of such a heady confession, Hawk wished he had stayed in his room. He could've increased the volume on his television and drowned the sound of his father's anguish out. He didn't like this broken version of his father. This level of survivor's guilt was excruciating for him to watch.

"Giselle and I are fine. We'll be fine. We have each other." He reached out to pat his dad's knee. "I'll always take care of Giselle. You just take care of you."

Chase went back to the pictures, and Hawk hurried out of the room and into the quiet seclusion of his own bedroom. That was probably the realest moment Hawk ever had with his father.

That's why Hawk understood how Chase and Sera attracted each other. Each was severely damaged in different ways. It would have been easier if Chase was into self-flagellation, because that's all this marriage was—Chase beating himself down every day.

Hawk stretched as he shook that old memory off, and he walked over to the full-sized bed. He didn't have a safe to hide photos like his dad had in the old house.

Hawk taped an envelope underneath the bed, hiding the one photo that meant the world to him, Lizzie and Greg with him at the park. Like his father so many years before, he sat on the floor and gently traced Lizzie's face with his thumb.

The tangled web of depression layered over him. He returned the photo to its hiding place and stood. He didn't have time to wallow. Wallowing would make him like his father. Fuck that.

He reclaimed his seat at the computer and sifted through a few more photos of Giselle before he went back to work. This site wasn't going to build itself.

Neither would his life.

CHAPTER
26

December 2013

Giselle peered out at the packed audience from behind the curtain. She was supposed to be lining up with the other graduates. Instead, she held back, needing a few seconds of peace before taking those steps into her future.

She had worked her ass off at Lexington and managed to graduate a semester early. Summers when Kim would go home or to her parent's martial arts camp, Giselle would be grinding away. Any free time she had was spent honing her own fighting skills.

Having Kim as a roommate had definitely been beneficial. Besides becoming a damn good friend, Giselle didn't have any doubts about her ability to protect herself from anyone, including Sera.

Now she was gazing out at a crowd filled with the excited buzz of parents and family members and friends. Not one of them was there for her. She'd need to prepare herself for the polite applause when her name was announced, which would be a contrast to the shouts and catcalls that the other grads would surely get.

The only person who knew she was graduating early was Lizzie, but she'd been sworn to secrecy. The last time they'd talked early one morning before Giselle's daily run, her best friend had some interesting news to impart and Giselle didn't take it so well.

"Lizzie, what do you mean you're on strike?" Giselle demanded, when she reached out to have a conversation with the one person who was a true tie to Hawk. "You're not talking to us anymore?"

"No, that's not what I mean," Lizzie grumbled. "I want you to talk to each other. Damn it. It's been three-and-a-half years already."

Giselle grabbed the bridge of her nose, trying to alleviate the headache that was slowly thumping against her cranium. "Lizzie, you've got it all wrong. He doesn't talk to me."

A sound in the background signaled that Lizzie had taken a seat somewhere. "I know. Damn testosterone. He thinks he's protecting you. He thinks as long as he doesn't talk to you that Sera won't think you're important to him."

Giselle groaned at the meaning behind those words. "So how is this my fault again?"

"Tell him about Ninja," Lizzie exclaimed.

Giselle stilled. "Nothing to tell." Actually, that was a lie if Giselle had ever let one escape her lips.

"I can't believe you're trying to convince me that it's nothing," Lizzie shrieked. "Every time, and I mean every time, you mention his name, your voice gets all 'ooh baby'."

Giselle scanned the area to make sure no one was listening to her conversation. Giselle rose early each day to stretch out before running. Tory left the house for his job at TJH Global Investments before the sun came up, making it the best time to talk to Lizzie. It worked for both of them.

"What does that mean?" Giselle.

"Oh, you know," Lizzie responded, a triumphant tone in her voice that made Giselle bristle with irritation. "Trust me, you know."

Lowering her voice, she explained, "Once we cleaned up your brother's language, his hoodness became a bit sexy. I have to admit those looks he gives people every now and then, when he's telling them that if they don't keep moving he's going to kick their ass (like he is actually capable of kicking ass); sometimes that's hot," she confessed.

Giselle stretched forward until her head was level to the ground. And then she banged it, because she'd never unhear that. "Lizzie. He's my brother."

"Just saying," Lizzie continued. "So if you told him about Ninja and told him Ninja was cool, maybe they could be cool and he wouldn't feel so damn alone."

Giselle sighed, praying for patience. "Lizzie, Ninja's cool because I'm here and Sera doesn't want anything to do with me. If I come back to Chicago, I don't know whose side Ninja will be on. Our conversations don't erase years of loyalty."

Lizzie harrumphed. "I think Ninja is team Giselle, but I understand that you can't chance it. Hawk can't chance it. No one can take any chances. I think everyone is underestimating everyone, but I'll mind my business."

Finally. "About time."

"I'll even find a place for you to stay when you come back," Lizzie conceded.

Giselle raised her head, perking up at that bit of news. "The condos across from Burnham Park?

"Can't do it," regret laced Lizzie's voice. "Even with the projects across the street, that's a hot address. Nothing's available right now. But the Warner Consortium has a place in Hyde Park you can stay in for now."

Giselle closed her eyes, the images of walking up to Sera on the street and striking her across the face faded to black, replaced with a two-bus ride or a bus-and-a-train ride and squinting to make sure it was Sera wrapped up in winter clothes.

Regardless, she couldn't wait to be home again. "Thanks, Lizzie. I mean it. Thanks so much."

"Whatever," Lizzie grumbled.

Giselle grinned. "Don't be all grumpy, because the romance novel you're spinning isn't going to have a happy ending."

"Well, at least our Giselle is graduating," she exclaimed with her usual perkiness. "I hate that I have to miss it. Can I tell Hawk at least that?"

"Depends. How much will he worry if I'm in the city?" Giselle challenged.

Giselle heard a knock on Lizzie's side of the phone. "Miss . . . you're needed . . . ." Everything else was garbled.

Lizzie came back on the line, sighing, "Duty calls. Get your run in. We'll talk later."

Now feeling alone, Giselle wished she had begged Lizzie to come. She wished she'd told Hawk. She wished someone was there to celebrate.

Suddenly, someone enveloped her in a squealing hug. It didn't take Sherlock Holmes to recognize Kim's enthusiasm. "You're choking me. Aren't you supposed to be out there somewhere?"

The band began to strum up their instruments. Instead of quieting, the buzzing of the audience grew louder.

Kim winked. "Well, that's what happens when they let male students handle security." Lexington wasn't a huge school, and Kim's beauty was legendary on campus. Her compact lean frame, honed from years of training, looked great in everything. Plus, she was probably the nicest person Giselle ever met, besides Lizzie of course.

Giselle and Kim walked arm-and-arm back to the line that Giselle was supposed to be in. At the site of Kim's tears, Giselle held up her hand. "No, no. Don't. Don't do that."

Kim continued, "But I'm here at least a year and a half longer. Instead of spending all those summers hanging with the parentals, I could have been here," she wailed. "Why didn't I take summer classes, too?"

"Because you have a life."

Kim paused and bumped Giselle with her hip. "Well, you got me there." She raised and lowered her eyebrows in her really bad Groucho Marx impersonation. "So a train back to Chi? Promise me you'll come visit me."

Giselle nodded. "I promise." And then she remembered. "And if I get any mail . . . ."

Kim gave her a mock salute. "I'll forward it right away."

Giselle pulled her into a hug. "See you out there."

Kim gave a finger wave to the incredibly high-heeled teacher bearing down on them, who was supposed to ensure only graduates were in the staging area.

The graduation march began, and Giselle put on a fake smile as she fulfilled this last promise to Hawk. Her mind was shifting to what needed to be done. She had to take on Sera Brooks. Giselle would have to be as cold as Sera to survive.

In the Midst of Fire

CHAPTER
27

Hawk and Ninja were standing in their normal location on the block, settled against the Hawk's car. They were surrounded by five other high-ranking members of the crew. NuNu was entertaining them with tales of some girl he had picked up the other night.

"Dude, she was fine as hell—chocolate skin, and a fat ass. Sorta' reminded me of your momma, Hawk."

The group laughed as Ninja elbowed him in the ribs, as if Hawk cared who Sera wrapped her legs around. They always poked fun at him, looking for chinks in his armor. They should know by now, Sera was not it. She was his father's wife and his employer. She didn't factor into his emotions.

He'd always been the kind to hold his emotions close to his vest with everyone except Giselle and Lizzie. When Giselle left, he didn't have anyone. So he shut his emotions down, at least on the block. During the snatches of time he had with Lizzie, he was really free.

Four years ago, he thought the block would swallow him whole and spit out a ghost of his former self. Amazing what he could survive. Here he was talking to the very same men who assaulted him for the sake of brotherhood. NuNu had torn open his sister's blouse, intent on taking what she never offered. And thankfully, Ninja was the one who stopped him.

Now he had to hang out with these fools, like he was one of them, like he had their back. He'd kill any one of them, if Sera hadn't told him what the retribution would be if he got out of line. She'd make sure his father died, slowly and painfully.

Giselle would be next in line.

These were Sera's soldiers, her favorites, the ones she trusted implicitly: Ninja; NuNu; Sweetness, the ladies' man; Mookie, the youngest; Hitta, pure muscle and the most ruthless. Any one of them would slice him open, if that hateful woman asked them to.

"Come on, Hawk," NuNu cajoled. "That was funny. Dude, do you even have a sense of humor?" NuNu watched him closely.

Smiling, Hawk answered as he was expected to, "Only when I'm giving some to your momma, NuNu."

The crew gave a collective, "Ohhh."

"The faces she makes are hilarious," Hawk added.

NuNu dismissed his statement with the wave of a hand. "So, anyway, I'm talking to this girl, right, and her girl shows up. And I'm like, this is it. I'm 'bout to bang both of 'em. So I'm throwing some words at 'em."

Hawk let NuNu's words slide into the background as he concentrated on what was happening on the block. Something was different about today. The police were doing their normal drive-bys, but nothing new. The people on the block were the same ones who made an appearance at some point every day.

He paid particular attention to cars as they passed: nervous-looking white people, driving down Sedgwick in Range Rovers and Cadillacs so big they may have needed their own refueling truck; nervous-looking yuppie Blacks, who scurried around as if they wanted to be away from Burnham Park, lest someone believed they actually lived there.

Turning, he gave a quick look at the red-brick condos across the street. Those were always quiet. Nestled in between a three-story walk-up and overpriced market that sold necessities, and only at the highest prices they felt they could get away with. Highway robbery. Every now and again someone would holler at someone down the street.

Something was unsettling. The air was different—stifling.

In the Midst of Fire

He sniffed, hoping to figure out what it was.

Ninja inspected him. "What the hell you sniffing for?"

Hawk slowly turned to face the mysterious man. "Nothing, dude. Maybe I'm coming down with something, I don't know."

"Don't be passing that shit on to me."

Hawk gave a reassuring hitch of his head. "I'm good."

Ninja's eyes narrowed to slits as though assessing the risk. "Um hmm."

NuNu was still talking about the girls who took him back to their house up on the west side. Knowing NuNu, his evening probably ended with his spiking their drinks. NuNu didn't care about how he got some ass, just that he got it.

Hawk didn't make it a point to hang out with him. but there were too many rumors, too many women that looked at NuNu with fear in their eyes; too many women that crossed the street when they saw the man for Hawk not to believe there was some semblance of truth in the swirling accusations.

NuNu's lazy posture remained, but his eye twitched—the only indication that he'd entered the lying portion of his storytelling for the evening.

Hawk waited a few seconds. The minute NuNu said, "Swear to God," a whopper of a lie was certain to follow. You'd think the boy would realize his tell. Hell, they all had them. Mookie would scuff his shoe. Hitta would nod emphatically, as if he was trying to convince someone to believe him. Some—like Ninja—were better at hiding theirs than others. Hawk hoped his was more like that. Hidden.

NuNu lifted his right hand. "Swear to God."

A wisp of air whizzed by Hawk's left ear. Time stopped. Sound ceased. NuNu was standing, his hand still raised. But an arrow was sticking through it—a real arrow, like archery kind of shit.

NuNu let out an unnaturally long screech that echoed as if the block had been dropped into the Grand Canyon. Ninja, Hitta, and Hawk crouched, pulling out their pieces, scanning for the threat.

People scattered to their homes. Half of them probably didn't even know why they were running. With the kind of noise erupting from NuNu's lying lips, the best course of action was to get that ass to safety first and ask questions later.

Hawk's heart slammed against his chest. That arrow had whizzed by his ear. It could have exploded in his scalp. Was it meant to? Needles, knives, now arrows—had Sera gone back on her word? Hawk took deep breaths, as he maneuvered behind the I-Roc.

Using the heavy steel to block his body. He shifted his gaze to the buildings across the street. No movement. Only a man on the sidewalk with an arrow through his hand, screaming like a bitch.

That was . . . that didn't happen. It just didn't happen—not here on the north side.

"Damn it. Someone get NuNu out of here," Hawk shouted. "Now!"

Mookie dragged NuNu's narrow frame into the nearest building.

Ninja peaked over the hood of the I-Roc. "Man, what do you see?"

It wasn't a big secret that Hawk's sight was better than 20-20.

"Nothing's moving. Come on."

Ninja, Hitta, and Hawk ran past the cars, and kept low as they crossed the street and quickly made it to the condo buildings. Ninja took everything on the left; Hitta peeped through the window of the middle entrance.

Think . . . think. The only hiding place on his side was the courtyard of a house. Hawk walked up the to the wrought-iron gate and perused for movement. The gate was closed and locked. He waited to see if anything changed or shifted. It didn't.

Hitta and Ninja were shaking people down on the street, trying to figure out who in the hell declared war on the Knights, in broad daylight.

Police cars appeared from several directions. Hawk stashed his gun in the lower part of his back and rushed to the opposite end of the block. Three black guys running around with guns drawn would not be received well, but he would only ditch it if necessary. He met up with Ninja and Hitta a couple of blocks over.

Ninja's lips tightened like he was trying to keep a garbage truckload of words from spilling out. "They're taking NuNu to the hospital. I didn't get anything. You two?"

Both Hitta and Hawk threw their hands up.

"Hide your guns so 5.0 don't have a reason to drag us in," he commanded. "We have to give Sera an update."

In the Midst of Fire

Hawk put both hands on his head. "Shit, man. I felt it pass my head. Felt it! It was that close."

Ninja pulled his arm down so it landed by Hawk's side again. "Come on. We need to get back."

Hawk took a deep breath. Was this how he was going to die? An arrow through the head? The same feelings that came over him earlier had returned full force. Hawk shivered like someone had just stepped on his grave.

Stepped? Hell, they stomped on the bitch.

CHAPTER
28

The pounding on the door forced Sera to sit upright, her heart racing like a Ferrari on the Autobahn. She wiped a hand over her face to wipe the sleep from her eye. She wasn't used to sleeping during the day, but her allergies were flaring up. Instead of her normal allergy medicine, Hawk had "accidently" brought back another brand, which had her down for the count. Like he couldn't tell the difference between lime green packaging and the bright pink of the other.

Now the maniac pounding at her door was forcing her from a much-needed rest. "I'm coming," she yelled, snatched a T-shirt on her bed, and added it to her jean-clad body.

She opened the door to find Ninja, who almost bowled her over in his rush to get inside the apartment. She leaned out and looked down the hall. Hawk and Mookie were trotting towards the door. All of them, at her place, at this hour. Something had definitely gone wrong.

Sera slowly turned to Ninja. "What the hell happened?"

Although Ninja was standing still, his body was reverberating with energy. "Someone got NuNu."

"Got?" Sera turned to face the other two who had slipped into the room. "Close my damn door."

Mookie rushed to comply.

"And tell me what the hell is got?" Sera demanded. "Shot? Kidnapped? What happened?"

Hawk sank into the cushions of the couch, resting his forearms on his knees. Sera whirled to face Ninja. "I *said* what the hell is got?"

Ninja's eyes pierced hers, as he explained, "Someone shot him through the hand with an arrow."

Sera's head snapped to Hawk and Mookie. Both of them were looking down, as though the weave of the carpet held all the answers to what had transpired. Ninja's eyes were still focused entirely on her. "Who the hell uses arrows?"

Ninja pulled at his chin, deep in thought. "Olympians and rich people." Ninja's mouth drew up into a fierce grin. "No one that we've run into, have run with, or have rolled up on uses arrows."

He shook his head. "You're lucky if they shoot a gun straight. Arrows? That's some new shit."

Sera went into the kitchen, her mind bouncing. Her men were correct, which meant there was a new player on the block. She gripped the edge of the kitchen window and looked down at the alley. People were talking in groups, pointing to the block.

If she didn't protect the Knights' interests at Burnham Park, she'd be worse off than when she came crawling back four years ago. Dead weight didn't survive on the street. Dead weight was cut off and left to die. "Find them," she commanded. "Kill them. Leave their bones for the dogs."

Ninja gave a slight bow and eased out of the door. Mookie lumbered behind him.

Hawk glared at Sera, the resentment he normally kept under a layer of indifference rolled off of him and slammed into Sera so hard that she gasped. The air was so thick with hatred she almost choked on it.

Steeling her composure, she folded her arms across her chest. "You're not afraid of a little death, are you Hawk?"

Hawk pushed himself up to his full height. "Not at all. If something happens to me, I'm going to be the ghost that haunts your ass each and every remaining day of your life." Smiling, before cloaking his emotions once more, he added, "I'm looking forward to it."

CHAPTER 29

Hawk needed to disappear.

He slipped into a pair of gym shoes and jogging pants and hit the block for a run. In four years, he'd never run in the neighborhood. It's not what people did, unless the police were on their heels. But he wasn't from the neighborhood. And he'd almost gotten shot with an arrow today.

He headed over to North Avenue beach and jogged along the Lake Michigan concrete path. The area was littered with joggers, bikers, and tourists who only managed to get in his way. He tried to let the soft breeze from the lake calm him, but it was impossible.

One inch and that arrow would have been planted in his brain. He could've been dead; a vegetable—whatever. Brought on by the fact that he was involved in something that had no defined rule, he hated depending on Sera for anything, much less to keep him alive. Every day it was getting harder to maintain the cloak of indifference.

Right now, if life was fair, he would be walking across the stage with his bachelor's degree in hand. Giselle had tried to make that happen on many occasions.

Soon, though. The moment he saw a Facebook photo of her with a cap and gown, he was walking out of that apartment and never looking back.

This double life had worn him to the core: long nights of programming, days of forced politeness. And it had changed him in ways he hadn't recognized.

In the beginning, Lizzie would hate meeting up with him.

"When did you start cursing like this?" she asked him one day when they were at North Avenue beach. "Every other word is an "F" bomb. What the hell?"

He thought about those words for a moment. "I'm sorry," he whispered, stroking a hand over her silky arm. "It's just trying to be like the other guys."

"By pretending that you don't have a real vocabulary?" she queried, her hazel eyes flashing with anger.

"Trying not to stick out, not to get shot." Hawk rubbed his faded hair. "I don't even realize I'm doing it anymore."

Lizzie was quiet for a minute; then she locked a gaze on him. "You're changing."

Hawk rested his chin on her head. "I'm trying not to."

A cheer erupted from the patrons seated in a restaurant on the beach. The clinking of glass along with the raucous laughter gave indication that Chicago was celebrating another summer.

This Chicago could do exactly that. In the projects, summer meant an increase in violence. Burnham Park apartments was no different.

Hawk slowed his stride on the concrete path, then headed over to the sandy areas. He plopped down and focused on the waves flowing in and out.

A pair of children were running around the sand with a golden retriever. The dog barked occasionally, happy to be playing a game of tag.

Happiness is such an elusive emotion these days. He watched those around him who personified the sunshine streaming from the sky. One thing he knew for sure—he didn't realize how good he had it until it was wrenched away from him.

He was damn proud of his associate's degree, and it was a right step toward finishing his degree in marketing and making the kind of money that could sustain a household.

It didn't compare to the millions that Tory had in his bank account; but Tory had started with an overflowing bank account. Hawk was forced to do everything himself.

In the Midst of Fire

He had applied to a school in North Dakota and got in by himself. And now he had to find a way to convince Lizzie to leave her mother, her husband—and for all intents and purposes—Gregory's father and his money behind, and take a chance on being with Hawk.

As soon as he figured out the housing situation and the finances to back his play, he'd approach her with his new plans. She had to know that he could take care of his family. She had said it took strength to stay put to secure Giselle's future. Giselle wasn't the only one whose future he was determined to secure.

Leaning back on his elbows, Hawk closed his eyes and lifted his head to the sun, letting the warm rays caress his skin. His thoughts shifted to his future right before someone plopped down next to him. He stiffened, preparing to fight, but didn't move.

A familiar voice penetrated his psyche. "You should be more careful. Chicago isn't as safe as it used to be."

Immediately, his body relaxed. He smiled. He yearned to open his eyes and shout for joy, but years had passed.

He knew that if he opened his eyes, he'd follow that voice anywhere. And he would lose more than he had gained. Keeping the status quo kept his father alive, Lizzie, their son. Changing anything would guarantee someone would die. He didn't have the luxury of making those kinds of decisions. He lost that luxury years ago when Giselle left.

Even with that thought, not opening his eyes was costing him his very soul. For a second he luxuriated in the feel of the ache. He thought he had lost his soul the day Giselle had walked out of his life; or maybe when he was forced to threaten innocent people; could have been when he walked away from Tate's lifeless body and went on about his day.

It was comforting knowing that somewhere deep, the essence of him still existed, that his soul could ache. The pain felt good.

Hawk heard a screech and a splash. It brought him back to the issue at hand. "What do you want?"

"You look good."

Hawk smiled. "That doesn't answer my question. You have no idea what it's like in Burnham Park. This game you're playing . . .

"It's not a game."

Hawk continued as if he hadn't heard the response. "It'll get us all killed." He quickly hopped up and turned to continue his jog.

Hawk paused as he inhaled the seaweed from the lake and the sweet mango scent of his companion. "I'm glad to know you're here. Now leave. She will kill my whole family just because she can. You . . . You? She'd relish in making me suffer if she saw you."

He picked up speed, letting his Nikes slap the concrete in rapid succession, letting the laughter, chatter, and happiness fill his senses instead of the person he was leaving behind.

CHAPTER 30

Sera stomped down Sedgwick. Tension filled the air. NuNu's hand required major surgery, then some form of physical therapy. Thank goodness for County Hospital or his hand would be useless for anything other than waving in parades.

Now, they only had to figure out who would dare do such a thing.

Familiar faces were giving her the side eye. Most people thought she was crazy since that Kevin incident. The story had blown from him screaming while she cut him (which she did) to her laughing manically while she cut (which she didn't remember happening).

It worked well for her since folks tended to leave crazy people alone. Was this assault on NuNu personal to him or her? Either way, she'd have to respond; otherwise, the Knights and her enemies would think she was weak.

"V, what's up with you?" She ran towards him and gave him a hug. "It's been a minute. Where have you been?"

"Down South. Just got back yesterday." Vincent scanned Sera's body before adding, "Heard you had a little trouble?"

Sera examined the nuances of Vincent's response, but read amusement in his eyes the color of a Hershey's kiss. "Did you hear? Or did you kick off that trouble?"

"Wasn't me. Wasn't my style." Vincent placed his foot on the low metal fence surrounding a tree. His head tilted in her direction. "But then, you already know that."

She figured it wouldn't be that easy. "What have you heard?"

Vincent inspected his Adidases, forcing her to wait for his response. "I don't think it's any of the usuals." He assessed her closely, almost as if he was accusing her of some unspoken crime, "Y'all must've pissed someone off real good."

Sera scanned the street. Cars rumbled past, bouncing over one errant pothole or another. Children were screeching as they chased each other around. Brave little souls, especially given what had happened earlier today.

"This has to be a completely new player."

Vincent smirked, "A good player with an arrow. Ain't a lot of those around here." He turned as a school bus bounded down the street, probably on its way to the garage, since it was emptied of passengers.

He focused his attention back on Sera, "You know, I would be happy to protect you . . . if?"

He let that if linger. Sera could fill in all the blanks following that if: if she became his girl, if she let him love her, if she loved him. He'd been throwing that if out in the air since she was sixteen. She hadn't snatched it up yet.

"V, we've worn a hole in that discussion."

He tugged her shirt to bring her closer to him. "That old pretty boy ain't the one for you. You should see him running through the hood as if the hounds of hell are at his heels."

Sera's jaw tightened as he threw back his head and laughed. "He can't handle you."

Sera leaned forward, whispering, "He handles me just fine."

Folding her arms over her breasts, she glanced up to see some of the older busybodies in their respective windows watching their exchange. Nosy bats needed some business of their own.

Vincent's smirk turned to a snarl. "You settled and don't even know it. You need someone who can watch your back, count your money, and keep those asses in line. I'm that nigga."

In the Midst of Fire

He leaned over slightly to the left as if wanting to make sure each sound that escaped his lips made it directly into her ear canal. "That little security detail you put together is a'ight. But they ain't about you. They 'bout watching the block. You want someone that's going to be. About. You."

He pointed, punctuating each syllable. "I'm that nigga. And the sooner you realize that, the sooner was can stop this bullshit game we've been playing for years." Vincent grazed her arm with his knuckles. "You're mine, ma."

Pulling back, Sera gave Vincent a onceover. She turned to leave and took five steps when Vincent yelled after her, "What's he gonna do with all that fire?"

Fuck. The busybodies' phones were probably blowing up.

Sera spun back around to face him. "Not your problem, V." She stomped down the street. Vincent always managed to piss her off. They could talk for ten seconds or ten minutes, and by the end, she was ready to punch him. Always.

The fact that he was right didn't matter. Chase was soft. That's what she liked about him—soft hands, soft demeanor, and controllable. Vincent represented everything she was trying to escape.

She'd seen him choke out a dude with his bare hands—relishing the act as the man took his last breath. On the flip side, he'd seen her knife work on more than one person. They were definitely a deadly match.

In all truth, Vincent would be a hell of a lot more useful than Chase. Vincent held a top spot in the Knights' organization. He always kept his ear to the ground to immobilize any threat to her.

She had to know if what happened today was because of something NuNu had done, or if her past had come back to haunt her. No, that couldn't be. Maybe NuNu was more trouble than he was worth.

It might be time to cut her losses—literally.

CHAPTER
31

North of North.

On Sedgwick that's all it took. South of North Avenue there were pockets of prosperity, but also pockets of destruction and despair. However, walking north towards Lincoln Park changes perspective. Seems minor, but every real estate agent in the business knew the difference.

Chase wondered about the little things that made such a big difference: a block, a wrong choice, a missed opportunity, a left turn instead of a right. Was life that fickle? that random? If he had driven his family to the circus instead of staying home, would Rose be alive today.

If he had stayed at the Bellagio instead of Aria, he'd be married to Cathy now instead of Sera. Or looking further back, maybe the universe was paying him back for every selfish choice he had made.

He shouldn't have married women solely because of their bank accounts or dumped them because of their lack of one. One in particular still haunted him. Lizzie's mother. He never should've dated her with their kids being so close.

Raquel Warner was an amazing woman—smart, feisty, and inventive. He thought she'd be his next wife. She had probably, mentally, already picked out the ring. She'd been thirsty to remarry after being alone for so many years.

For some reason, she never managed to walk down that aisle. For her, it was all about Disney-inspired love. For him, it was all about common cents.

She treated his children like they were her own. A marriage between them was almost the perfect situation—almost, until the truth came out. Truth always follows orgasms. And anyone who says differently has never had an orgasm . . . at least not one from him.

The last time they were together, Raquel began to spin the fairytale of their relationship.

"I mean it's perfect, really. I've known the kids so long, I feel like they're my own."

Chase smiled and kissed the top of her well-tousled hair. "You do really love my kids."

"Not just the kids," she whispered, "I love you, too. And one day Hawk and Lizzie will get married, and we'll be grandparents together. And all my money worries will be over."

Money worries? Chase chuckled as a sliver of alarm went through him. "What are you talking about? Your husband was loaded."

Raquel lightly raked her purple nails back and forth across his chest; the move didn't bring the kind of pleasure it once did. "For some reason, he didn't trust me with any of it.

He left everything to Lizzie. I have an allowance, of course. And there are stipulations in the will." She looked up at him, probably failing to see the panic in his eyes as she finished with, "For all intents and purposes, the real money is Lizzie's."

Chase felt the dots of perspiration on his brow. Yeah, Raquel was beautiful; but she was broke. With his tax issues, he needed to refill the bank accounts before he ended up back where he started . . . the projects.

Raquel obviously was not the route. It was a shame really. He did enjoy her so. But he'd already had the love of his life. Now he was strictly looking for companionship and cash. One without the other wouldn't do.

"You know, Raquel," he said, extracting himself from her hold. "I think you're a really special woman."

She sat straight up with the cover clutched around her chest. "Chase . . . ."

"Maybe we are going a bit fast," he confessed. "I mean, with the kids and all. Maybe we should take it slower."

She tensed. "It's the money, isn't it," she queried. "You didn't say anything about how quickly we were moving a second ago. Matter of fact, a second ago you were going like a piston in a brand new Porsche."

Chase closed his eyes, realizing he should have handled everything much differently. "Listen, you don't understand. I just think that maybe our families are too close. You're like a second mom to Giselle. She lost hers so young."

Blowing out a breath, Raquel shot back, "Shouldn't that work in our favor?"

Chase's mind churned, trying to come up with an excuse that would sit well with her. "My track record since my first marriage hasn't been good."

He paused and ran his knuckles down her face. She leaned into his touch. "I can't risk the kids."

Her voice quivered ever so slightly, causing his heart to harden. "Chase, is it the money?"

Kissing her forehead, he answered, "Let's give it until the kids leave for college. Leave it until they're on their own. Then we can do this right." He grasped her hand. "Just give me time."

Three months after that, he married Sera—the poorest one out of the bunch.

Now he's looking up at the grand homes that he'd never reside in again. He didn't deserve to. He had lived behind the promise to his grandmother. Actually, he'd hidden behind it like a shield.

He used it to absolve himself of guilt for the way he managed to stay out of the projects. She would never have supported the lying and manipulating he'd done over the years. Hell, she would've popped him upside the head for thinking half the stuff he'd done.

The sun showed signs of sinking, and he preferred to be in the safety of his apartment—her apartment—before darkness crept all the way in. Turning around to retrace his footsteps, a young woman ahead of him made him pause. She looked familiar.

As her walk turned into a jog, his mind screamed the name that he

In the Midst of Fire

dared not to think about all this time. Her skin tone, the cinnamon-colored natural hair, her gait. everything added up to one thing . . . .

Giselle was home.

Picking up his pace, he shouted, "Giselle."

The woman didn't turn around.

The closer he came he noticed the bob of a cord from her ears to her waist. Headphones. Chase would never catch up to her at the slow pace he'd managed. He broke out into a full run. Half a block in, he was panting like an asthmatic dog in the middle of a heat wave. Damn, he was out of shape.

One block in, a stitch in his side nearly caused him to collapse. Giselle was back! He wasn't going to let unbearable pain stop him.

"Giselle, Giselle!"

She stopped at a light on North Avenue. Finding another gear, he forced his body to go faster than it had in about ten years. He finally caught up with her and grabbed her arm as he struggled to gain his breath. "Giselle."

The woman turned, snatching her arm away. "What the hell?" She yanked her earbuds out. "Get away from me, you freak."

Fuck. That wasn't Giselle. But from behind, from behind, she looked . . .; it could have been Giselle's twin. Well, other twin. People stared. Two bulky white guys, with so many muscles their shoulders touched their cheeks, rushed towards them.

Flabbergasted, Chase said, "I'm so sorry." Pant. "I thought you were someone else." Pant. Pant. "Sorry." Backing up with his hands held up, indicating he meant no harm.

Burly guy number one lumbered close. "Dude, you can't just grab women on the street like that."

Chase couldn't eek one more word out of his mouth, so he plopped down on the concrete trying to catch his breath.

"Dude, is he having a heart attack?" asked burly guy number two.

Chase shook his head and tried to manage his breathing to slow down his heart rate. The lady who appeared ready to punch him a minute earlier was now bending down beside him. "Do you need an ambulance?"

"No. No. Fine," he managed. After a minute, he added, "I'm so sorry. I thought you were someone else."

Giving her his most engaging smile, he continued, "It was never my intention to scare such a beautiful young lady."

Burly guy number one cracked up laughing and held out his hand. "The old guy is flirting. That definitely means he's okay."

Chase took the man's extended hand and allowed himself to be hauled up to his feet. The small crowd dispersed.

Physically he was fine, but something inside of him broke. What if that had been Giselle? What did he have to offer his only daughter that was different than four years ago? Nothing. He had stayed in the exact same place, doing the exact same thing, leaving her to make her own way in the world.

What if he had a heart attack after that run? Hawk would be left with Sera, stuck in purgatory—forever.

He spent years wandering aimlessly in and out of the various rooms of the Burnham Park apartment. He hadn't tried to seduce a new rich widow. He hadn't visited any old haunts. He hadn't done anything. What should have been a minor setback had become his self-imposed prison sentence.

Losing Rose's house, and then losing Giselle, made him a loser. He'd been living like a loser ever since.

That was over.

CHAPTER 32

Chase stood in the kitchen looking for something to drink, when Hawk walked through the door. He wanted to walk to him, tell him about seeing almost Giselle.

Hawk didn't talk to him these days. Disdain pulsated from Hawk's eyes every time they connected with Chase. That made Chase pause. He wanted to have a plan, a real plan before he approached his son.

Hawk must have felt Chase's eyes, because he turned, assessed him with the kind of gaze that should have been reserved for a skunk that had already lifted his tail; then Hawk walked into his bedroom without saying a word.

Chase grabbed the bottled water out of the refrigerator. That was yet another way he failed his children. Where did Hawk learn the look he just gave? When did he pick up that level of hatred? Rose didn't have a hateful bone in her body, not a single one.

He still remembered the call that he received from Hawk the day of the accident, which had changed their lives.

"Dad?"

The wavering voice on the other end of the line made him sit straight up. He wiped his eyes and tried to focus on the numbers of the clock. How long had he been asleep? He just meant to rest his eyes for a minute. Now, his son was calling. Sounding . . . scared. Hawk was the more daring of his children. Scared was not part of his vocabulary.

"Dad?" The strength was waning, and in its place a water-filled whisper sniffled through the phone.

"Hawk? Hawk!" He bolted from the couch. "What happened? Hawk, what happened?"

"Sir?" Hawk's voice was replaced with a different male voice, full of sympathy while still reeking with authority. And it terrified Chase to the point where he was shaking while he paced.

"Yes. Y-yes … Yes. I'm here," Chase stammered.

"Is this Chase Glen?"

"Yes, what's going on?" Chase demanded. "Please tell me what happened to my family."

"Sir, there was an accident."

Chase's mind raced. Something obviously was wrong. Hawk called him. Rose had not. Rose. Giselle. "My wife? My daughter?"

"Sir."

"No," Chase snapped, running his hands over his faded hair. "I want to speak to my wife and my daughter, right now!"

"Sir, your family is at Cushman Hospital," the man said. "Is there someone who can bring you?"

"Is my family alright?"

"We can send a car."

"I don't need a damn car. I've got my own goddamn car," he yelled. "I need my goddamn family."

Chase slammed the phone down before the man could say anything else. He had to believe his family was alive and well. He had to believe that it was just minor scrapes and scratches. If there was a God, his family would greet him when he walked through the hospital door.

He thought his grandmother's death was how bad his life got, but he was gravely mistaken.

Seeing his wife's lifeless body, without her joy, without her spirit, without her essence, was enough to fell him. Looking at his children, broken in body and spirit, drowning in a despair that sucked them down like quicksand, had only made him want to succumb to his despair.

Picking out a casket, watching waves of people from the area, and listening to family friends offer him condolences, left him bereft, trying to gather the pieces of his shattered life and glue them back into some semblance of normalcy.

Everything was compounded by a steadily dwindling bank account and the realization that he was not man enough to protect Rose; nor was he man enough to ensure her legacy, Rose's inheritance, was stable enough to support her children. And that was his only job.

How do you look at your children and tell them you don't have a dime to your name? And subsequently, those children, who had been born and bred into a life without worries, were now as destitute as he was.

Yeah, life could get worse.

Had Rose's death stolen Hawk's joy? No, no. Some of his happiness had lost its sheen, but over the years Hawk had Lizzie.

Hawk's breakup with Lizzie was another disappointment set on Chase's doorstep. If he hadn't been broke up with her, or if he hadn't screwed Raquel over, Raquel wouldn't have demanded that the two children separate, even though they were truly in love—almost as in love as he had been with his Rose.

Hawk lost his girlfriend. Giselle lost her best friend. Chase had lost every bit of cash reserves. Then he lost Giselle, and it seemed Hawk as well. No one had anything that mattered.

Chase went to the living room and dropped on the couch. One issue at a time: The first issue was managing to get his son out of the projects. That was priority No. 1. Reconnecting with Giselle was priority No. 2. Getting some type of job would be priority No. 3.

CHAPTER
33

Hawk smiled at the excited voices of children at play, children without a care beyond getting up the ladder and back down the slide. He drew a circle in the gravelly dirt with his foot, thinking about the decision he made.

His father had been acting weird when he left, but Chase he couldn't figure out if this was another version of the Chase that had emerged when they moved into the projects or if something else happened.

How could Hawk possibly turn back time and just run away with Lizzie the minute she found out she was pregnant with Gregory? He should live life by his own choices, and not be pulled around by his dick based on the decisions of others.

A light female voice interrupted his musing. "Well, Mr. Graduate. How are you doing?"

Normally his heart would soar. Today it dropped. Lizzie's son Gregory ran past with a quick wave on his way to the slide and his friends.

Hawk barely managed to lift his fingers to return a wave before he answered, "It's an associate's degree. No big deal."

Eyes sparkling with pride, Lizzie handed him a small gift-wrapped box. "I beg to differ. Yeah, it took your four years, but you did it. And you did it without any help or support from your dad or that woman."

Hawk opened his mouth again to protest. But before he could say one word, Lizzie went on, "And you've sent Giselle money"

Hawk raised his eyes to the heavens for help. "Lizzie. It's—"

"Nope." Lizzie shook her head to stop his denial. "It's an accomplishment that we're going to recognize. Now open your present."

Conceding defeat, Hawk peeled open the wrapping paper to reveal a pair of University of Phoenix socks. Unfettered laughter pushed past his normal reserve, until he was doubled over with it.

They had discussed how he couldn't wear any paraphernalia from his school. Yes, she'd found a way to do it so that no one would know. *God he loved this woman.*

Lizzie slid onto the bench next to him. He pulled her into an awkward side hug, while watching to make sure Gregory was distracted by his playing. Though it pained him, he asked, "And how are you feeling today."

She scrutinized him a moment before whispering, "I'm doing well, really good."

Hawk itched to reach out for a full body-to-body hug, drag her into his lap, and kiss her senseless. Instead, he merely rubbed his hands together and commented, "He deserves a brother or sister. It's time."

Lizzie merely looked at him as though trying to figure him out.

Hawk kept up with Giselle online. Even though her posts were few and far between and never gave the details he yearned for, it was enough for him to create a countdown clock. He knew she'd be free soon. As soon as she was free, he would be, too. His father be damned.

Free to do what? He had no idea. Even if he saved enough to float him, Lizzie, and Greg until he found a decent job, what the hell was he going to do with an additional mouth. The reality was, he wasn't sure if he would have been able to support Lizzie and Gregory alone.

"And your husband?" Hawk ventured, even though the thought to mention Tory made him clench his teeth. "He has to be excited."

Her grip tightened on the bench. What was that about?

Her shoulder relaxed and she gave him an unconvincing, "Yes, he is."

Hawk remained silent, watching his son play on the jungle gym. Never one to walk when he could run, Gregory almost wiped completely out while running. Hawk stood a bit as the boy stumbled, then sat down as Gregory righted himself and kept going.

Hawk could barely stand the pain slicing randomly through his soul. He had almost walked away. But that would've been like pulling his beating heart out of his chest. There was no winning this constant struggle within his mind to set them free or keep them close. So he had stayed.

"It must be hard for you," Hawk whispered.

Lizzie brushed a leaf from her lap and shifted her gaze to Hawk. "What must be hard?"

"Living this life. Letting me come here to see him." He rubbed his hands together, trying to generate energy for the conversation he didn't want to have. "This wasn't our plan."

Shrugging, Lizzie replied, "Plans change. He loves it. So it's not a hardship."

Hawk absorbed the nuances of emotion flittering on her face, seeking any indication of how she must be feeling. "Is it a hardship for you? coming here?. Does it cause problems?"

Lizzie gazed up at the sun, taking seconds with her reply. "Would it be easier if my husband fathered my son?" Taking a deep breath, she studied her wedding ring. "Of course. But he knew going in that he wasn't the father. So . . ."

Hawk watched the little boy who mirrored him in looks at that age, except he had Giselle's energy. Poor Lizzie didn't know that he would only get busier as he got older.

Hopefully, he also took after Giselle when it came to intelligence and dedication; as opposed to himself, who played his way through school. If so, he would go far, much further than his father ever had. At least, he hoped Giselle was living her dreams. One of them had to.

"Lizzie, tell me the truth."

Lizzie frowned.

"Would it be easier if we stopped doing this? if I stopped coming around?"

Lizzie's sad smile broke his heart. "I thought so. At first, it hurt so much to see you and not be with you. But at the same time . . ." She brushed a gentle hand over his face. "You were my sun. Every happy thought, I wanted to share with you. Every sad thought . . . even if you caused it, I wanted to share with you."

Hawk stilled, but didn't comment, as her words mirrored his thoughts exactly.

"I can't live without you in my life. I just can't." She gently hooked her pinkie with his. "So if this is the only way for it to happen, then so be it."

Hawk stared at their joined fingers. "I should leave you alone. I should have let you go years ago."

"I should leave you alone," Lizzie replied, her voice cracked. She cleared her throat before continuing. "It can't be easy walking over here, sneaking around so that no one will know, keeping his very existence from your dad, not being able to share every milestone with anyone but me."

Hawk held up his hand to halt any further discussion, but she merely took it in hers and pulled it down into her lap.

"To have to discuss my life with my husband, knowing that it was supposed to be you. Most days, I know I'm causing you unbearable pain. I don't know the right answer or the right mix."

Hawk felt something in his chest crack open, and the love he had kept tamped down for years burst through. "You're the right mix for me—always."

For a very precious second, Lizzie put her head on his shoulder. Hawk inhaled her floral scent. Money wasn't everything. What they had together was way more. Would Lizzie agree and leave with him?

A child shrieked, and a nanny screamed, breaking the mood.

Lizzie and Hawk jumped apart.

Lizzie gave him more than he bargained for when she uttered, "Well, you're the right mix for the twins that I'm carrying."

Twins. Hawk gave his head a mental shake. "Wait. Twins."

Grinning, Lizzie answered, "Yeah, I hear they run in your family."

Hope and love warred with fear, as his top emotion behind that admission. "We used protection."

"Why do you think we always used my condoms?"

Standing, Hawk wanted to scream at the injustice of it all; and at the same time, he wanted to drop to his knees and revel in the beauty of the children she carried, their children. "Lizzie, how could you? I've been struggling for years, years trying to find a way to support us. Three of us, and you do this. You know I can't ...."

Lizzie sat motionless. When she raised her eyes, they reflected years of pain that he'd never seen. She aged before his eyes. "We've done it your way. For years, I let you try to 'figure things out.'" Lizzie pointed to Gregory. "I let my son live a lie. I'm so proud of who fathered my child, my children."

He kneeled beside her on the bench, unable to face her while trying to get his bearings. He felt eyes on them, but he didn't dare turn around. "Lizzie, I—"

"Shut up and listen," she snapped. "I made mistakes, too. I never should have married Tory. I can live with that," taking a deep breath while Hawk held his. Lizzie hissed, forcing power in each whispered syllable. "But it's time you either piss or get off the pot. You're either their father or you're not."

Hawk stood. He had nothing to give her or them at this point. As he lifted his eyes, a bunch of adults shifted their gaze, pretending that they hadn't watched the exchange, even though Lizzie spoke low enough to impede eavesdropping on the conversation. She deserved a response, something better than "one day."

"Listen, Lizzie…"

A sensation crept up Hawk's arm before the deep voice echoed around him like the tendrils of an octopus wrapping around him to make Hawk their dinner, a voice belonging to a man that he'd spent countless miles trying to avoid.

"So this is where you're always disappearing to?"

Fear drowned out the happier sounds from the children in the park. Hawk turned, prepared to fight, prepared to kill, if he was given no other choice. Damned if he wasn't going to protect his family.

CHAPTER 34

Chase sat on the couch pretending to watch *The First 48* on television. Sera puttered around in the kitchen, fixing lunch. The rain beat a drum solo against the window. He closed his eyes. Rain always made him think of his Giselle.

Giselle was a naturalist. She was the first one to run out and play in the very rain that kept most people indoors.

No matter what age, the pure joy on her face, as she tracked barefoot in the backyard, was something to behold.

A constant dull ache was a constant companion to losing a child. It stayed, thrumming like a steady heartbeat. Each syllable pulsated, "Fail-ure. Fail-ure."

Hawk's presence would help, but even his pupils beat to the same ache. "Failure." The only person who looked at him with something other than disdain was Sera. She was all he had left.

He was a kept man. Though she didn't keep him at the levels of his previous wives, she never asked when he was going to get a job.

She didn't ask where her money went. She didn't ask anything. His presence seemed to be enough for her. Her eyes didn't dim with disappointment like his exes.

All he deserved was Sera. She was as damaged as he was. His children deserved something better from life than him as an anchor holding them down. So the day Hawk told him Giselle had left, Chase felt an instant of relief.

Hawk would always look out for his sister. Hell, he did a better job as her father than Chase. That didn't mean that it didn't hurt, every single day. And it didn't keep him from missing the sight of GiselleGiselle twirling in the rain.

He had only spoken with his daughter twice since she left. That first time she hung up the minute she heard Sera's voice. The second time had been two days later.

He answered the phone, "Giselle, baby?"

Wariness was in her voice when she said hello. What had he done to put that there?

"Why, baby?" he asked. "What happened? Why did you leave?"

Giselle snorted. "You mean she didn't tell you."

"Who?" Perplexed, Chase went through his mental Rolodex, but the only name he came up with didn't make sense. "What? Sera? She was home with me when you left. She's as shocked as I am."

A dry laugh crackled over the phone. "I'm sure she's surprised I escaped."

Chase pulled the phone from his ear and looked at it as though there were little men inside changing Giselle's words. "Escaped? From what? What are you running from?"

Icicles formed on the phone as she coldly blew out the words. "You saw Hawk. How can you ask that?"

Shaking his head quickly for clarification, he repeated the story Sera told him. "I don't understand. He got into an accident."

"You can't possibly believe that," Giselle said, her voice raising an octave or two. "We were jumped—on Sera's orders."

How could Giselle put Sera in the middle of what happened? "No. No. Sera wouldn't do that." Sera couldn't have, wouldn't have. It had to be a misunderstanding.

"Leave her, Dad. Come to Pennsylvania," Giselle implored. "Bring Hawk. We can start over."

"Leave? Come on, baby," he whispered, imploring her to understand. "It's not that serious. We can work it out."

The anger and coldness left her voice, and was replaced by sadness so immense that he felt it all the way from her place in the shadows. "No. We. Can't."

She ended the call. The next day her number was no longer in service. She was done with him—all from some type of misunderstanding.

The memory of the last time he spoke with Giselle swirled into nothingness. But the rain remained and reminded.

CHAPTER 35

Hawk had always been careful, always. He walked everywhere, he doubled back, he didn't follow a pattern. How could Ninja have followed him? God.

"Lizzie, don't ask any questions," he warned, then realized that his tone could easily put her in a fearful state of mind. He added, "He's a friend." Smiling, thinking inwardly, sort of ."It's fine."

Just then, his son came running up. But he stopped short, evidently sensing the tension. He asked, "Mr. Hawk?" His voice was as unsure as Lizzie's expression.

Hawk turned smiling, "Hey, man. I'm sorry, but I can't stay and play right now."

"Why?" Gregory's gaze continued to vacillate between Hawk and Ninja.

"Well, my friend was nice enough to come pay me a visit."

Gregory tipped his head, then generously conceded, "He can play, too."

Ninja's eyebrows rose as he answered Gregory. "Well, that's mighty generous of you, Li'l Man."

Lizzie walked up and held out her hand. "Hi, I'm Lizzie."

Hawk wanted to grab her and push her out of the park, but the damage had already been done. Funny, before he got his ass kicked on the way to the store, he was like Lizzie, willing to give people a chance.

He believed in the inherent good. But these past years, he watched how insidious evil was, how it slithered around the edges of life, waiting for its chance to strike—then retreated and started all over again.

He spent considerable effort keeping that part of his life from Lizzie. So how could he expect her to know that the last thing in the world she should be doing is introducing herself to Sera's right hand, when at one time, he was just like Ninja.

However, he was pretty sure he wouldn't be giving Ninja the onceover that Lizzie was giving him. Lizzie belonged to him; but something funny was certainly going on here, and a tinge of jealousy caused his shoulder muscles to tense.

Ninja gently lifted her manicured hand to his lips. "Ninja. Pleasure to meet you."

Grinding his teeth, Hawk focused his energy on telepathically pushing Lizzie towards her car

"Well," Lizzie replied, giving him a coy smile. "Aren't you cuteness personified? and debonair?"

Ninja, still holding Lizzie's hand, commented, "Hawk, you keep looking at us that hard, your face is gonna get stuck like that."

He slowly released Lizzie's hand and turned to Hawk's side. "Didn't your mother teach you manners? Obviously, this pretty young thing has what you lack."

Hawk didn't like the small smile playing at the corners of Lizzie's full lips and why it was there in the first place? Whatever it meant, she needed to put an end to it., like now. "Lizzie."

Lizzie responded with a distracted, "Hmmm."

"Lizzie!"

This time she turned and he hitched his head towards the street.

Lizzie grabbed Gregory's hand, "It's time we left, anyway. We'll play with Mr. Hawk another day."

Gregory's face tightened in a scowl. Hawk kneeled down and whispered to him about a promised future basketball game.

Ninja kept his focus on the two of them as they passed. Lizzie shot Ninja another curious look, tilting her head to the side as if trying to figure something out.

Ninja commented, "That's some good work right there."

"What?" Hawk asked, coming to stand next to Ninja.

"That's your son, right?"

Hawk's face tightened. "No, he's not my son," he said through his teeth. "He has a father, a very rich one at that."

Ninja gave Hawk a sideways glance. "Funny, he looks like he could be your twin. The male version, not the female one," he clarified. "How is she, by the way?"

Hawk's teeth clenched, but he ignored the reference to Giselle. "Well, everyone has a twin around here somewhere."

Ninja's grin was both a question and a challenge. "And the mother?"

Hawk's gaze narrowed. "An old friend. I have friends. Some go by their government names."

Nodding, Ninja put his gaze on the retreating forms of the two people Hawk had vowed to protect. "I guess we all need some of those."

As Hawk prepared to walk home, he inquired, "What are you doing here?"

"Well, you do some strange stuff sometimes, jogging and shit. I was curious. So …"

Hawk stopped midstride. "I deserve a little time away."

Ninja scowled. "*Deserve?* What the hell is deserve?" Ninja's thin finger jabbed Hawk's chest. "You're not in some office somewhere. You don't get to deserve anything but what the Knights give you. You don't deserve a break."

Ninja's eyes chilled to an emotionless, deep cold. "And when your people can't reach your ass, you don't deserve privacy. Dudes getting shot—with arrows—and you're playing ghost."

Ninja took a step closer to Hawk and eyed him like he was the scum stuck on the bottom of a homeless man's shoe. "So while you talking about what you deserve, what about what we deserve for watching your damn back when you out kicking it with light bright and not watching ours."

"I am not a piece of fuckin' concrete." Hawk puffed his chest. "I get to leave the block."

"So you left. Feel better now? How does watching your old life feel? Does it give you hope?" He nodded in the direction of the park entrance. "And when are you going to let that go?"

Hawk's hands balled into fists. "Ninja, stay outta' my shit."

Ninja tugged Hawk towards his car. "I can't be walking like you, dude. I need my ride."

"How did you find me?"

"GPS."

"GPS?"

"Hell, yes, I tagged your ass. I couldn't be jogging behind you or walking for miles. Not even."

Hawk stopped right before getting to the car. "You can do that?"

Ninja raised his left eyebrow. "Obviously."

"But you haven't before."

"Weird shit wasn't happening before," he shot back as if Hawk was a slow learner. "Plus, we have to scoop NuNu from the hospital. Sera wants to have a talk with him. Trying to figure out if it's us or just him."

"You know NuNu's always mixing shit up with the ladies. One of them might've come after him. With a damn arrow."

"You don't need me for that."

Ninja scoffed, giving Hawk a look that spoke volumes. "We're moving in twos now. Always. So how you gonna sneak off to see your girl and the son that's not your son?"

A horn blew, trying to figure out if they were going to finish their conversation or get into the car to give up the parking space. Ninja stared at the driver until he pulled off.

Hawk's heart pounded in his chest, but he kept his growing anxiety inside. Fear was as deadly as strapping a bomb to your loved one yourself, then giving the trigger to a toddler. "What are you gonna tell her?" Hawk held his breath waiting for Ninja to respond.

People swerved around them. Usually joggers, strollers, walkers, whatever, would bump into Hawk like he hadn't been standing in the same spot. No one dared to bump into Ninja. Matter of fact, a young lady who had been diligently texting on her phone stopped two steps behind Ninja, looked up, and walked around.

"I think I'll take one of your plays for this one. Keep it to myself, unless I need to share." Ninja narrowed his eyes with emphasis. "I don't have a beef with you, Hawk. Stop acting like I do."

"You're the one who told me not to trust anyone on the block," Hawk argued, trying not to show his relief.

Ninja agreed. "True that."

"So now you're asking me to trust you?"

"Hell no," Ninja shot back, laughing. "But we made a deal a long time ago not to lie to each other. If I need to come after you, it won't be a secret. It won't be on some punk clandestine shit. It'll be real and deadly. That's how I've always worked. I'm not changing now."

Hawk felt a weight off his shoulder. His secret was safe—for now. If Ninja went after him, he'd deal with that if the time came. That would be his punishment for not figuring a way out of this hell sooner.

"And it'll be you, not some chick from your past or the son that's not your son." Ninja's gaze was as intense as Hawk had ever seen. "I'll put a bullet between your eyes and your eyes alone. The only person that'll care about this shit is Sera. Apparently, she has enough on you or you would've left a long time ago."

Hawk remained silent.

"Yeah. Thought so."

In the Midst of Fire

CHAPTER 36

Sera scowled at NuNu, as he squirmed in his spot on the couch. She didn't speak. She didn't move. She just watched him.

Over the years, she had upgraded her apartment to hood-fabulous. NuNu gently rubbed the butter-soft brown leather of the couch. This couch was only two years old and a far cry from the furniture Sera had when she first moved back to Burnham Park Apartments.

She was happy to get rid of the old one that she'd found on the street. It carried too many memories that never were far from her mind. Back then she went to school every single day to keep her "alone" status a secret for as long as possible.

Soon, she ran errands for the Kingdom Knights and began making money to sustain herself. Sera didn't cause any trouble.

Well, not intentionally.

That year, one of Sera's mother's ex-boyfriends caught her alone in the hallway. He knew that Trinity was long gone. He pushed Sera into the apartment, intent on making her replace her mother in his life.

The memory of that day was so strong that she shifted from her current issue with NuNu and was instantly transported to the time when that man's rough hands gripped her breast so hard that pain shot up her arm. She had screamed. Someone must have heard. She could damn near hear people breathing in the hallway. No one lifted a finger to help.

When he first threw her up against the wall, she kicked, punched, bit; but she couldn't overpower him. So she went limp, giving the illusion that she had given in.

The glee in his eyes and the way he licked his lips were a stark contrast to the shock that flashed in those beady brown orbs when she brought her knee up so hard into his crotch that he fell to the side. She limped to the kitchen. He crawled after her, grabbing her leg. But he was too late.

She didn't remember what she cut first. All she remembered was crying, blood, gurgling; and soon he wasn't moving at all.

Sera called Vincent, another member of the Knights whom she'd known since grammar school. They were the same age, but she was certain, with all the fighting the Knights were doing to establish their territory, that he'd seen a dead person before. He'd know how to handle such an unfortunate situation.

Vincent came in, sized up the situation, made her take a shower and then leave the building. The guy's body was found in a burning vehicle in an empty lot. Back then, empty lots were on every street for a one-mile radius.

Today, they were skinny houses and condos. And NuNu was pulling the same shit that her mother's ex-boyfriend had tried to pull.

Sera had killed a man for the same that NuNu did to women. And she had ignored it, like what had happened to her was a minor thing. That was her mistake. She would rectify that, tonight.

The couch that NuNu now occupied had been purchased at Macy's. That was one thing she did that she was proud of; she upgraded everything in her apartment.

It might not be as large as the Lincoln Park house, but no one could say today it wasn't HGTV-worthy. Watching NuNu pick at the leather raised her ire. Clearly, he didn't show people or things the proper respect.

NuNu opened his mouth to say something, then must have thought better of it because those thick lips clamped shut. Apparently, he wasn't as dumb as he looked or acted. What could he say at this point? He was sitting there with his hand wrapped in gauze—which made it five times its normal size—and a huge question in the air? Why?

NuNu was loyal, always loyal. He had never done anything to directly threaten the Knights. In a neighborhood such as theirs, in a business such as theirs, loyalty mattered.

They had to be able to trust others with information that could send everyone to jail faster than the judge could bang a gavel and proclaim a five-to-twenty bid. Sera always believed she was too cute to serve time in Cook County Jail. However, in her line of business, options were limited. She'd be in the company of friends.

Laughter wafting in from the open window brought her back to reality and the issue at hand. NuNu's thirst for women was well-known. That wasn't the problem. His lack of finesse with women was the issue.

The use of force, his depraved indifference to a woman's right to choose, maybe she had let it go for too long, Yes, NuNu was loyal, but he was also a liability.

The heavy motor of a bus lumbering down the street overpowered the sound of *Family Feud* playing on the flat screen. The faint smell of exhaust fumes tickled her nose. As Sera sneezed, NuNu's muscles jumped. She took that to be significant as she leaned forward, demanding, "Why you?"

NuNu's Adam's apple bobbed as he swallowed. He plucked at the couch with his nail. "I don't know."

Sera's temperature rose with each scratch he was putting on her expensive couch. "Stop scratching my damn couch!" Her right hand shook with the need to slice this dumb-ass man. And that instinct came honest.

Swearing never to be as vulnerable as she had been when she'd been attacked, she started throwing knives. While most people would use empty lots for gun target practice, she threw those metal blades until her arm was so sore that she could barely lift it.

The shooters would laugh at her as she practiced every day; standing, constantly in motion, right and left hand. It took her years to perfect her aim. Now she could be in the back of Hawk's bedroom and throw a knife directly into NuNu's head before he could say sorry. No one laughed now.

Interrupting her reverie, NuNu explained, "Sera, it's not me. I don't know anyone who'd do this kind of shit."

She doubted he did. Blind loyalty usually came hand in hand with low IQ. "What have you done lately?"

"Nothing."

Sera watched a bead of sweat squeeze out of his pores as he answered, "Swear to God."

Her back tightened with tension as she walked closer to NuNu. She trailed her fingers up the arm and along the back of the couch. She grazed the back of NuNu's head causing him to flinch. Fear was a great motivator.

"You know, I tend not to bother with issues that don't impact the business. I knew you had some problems, but the last couple of days have been eye-opening for me." She leaned in so she was only two inches away and whispered, "You're a bad boy."

Sera reached into her waistband and slid out a knife, then softly dragged it across his throat.

As NuNu swallowed again, it nicked him, causing a little trail of blood to follow the knife up his ear.

A few more beads of sweat burst across the man's forehead. She inhaled deeply, relishing the fear-generated perspiration. Power was one hell of an aphrodisiac. She gave his left cheek a broad stroke with her tongue and then blew. NuNu cowered into the corner of the couch.

"You've always been a bad boy. If you did to me, what you've done to some of those women on the street, do you know what would happen?"

NuNu focused on the carpet is if it was made of gold. "You would've cut me."

Sera dragged her blade across his cheek, causing a whisper thin cut to appear. She watched the blood bead. Using her left hand, she wiped it across the split skin and examined the blood.

She moseyed around to the front of the couch and perched on the coffee table. NuNu's gaze darted around the apartment, not settling on one particular thing.

Sera tilted her head to the right as she observed him. Fear and anger filled the small space between them until she commanded.

"Look at me." When NuNu didn't respond as quickly as he should have, she shouted, "Look at me!" so forcefully, spittle flew from her mouth.

NuNu's head snapped up and he looked into Sera's eyes. She tried again with a deceptively soft voice. "What would have happened?"

His eyes were bucked as he uttered. "You would've killed me."

"Good boy." Sera leaned back. "Here's the problem. Because of your issues with women, I don't know if I'm in the middle of a war or just one pissed-off bitch."

A burst of laughter bounced through the window, breaking some of the tension. Sera turned back to the window. "You understand my dilemma."

Silence.

"Do. You. Understand. My. Dilemma."

NuNu's voice croaked as he tried to speak; then he cleared it and tried a second time. "Yes."

"So you figure out who you've pissed off to the point where they may be shooting arrows at your ass." Sera squinted, focusing in on fear pulsating in NuNu's eyes. "And I will do the same."

"And if I find proof that you've been . . . inappropriate . . . let's say, with one more woman," Sera growled. "I'll leave you locked in a room, tied up with every female you've even thought about groping, and see how creative they can be with killing your ass."

CHAPTER 37

Sera's normal loose gait was a tight, staccato march. The normal sounds of children playing, grown folks in the throes of heated arguments, and traffic bustling down the street took a back seat to her mind racing, trying to figure out who was playing Robin in her Hood. And she was fucking horny. Unfortunately, Chase's depression phases included the inability to get it up or keep it up.

The rain that besieged the neighborhood that week didn't help her mood.

Her thoughts were interrupted by a flash of red and blue in her peripheral. As the police car pulled up beside her, she stopped and folded her arms at seeing a not-so-welcome face. "Officer."

Officer Scalero was an asshole. He thought that every woman in the projects should want his streaked drawers because he had a steady job and benefits.

Sometimes it worked for him, even though doing so was illegal while he was carrying a gun. But when it came to her, she required a bit more . . . depth.

Officer Scalero looked her up and down and smiled. "Looking good, Sera."

In the Midst of Fire

She stuck her tongue in her cheek hard enough to push out her dimple permanently. "Thanks. What can I do for you?"

He inched his torso further out of the driver's window. "Man, would I like to show you."

As Sera turned to walk away, the officer baited her, "So who's shooting arrows at your people, Sera?"

She paused, turning around slowly. Her right eye somehow developed a tick, but she refused to address it. "Isn't that your job to find out?"

"Well, y'all keep us so busy with actual guns here in the 18th precinct over in 7, 15, 9 that arrows fall way down on the list."

Rolling her eyes, Sera snarled. "Anything having to do with your actual job falls down on your list." She turned again shouting over her shoulder, "Catch him, Scalero, before I do."

As she took two steps, she ran head first into a mountain. Deep woodsy cologne filled her nostrils, causing her to lift her head. Vincent. He grabbed her, angling her petite form so that his back was to the cop, effectively shielding Sera from the direct view.

"Hey, Chère."

Sera's tension started to level out. This was the banter she was used to, the banter she loved. "You're not French, V."

He lifted two pushy eyebrows up. "No, like the French, I enjoy a classic work of art like you."

Sera snorted out a laugh. "Really?"

Vincent smiled and trailed his finger down her right arm. "Every curve of your body should be worshipped."

Sera didn't know what it was about Vincent. She had turned down a lot of men in the building. Some took it well. Some got a knife where smooth skin should be. Vincent steadily pursued.

At one point, she considered taking him up on his offer. They would've made one hell of a team. The problem was they were so alike in so many ways. But he was good for her. At least he was good for her ego.

"Trust me, my husband handles that on a nightly basis."

Vincent's nose flared. The muscles rippled along his jaw line. "Baby girl, that man wouldn't even come close to doing to you what I could."

Sera's gaze traveled down his thick legs and stopped where they always did . . . at his feet. Someone that tall and thick should have bigger shoes. *Impress me.*

"Well, believe me when I say what he can do is more than enough for me," she lied, reflecting on the last moment they had together when Chase's distraction led to a disappointing episode that he tried to make better with her vibrator. Nice, but not the same.

"You put all that effort into finding a man to help you get out of here, then ended up right back where you started," Vincent sneered. "Don't you feel even a little bit disappointed?

And this is where the conversation went downhill. Vincent's ego. "I didn't marry him for his money."

Vincent's Hershey Kiss eyes twinkled. "No, you married him for that high-class address. And that you got to enjoy for all of three months."

Vincent hitched his head back towards where the police car had just been. "It doesn't do anyone any good to threaten Scalero like that. You know better than that."

Biting the inside of her cheek, Sera conceded. "Yeah, I know, but it's Scalero."

Raising both eyebrows, Vincent stated, "Yeah, and he has a badge behind him."

Sera waved him off. "Yeah, yeah, yeah."

Vincent chucked her under her chin, making her smile. Over his right shoulder a group of birds suddenly took flight.

She paused to enjoy how they rose in union, how they'd been so quiet and then suddenly blocked every ray of sunlight. She followed their pattern and then it hit her all at once. Something had scared them.

Vincent shouted. She snapped her attention to him and blanched at the arrow sticking through his arm. He tackled her as another arrow whizzed by. Her body ricocheted off the sidewalk, and pain exploded in every possible muscle and bone.

Children and adults were shouting, running. All she could do was focus on the arrow sticking out of Vincent's arm. It had bounced when they fell to the concrete. Shouldn't it be gushing blood like in the movies?

In the Midst of Fire

She wanted to pull the arrow out, but Vincent had wrapped her body so tightly, breathing was damn near impossible. Sera looked up in time to see Hawk and Ninja running towards them, shouting something she couldn't make out, right before the darkness on the edge of her vision closed, rendering her unconscious.

CHAPTER 38

Chase gasped as Hawk burst through the front door with Sera draped in his arms, followed closely by a staggering Vincent, and Ninja. Chase barely glanced at them, as he focused on the limp body of his wife. Hawk lowered her to the couch. Chase collapsed on the rug beside her, eyes frantically checking for blood.

Chase wanted to touch her, but she was so still. It was almost like the last time he laid eyes on Rose, that fateful night when his whole life changed, when their whole life changed.

When Rose died, he raced in his car to the hospital, clinging to the fact that it was Hawk who called him first. Hawk was fine. Giselle and Rose had to be fine, too.

God wouldn't be cruel. He wouldn't take away the one person who saved his very soul, as he was teetering on the tight rope between succumbing fully to the street and being the man his grandmother raised.

Rose's light drew him away from the darkness of the streets. Her light expanded his vision. With her light, he could see further than the block, further than the drug dealers, further than the hustlers.

She illuminated a completely different life.

So when the doctors told him she had died, he didn't believe them.

In the Midst of Fire

He couldn't. Not his Rose. When he stood in the morgue, he couldn't quite reconcile the vibrant woman who danced in fountains with abandon to that perfectly still entity.

It wasn't Rose. It couldn't have been Rose. Rose was energy, adventure, excitement. That body was devoid of all that.

Chase had reached out slowly, touched Rose's skin. The cold that invaded his fingertips chilled him to the core of his heart. He pulled her hand out from under the sheet and looked at the tattoo on her ring finger.

She once said that jewels come and go. Their love was like a tattoo etched permanently in the skin. That's what she did, etched a design on her ring finger.

When he saw that hand, that finger, that design—and her fingers didn't curl to intertwine with his, as they had done so many times over the years—he fell to his knees, subjugating himself to whatever good or evil spirit could bring life back to Rose.

His prayers must have fallen on deaf ears because one week later he found himself in front of her casket in a cemetery, listening to a preacher try to share Rose's essence, using the limited vocabulary of the English language.

Now many years and marriages later, he was kneeling next to another wife. He reached out to gently touch the side of her face with a trembling hand.

Warmth. Her chest rose and fell only slightly. He nearly fainted in relief.

Closing his eyes, in an attempt to control the emotions coursing through his body, he heard Hawk inquire, "Dad?"

Shaking his head to try to shake the memories loose, Chase tried again. Did Hawk Just say something? "I'm sorry. What?"

"Closest we can tell, she hit her head on the concrete and knocked herself out," Hawk explained.

"She fell?"

Vincent responded. "No, I was shot with an arrow. I was protecting Sera. That's when she hit the ground."

Chase looked up at the burly dude he'd seen on the block a few times. Even he knew by now that the behemoth had a thing for Sera. "So to protect her, you threw her to the ground."

Vincent shrugged. "I didn't have a choice."

Chase pushed himself to his feet, anger pulsing blood through his body until he could feel each beat of his heart. "You're huge. You could've killed her."

"No, I just reacted. That's what a man does when it's time to protect a woman."

Chase pointed at Vincent's arm, which was still sporting that arrow. "We can take care of Sera. You need someone to handle that."

"I just need Sera to be okay."

Chase squared his shoulders and looked up at the man who couldn't seem to take his eyes off of Sera. "No, *I* need my wife to be okay. You need to leave."

The giant's eyes bored into Chase, but he wasn't buckling to Vincent. Instead, he took a step forward. "I didn't think I needed to repeat myself."

He wasn't about to have his card pulled by the loser in the battle for Sera. Vincent had years to get Sera if he wanted her that badly.

Obviously, she had made a different choice.

Now Chase wasn't crazy enough to believe he could take Vincent. But he was smart enough to know the first thing he was going to do was pull that arrow out of his arm and see what happened next.

"Vincent, dude. Come on," Ninja said, stepping between the two men. "I'll drive you to the hospital."

Vincent's gaze remained locked on Chase. Chase narrowed his eyes to slits. If he was going to get his ass kicked, fine.

Ninja waved a hand in front of Vincent's flushed face. "I'll even take you to Northwestern if you wanna' go high class."

Vincent's eyebrow shot up to his brow, then he looked down at Ninja and chuckled. He hitched his head at Chase in a dismissal, then walked backwards out of the door.

Chase took a deep breath and glanced over at Hawk. "Are you okay?"

Hawk nodded.

She needed a hospital, but he hadn't been in an actual hospital himself in years. The night when Rose died was the last time. A doctor's office for a basic check-up—yes. A hospital? No way.

Sera hated hospitals as well. She never talked about why. She had only told him she had a bad experience in one. Hence, the reason they'd brought her home instead of calling the ambulance.

Chase's heart and head fought over what he should do versus what he wanted to do. Maybe they could wait it out, maybe just fifteen minutes more.

If not, he would have to darken the church's doorstep once more and ask the God who denied him with Rose, to help him with Sera. If no answer came for a pure soul like Rose, what did he think was going to happen with a slightly crazy, knife-wielding bad ass from the block.

He stared intently at his wife, willing her to awaken by the power of his thought. Knowing in his heart, that sometime no matter what was done, people died.

He lowered himself to the floor and placed his forehead against her hand. Live, my Sera. Live.

CHAPTER 39

Hawk tried to rub the concern off his face. They had struck again. Did they mean to hit Vincent this time? Or was it Sera they wanted? Either way, NuNu and Vincent had one common denominator—Sera. Seems like the Knights were in the middle of a strange kind of turf war, one that they didn't start nor could they figure out how to finish.

The only good thing was that no one was dying. NuNu's hand, Vincent's arm, either someone was a bad shot or someone was just toying with them. The scenarios meant one thing: the block was hot, and they didn't know who had lit the flame.

Hawk's stomach turned as his father gently bathed Sera's face. Why didn't his father see the devil encased in that body. How could his father love the woman who had destroyed their family? Hawk leaned over and rested his elbows on his knees. "Do you ever miss Giselle?"

Chase paused midstroke and whispered, "Yes."

"You never talk about her," Hawk commented. "You don't mention her, ever."

Chase pursed his lips. "She never calls here." He turned to look Hawk in the eye. "Ever." Then he continued with his ministrations. "I don't even have her number. She chose to leave me behind, leave us behind. Her decision."

In the Midst of Fire

Decisions. Lizzie had given him an ultimatum the last time they were together. Hell, she'd shared quite a bit. Twins.

He needed Giselle, but things were even worse now than they were when she left. Before, it was only Sera they had to worry about. Now, a ghost was hiding in the background sending a semideadly message to Sera's crew. Whether she was there or not, a stepdaughter counted as crew. He had to protect her at all cost.

Look at the cost of protecting Lizzie. He thought he'd done the right thing by not fighting for her, not dragging her by her hair away from her legacy and straight into poverty. However, the pain in her eyes the last time at the park. God, that hurt to know he had been the one to put it there. The situation was as bad as the one with Giselle, if not worse.

Maybe he was selfish for holding on to the belief that Tory only had his family on loan. Now, God, the universe, someone was calling his marker. He had to find someplace for his family to go.

"Do you think it was the right decision for us to stay here as long as we have?"

Sera stirred.

"Ssshhh," Chase said, shooting him a warning glance. "We will talk about this later."

"Sure we will," Hawk scoffed. The last thing he wanted to see was his father mooning over Sera, so he left. Outside, he inhaled the lingering exhaust from the bus further up the block.

The tension was still thick. It rolled off everyone still on the sidewalk. This wasn't normal shit.

Before when someone got shot, everyone scattered, went home, checked themselves for holes, and came back out to resume the activities they'd abandoned. The younger kids would stay in the house longer. He'd seen it with his own eyes.

Now, people were talking to the cops. Without Vincent, nothing much the cops could do. The Knights weren't going to call in anyone for an arrow wound. Whatever he survived, he handled.

A cop ambled Hawk's way before his phone vibrated. He turned and walked the other way and answered. "Hawk."

"Hey, I was just checking to see how you were doing. It's not like you to not meet us at the park."

Hawk let loose with a string of profanity that made the cop's step slow to a near halt. In the past four years, he never missed one day that he was supposed to see Lizzie and Greg.

He couldn't tell her someone was shooting arrows at his crew. She'd be more worried for him than she already was.

"Babe, Sera got into an accident."

Lizzie's gasp echoed, before, "You didn't . . . .,

The tension uncoiled and Hawk laughed. "I haven't done anything in all of these years. Why would I start today?"

Lizzie hesitated. "I don't know. Just thought . . . " she whispered, then shifted into. "Greg's asking about you. You were supposed to play basketball with him."

"I can be there in . . . what . . . twenty minutes."

"That's okay. We'll be fine." The disappointment in her voice wasn't hard to miss.

Hawk didn't need Lizzie's judgment to know what a failure he was. And he surely didn't need it today. "Don't do that."

"Do what?" She inquired with a voice so innocent that it rang fake.

"Play the martyr," he spat. "How's your husband and your bank account?"

"Don't do that," she shot back.

"Do what?" he replied in a tone that matched her fake innocence.

"Play the asshole."

Hawk ran his hands over his head and mumbled. "Sorry. A lot going on."

Lizzie sighed. "How's Sera?"

"She'll live," he replied, then mumbled, "unfortunately."

"I wanted to tell you in person. Tory got a job offer." Lizzie tried to sound upbeat, but something in her tone told the story. "I'm . . . well . . . we're moving to Paris."

He stopped in the middle of the street until a horn honked, spurring him to action. What had Ninja called Greg? The son that was not his son. No truer words had ever been spoken. And if they moved to Paris, Greg would never be his son.

"Hawk? Hawk!"

"I'm on my way," he ground out through his teeth. "You'd better be at the damn park when I get there."

CHAPTER 40

Giselle sat on her back deck watching the moon as it bid hello to the neighborhood.

Night was her favorite time, when the moon brought its own brand of lightness. As she was leaning back against the frame of the window she'd just climbed out of, two males made their way down the alley.

Sometimes she missed her old neighborhood. But she had to acknowledge, while Lincoln Park was beautiful, it didn't have any character besides "rich." Here, energy pulsated through each and every individual; every brick and blade of glass.

Her phone rang. She checked the caller ID and ducked back through the window into her apartment.

"Hey, Ninja."

"Hey there, Hawk's Little Sister."

Ninja had no idea the timbre of his voice made her vibrate in a totally different way. But no matter how she looked at the situation, she couldn't see any way that a relationship with him would work.

They were who they were. He was Sera's right hand. And she was the estranged daughter of the man Sera had married. She felt the possibility of "more" every time he called.

She wanted to explore that possibility, but that would mean coming back to the place where she was unwelcome. And she would surely be hunted down by NuNu, if not Sera herself. That's what made her keep a distance. She wondered what made him keep his.

Giselle tried to avoid what Lizzie had described as the 'ohh baby' voice, as she asked, "How's Hawk?"

Ninja chuckled, "Still not asking about me first? I must be doing something wrong."

Feigning innocence, she responded, "I don't know what you're talking about."

"You will."

Ohhh, baby. Just the possibility of the things he could do right made Giselle inhale and cross her legs to try to stop her privates from pulsating.

He hadn't pushed the physical, not at Lexington, not any day since. That day, he stepped back and watched her, with the tension crackling to the point where Giselle's shoulders were stiff and she thought she was going to have to strip off her own skin.

She wouldn't give him the satisfaction though. If he could be cool, she could be cool.

That first day, they had gone to a coffeehouse off campus and talked, as they waited for the time for him to make it to the airport. He was more than she expected.

He was a thug. He was that; but he was intelligent, well-read, and a chameleon.

She had asked him, "Why do you work for Sera? I mean you could be anything, do anything. You know there is more to this world than Burnham Park Apartments."

Ninja quietly explained, "I left my brother there, my little brother. Once I left, the Knights didn't hesitate to pull him into the fold."

Leaning forward, Giselle was waiting for the rest of the story. "And?"

Ninja leaned back. "He died. Listen, I did some things back then. I still do some things. I'm not innocent, not by a long shot."

Giselle didn't get the sense that he was going to elaborate on some things. "Could you get out? Is there a way out?"

"Always." Ninja played with his coffee cup. "You just have to be willing to pay the cost."

Giselle couldn't believe he was only giving her two sentences at a time. Damn frustrating. "Well, are you willing to pay the cost?"

"Not today." Ninja's eyes bore into hers. "Maybe tomorrow."

Giselle had let discussion about his life choices drop all those years ago. Apparently, he still wasn't willing to pay the cost because he was still a Knight.

She wished she had a mother to teach her how to pull a man into her web like a black widow spider; not change him, per se, but change his trajectory, make him willing to pay the price for her.

Rose Glen was long gone, and Sera was more like one of those preying mantises. Her dad was going to wake up one morning, and that hateful woman was going to bite off his ear.

"Soo, umm, how is Hawk?"

She could almost see his smile through the phone as he answered, "He's good. Same old. Same old."

Giselle scratched a nonexistent itch on her elbow. "That's good."

As casually as if he was talking about the weather, Ninja dropped, "You didn't tell me about the boy, though."

Giselle mentally went through her memory before she probed, "What boy?"

Ninja made a noise deep in his throat before he responded, "Interesting."

"What boy, Ninja?"

A siren blared as an ambulance rushed down Sedgwick Street. Giselle froze. Her luck couldn't be that bad. She hoped he didn't hear it; that somehow, someway, he missed it.

She was in trouble the minute Ninja declared, "Funny, in all the years you were away at school, I never, ever heard a siren, ever."

Shit. He'd heard it. As it came closer, Giselle ran to her bed and tried to wrap herself in a blanket, even knowing it was too late. Her place wasn't that big, and the window was wide open.

"You know what's even funnier," he added.

In the Midst of Fire

Anger edged into Ninja's tone, even though his voice was dead flat. If his voice was like this over the phone, she couldn't even imagine what it would be like face to face.

Giselle closed her eyes and smothered her face against the pillow before answering, "No."

"In all the conversations we've had, I've never, in any of our conversations, heard the same thing on *this* phone line that I'm hearing in my own neighborhood."

Giselle held her breath as the ambulance continued to pass her apartment and the sound echoed through the phone.

"So tell me, Giselle. Where the hell are you? Because we both damn well know the answer isn't Lexington University."

CHAPTER 41

Hawk rushed into the park, breathless. Greg was playing on the slide. Hawk's attention shifted to something more urgent—her. He hurried in her direction and didn't bother with niceties.

His feet hurt from running in the wrong shoes, and his pseudo-girlfriend was trying to move across the world with her son. His son. Their son. Their twins. And her damn husband.

"Your husband doesn't have to work a day in his life. Why is he suddenly taking a job offer on the other side of the planet?" he snapped.

"Shhh." Lizzie grabbed his arm and yanked to get him under control. "You're going to have this whole park in my business."

"Like I give a shit," he shot back.

Greg ran up and screamed, "Mr. Hawk." Then he froze, his attention shifting between his mother and Hawk. "Mr. Hawk? Why are you mad?"

Hawk cracked his fingers, took a deep breath, and managed to smile down at his son. "Do you want to play basketball?"

Greg nodded, but dragged his feet as they walked toward the nearly empty court. Hawk looked over his shoulder to find Lizzie staring after them, appearing forlorn. She had nerve. She would take them all, even the ones that weren't born yet.

Hawk lifted Greg up and positioned him to shoot. Greg made it and crowed. Hawk laughed. Greg was the cure for everything that ailed him right now. Giselle was gone. His father was useless. Lizzie was . . . well, slowly killing him.

All of that was fine because he had Gregory. So what if Gregory called him, "Mr. Hawk," instead of dad. Gregory was always excited to see him, to do things with him.

And now, if Gregory left, and the twins right along with him, Hawk would have nothing—truly nothing.

"Mr. Hawk? Are you going to cry?"

"No." Hawk had years to cry. Now he needed to figure shit out. No. Not his family.

"Mr. Hawk, are you coming with us to Paris?"

Hawk wanted to reply, "hell no and neither are you," but he'd pretend that he would allow that for now. "No, Gregory. I won't be going with you."

"Oh." Gregory took two hands and dribbled the ball. Hawk watched as the ball hit the small pair of gym shoes then popped away.

Gregory ran after it and brought it back.

"Mr. Hawk," Gregory revealed in the saddest version of a whisper he had ever heard. "My mommy doesn't want to move either. She told my dad."

"How do you know that?"

Scuffing his shoe against the asphalt, he admitted. "I was supposed to be upstairs, but I . . . ."

Hawk did a double take. It never occurred to him to ask Gregory about what went on in his house. "Oh? What did your dad say?"

"He said we had to go." Gregory stopped dribbling and sat down on the ball. "Mommy cried, Mr. Hawk. She cried a lot." He craned his neck to look over Hawk's shoulder at his mother. "Please don't tell Mommy I told you."

Hawk reassured him with a gentle pat on the back.

Lizzie ambled up to them. "That was a short game." As she peered at Gregory, she frowned. "You okay, honey?"

Gregory nodded, then looked at Hawk.

"We were just having a man-to-man talk," Hawk interjected.

Gregory nodded, standing as he repeated, "Yeah, man talk. Mommy you can't be here for man talk. You're not a man." He looked to Hawk for reassurance, once again.

Hawk tried not to smile.

Lizzie rolled her eyes. "Right, man talk." She gave Hawk an evil look, then stormed away.

"Why can't you come with us, Mr. Hawk?" he challenged, sounding perplexed before his little head tilted. "I was going to ask Dad, but Mom said I shouldn't mention you around Dad. You're our secret. Why are you a secret, Mr. Hawk? Is my daddy mad at you?"

Hawk looked down at the little version of Giselle, who had to know the answers to every single question in the universe. And right now, Gregory was asking the kinds of questions that Hawk couldn't answer.

"I don't think he's mad at me," Hawk reckoned, running a hand over his son's head. "He shouldn't be."

Hawk sat down on the basketball court in the space next to Greg. Shouts of happy children running around the playground were mixed with a half-court game going on several feet away.

He didn't know how to explain the complexities of life to this barely four-year-old.He didn't know how to explain about unplanned pregnancies, inheritances, crazy stepmothers, disappearing sisters, sprung fathers, and everything that brought them to this point.

"No, your father isn't mad at me. Sometime when you're older, you'll have a friend your parents won't like. They're not bad. It's just that your parent would prefer if you hung out with other people."

Gregory agreed. "Like my friend, Steve. His mother let him dye his hair green. The other mothers didn't like that. I can't go over to his house anymore." Greg looked up at Hawk, hope etched in his eyes. "But he can come to mine."

Hawk shuddered to think there was a boy walking around with green hair. But it was a good enough comparison.

"Yes, like your friend," Hawk continued. "See, when you're little, you have to tell your parents who your friends are, so they can keep you safe. When you're older, you can share that information or keep it to yourself."

Gregory nodded. "What did you do that my dad didn't like?"

Hawk grimaced. *Knocking up your mom wasn't an appropriate answer.* "My dad made some bad decisions that got him in a lot of trouble."

Gregory's eyes widened. "Did he go to jail? Steve's dad went to jail for having a white collar."

Hawk snorted out a laugh. "Well, that's not really what that meant. But anyway . . . he didn't go to jail, but he got in a lot of trouble. Most people don't want to hang around with troublemakers."

"But you didn't do it, Mr. Hawk," Gregory surmised.

Hawk stared into Gregory's chocolate eyes. "Well, I've done a few things in my day. Your mom doesn't mind. Your dad does."

Gregory looked hard at Hawk. "I don't mind, Mr. Hawk. You're a really nice person."

Hawk felt his voice catch. "Thank you, Gregory.

Gregory plucked at the sole of his shoe. "I'm sorry you can't come to Paris with us."

Hawk smiled sadly, realizing that even his son's heart was breaking. "I promise we'll see each other again."

Gregory's eyes lit up. "You promise?"

Hawked leaned over and tickled him. "Promise."

Lizzie eased up on them, saying. "We have to go."

Hawk got to his feet and said to Gregory. "Hey, champ. Practice your dribbling while I talk to your mother."

Gregory continued his two-handed dribbling, something that Hawk hadn't managed to train him out of in all this time.

Hawk stared at Lizzie. He wanted to grab them both, elbow all the people around them out of the way, and carry them off to somewhere safe, where they could all be together. Instead, he stated, "This is not happening."

Lizzie watched a few seconds of the game on the court. Hawk heard a loud "oooh" that accompanied someone making a bold move which had garnered everyone's attention.

"You are not taking my family to Paris."

Lizzie touched his cheek. "I'll call you next week."

Hawk lifted her chin with his finger. "Does that mean you'll stay?"

Lizzie backed away. "For what? What am I giving up Gregory's security for? the twins' security? my security? For a wish and a prayer?" She jabbed a finger in Hawk's chest. "Four years. I waited for four whole years for you to figure it out, figure us out. I don't have the luxury of staying. I have too many responsibilities."

"And I don't?" Hawk roared. Lizzie turned, but Hawk maneuvered in front of her.

Lizzie shook, her eyes snapping in anger. "Four years. I've been waiting for you for four years. I know you stayed for Giselle, but Giselle . . ."

"What? Giselle what?" Panic clawed up Hawk's spine. "Is Giselle okay?"

"She's fine." Pointedly, she declared, "which you would know if you talked to your damn sister."

The urge to kick something was so strong; instead, with a steady voice, he baited her. "I guess Mrs. Warner is ecstatic."

Lizzie ducked her head. "She isn't going."

He bent down, trying to make eye contact, which Lizzie avoided. "You're lying."

Lizzie's eyes snapped to him. "I've never lied to you."

"Well then tell me the whole story." Hawk folded his arms.

Blowing a deep breath, she pointed for Gregory to go back to the slide. Apparently, he'd been inching closer and closer. He trudged over to the slide.

"Mother found out that I was pregnant again. No big deal really, but since Tory is—well, Tory—she knew he wasn't the father. And—"

Confusion clouded Hawk's mind. "What difference does that make? You're keeping up appearances. You're a good wife."

"The difference is that your father and my mother had a thing going on at one time," Lizzie revealed.

Hawk nearly slid to the ground, as he absorbed the shock of that statement. "No!" Thinking back, he couldn't recall anything about Mrs. Warner and his dad. They must've kept that under Saran Wrap, 'cause I never caught wind of that.

Lizzie winced, "So, she kind of hates your father. When she made us break up, it wasn't because of that tax thing."

In the Midst of Fire

She frowned, amending, "Well, it was, but it was because he dumped her when he found out she wasn't the one with the money. And when he married Sera with her being broke and all, Mom flipped."

Hawk blinked about five times. "She told you this?"

The guys on the basketball court got louder, interrupting what was turning into the juiciest story that he'd heard in years. He touched her arm, guiding her so they moved closer to the slide, which was further away from the excited game.

"She got drunk and told everyone about that," Lizzie admitted, "including Tory's father, at a family dinner. We were toasting the twins, and she tells the family that they were probably yours."

Hawk took two steps back. "God."

"Yes!"

"So Paris?"

"Tory wants to move to Paris to get away from my mother, his father, and the embarrassment. It'll be easier for everyone if we aren't here."

Hawk couldn't imagine a worse scenario than Lizzie had painted. It was a shit storm without so much as umbrella.

Hawk stepped forward and held her hands in his own. "Easier for you?"

"It's breaking my heart even more than having to say, 'I do' to a man I don't love," she whispered.

Hawk toyed with her fingers. "You're not going. I will fix this."

Gripping his hand as tight as a vice, she demanded. "Give me a reason to stay."

Hawk scuffed his toe in the dirt. "I'm working on it."

Lizzie waved at Greg to come over. "By the time your plans work out, Greg will be graduating from college."

"Don't do that, Lizzie."

Lizzie whipped back around, her eyes filled with tears. "You leave me with no choices, then ask me to make different decisions. How about you not do that Hawk?"

Hawk countered, "I just need one month and I'll be free."

"You're free now."

"I'm not—"

"You will be . . . soon, free from everyone. Then you can get the life you've been working on for years."

Hawk hollered after her. "I'm not giving up." Even when Lizzie was out of earshot, he continued mostly to himself, "I'm not losing you twice. No way."

Gregory gave Hawk a cursory wave, as he stumbled to keep up with his mother who was dragging him from the park.

CHAPTER 42

Sera woke up and rolled over, only to find that Chase's side of the bed was empty. Yeah, he'd pay for that shit, too. She pounded the back of her head against the pillow, frustrated by the recent turn of events.

First, NuNu gets shot in the hand, then Vincent got shot right in front of her, like someone didn't give a shit who she was, like someone didn't know what she'd do when she found them.

She swung her legs over the side of the bed and stood in one smooth movement. Her bare feet didn't make a sound on the carpet as she walked to the bedroom window that faced the damn condos in which she believed the shooter was living or hiding.

Her lips lifted in an evil semblance of a smile. Vincent would smoke them out, and Sera would slice them from collar to cock.

"Chase!" Sera yelled.

He shuffled across the living room, turned the knob slowly, and stuck his head through the door. "Hey, honey."

"And where did you sleep last night?" she inquired, failing to keep the irritation from her voice.

"Babe, come on," he pleaded. "I was on the couch. I just thought you needed some space."

"Come in here."

He rubbed his hands against the same pants he'd had on the night before.

Chase stood next to her as she glared at the condos across the street. Nodding at the view, she demanded. "What do you see?"

Chase shuffled from his left foot to his right. Finally, he answered. "Um, condos?"

Sera's head whipped around so fast her hair slapped against her cheek. She gestured to the window. "There's an enemy in that building. Every arrow came from there."

Chase shoved his hands in his pockets. "Oh."

Sera turned back to the condos.

Chase grasped Sera's shoulder and pulled her back into him.

"I've been thinking . . . . "

Sera couldn't believe his gall. Lowering her voice, she sneered, "And what exactly have you been thinking, Chase?"

He started, cleared his throat, and began again. "You know, Hawk, being on the street; maybe, he could do something else."

Sera grabbed his shoulders and turned him to stare into his eyes. "Are you saying I'm incapable of protecting my own people?"

"No," Chase denied so fiercely his head looked like a bobble doll. "Security is your thing. You've been holding all of this down ever since we moved here."

Sera looked in his eyes to see if she could detect any signs of deception. Seeing nothing was amiss, she nodded, turned back to focus on the condos and continued, "Someone's testing me."

Chase reached over to put his arms around Sera. She stiffened and commanded, "I need you with me."

Chase kissed the tip of her left ear. "Every step of the way."

Sera settled in for a few seconds before forcing herself to stand upright and put up the walls necessary to keep Chase at a distance. Then she straightened her shoulders. She had priorities today.

First, working with Vincent to plan how they were going to go after the immediate threat, before she dealt with cutting her husband down to size.

Sera picked up her knife from the nightstand. Chuckling to herself when she realized that wasn't the best place to put it if she wanted her husband to actually come to bed at night.

The ringing phone distracted her, answering and listening to the caller rant incoherently about a new shooting, her level of pissed-offed-ness increased with every syllable she deciphered.

She could feel Chase's eyes on her as he slinked towards the door. Her eyes narrowed on him and he froze.

By the time the caller finished, Sera was shaking with rage. She slammed the phone down, screamed, and launched the knife across the room so hard it whipped past Chase and impaled the bedroom door.

Chase inquired, "Babe, what happened?"

Sera picked up the lamp at the bedside table and hurled it into the wall. She dragged the back of her hand across her lips.

"Babe?" Chase called from a safe distance.

"NuNu's dead," she shared trembling. "Bullet point blank in the head. An arrow sticking out of his heart."

Chase lost ten shades of redbone from the beginning of her sentence to the end.

Sera demanded, "Find Ninja. Tell him to get Vincent over here. Now."

Sera couldn't believe someone had dared to kill NuNu. Their enemy was escalating. She'd show them what escalating really meant, turning to her husband, who hadn't moved a muscle.

"Do we have a problem?" she growled.

Chase swallowed, looking from the knife in the door to the remains of the lamp on the floor then back to Sera.

"Track down Ninja. Got you." Chase scurried from the room.

Sera picked up the lamp from the other bedside table and slung the heaviest piece across the room. It landed on the chair and stayed intact. That pissed her off even more.

Someone was trying to make a fool out of her. She'd be damned if she'd let that happen—not this day.

Tomorrow either. *Twenty-five expensive-ass condos, housing people who thought they were above the law. Her law. Her block. Her rules. They*

would soon learn. Money didn't buy safety.
    Not even close.

CHAPTER
43

A crash in the apartment woke Hawk up out of a restless sleep. He shot straight up; and for a moment, things were silent to the point he thought maybe he had dreamed it, until he heard his father shuffling quickly around and Sera's scream.

Damn! Something else had gone down. Hopefully, it wouldn't add to his already insurmountable problems.

After his uncomfortable conversation with Lizzie, he had walked to North Avenue Beach to sit for a while. The waves that roared back and forth were suspiciously silent about providing answers.

They didn't help him figure out how he was going to keep his family in Chicago; nor did they say how he could manage to get to Paris and live there. If nothing else, Paris was expensive. Right now, the best he could do was a down payment for a small place on a random Caribbean island.

When he had made it home, he'd been greeted by the sight of his father curled up on the couch trying to make a throw into a full-fledged blanket. Hawk didn't even bother to ask.

Hawk went to his bedroom and tried to sleep, but only managed to toss and turn most of the night. At one point, he ended up on the floor, plucking at the carpet fibers.

He'd been stacking his money; but it wasn't enough, not for three kids and two adults. Not for any length of time. He'd need help; and there was only one person he even remotely trusted to help, and that was Ninja.

But Ninja had his own secret. His occasional disappearances from the block, which had nothing to do with a recent death, left Hawk suspicious. But the Hawk trusted him more than anyone else.

The front door burst open. Vincent's lumbering steps echoed in the house. Ninja's authoritative voice followed, but his words were unintelligible.

Something else must have jumped off. Really, how much is he supposed to deal with at one time?

Hawk yanked on a T-shirt. Opening the door, he first saw steam erupting from Sera's head. *Damn. What was it this time?*

Hawk watched each face until Chase answered, "NuNu."

Hawk turned back to the group. "NuNu's back in the hospital?"

"Well, the morgue's in the hospital," Vincent responded dryly. "So yeah, he's in the hospital."

Hawk staggered. "Wait. What? How?"

"A gunshot to the head and an arrow to the heart," Chase answered.

Arrows were one thing. And yes, people got shot all the time. Fortunately, in the years that he'd been in this neighborhood, killers had developed good aim and actually shot the people they were gunning for.

Someone must've had a hard-on for NuNu—for real. There were other members of the crew who could've been shot—Mookie, Hitta, people with some actual weight.

"Umm, so NuNu was hit with an arrow." Hawk addressed Vincent. "Then shot and hit with another arrow. And you got shot with an arrow."

Vincent's eyes narrowed as he focused on what Hawk was inferring. "Yeah, problem is, we don't know if my arrow was for me or for Sera."

Hawk gawked at both of them, thinking, did that even matter? If NuNu was the example, they were all going to end up dead. And soon, if they didn't find out who was behind all of this.

Collapsing on the couch, Hawk scanned the anxiety-filled faces of the people who had collected in Sera's apartment. He was a target. They were all targets. Rubbing his face, he let out a major sigh.

In the Midst of Fire

Sera paced in front of the window. Shouts erupted from two people in the hallway. An arguing couple was having a hard time of it on the other side of the door. Sera yelled, "Shut the hell up."

Talking in the hallway ceased immediately. Hawk preferred the hollering in the hallway. That was normal. This quiet was unnerving.

Ninja collapsed on the sofa and the resulting sound made everyone turn towards him. Sera's phone buzzed on the coffee table. Messages came through one after another.

Hawk didn't have time for this. He needed someone to find and kill whoever was taking shots at them, so he could concentrate on the right words, the right turn of phrase, the right lottery numbers to get Lizzie to stay. "What do we do?"

Vincent stepped to the center of their small circle. "It's time to see who the hell is living across the street. Ninja's going to do a background check on all the residents and see if anything comes up that bears our attention."

Ninja pushed himself off of the couch. Hawk assessed him closely. Something was off. Normally, Ninja enjoyed any challenge that put him in front of his beloved computer.

He vibrated with energy at the thought of pitting his brain against his computer. Hawk didn't think Ninja would be upset about NuNu, but stranger things have happened. "I can have a preliminary assessment this evening," Ninja responded to Sera. "But it depends on how up front or how deeply hidden the information is."

Sera snarled, then stopped in front of him. "You find me that motherfucka over there. I'll deal with him."

"Calm down now." Vincent placed his hand on Sera's shoulder. "We'll get him."

Chase cleared his throat and pointed to Vincent's hand. Vincent hesitated a moment, then dropped the offending hand to his side, flexing it in a way that showed his irritation.

"Is this going to be a recurring issue with us?" Vincent curled his hand into a fist. "You know I'm not doing your woman. Stop trippin'."

Chase glared, as he shot back, "But you want to, so keep your paws off of her."

Sera threw her head back and screamed, "Shhhiiittt. We're all targets of some deranged murderer, and you're both pissing on my leg, marking your territory." She jumped on top of the coffee table as if to show her dominance, "Let me clear this up. I own me." She thumbed her hand toward her chest. "*Me!*"

Vincent and Chase glared at each other. Ninja edged towards the door.

Sera waved Ninja off. "Get out of here. I want information, and I want it quickly."

Ninja saluted and walked out.

Hawk put his head in his hands. If he left, where would he go? And would trouble follow him? He'd love to go to Lexington University to see Giselle, to get a breath of fresh, free air. It must smell so good where she was. Here, it smelled like poverty, desolation, and death.

Plus, with two weeks until Lizzie's departure, he needed to concentrate on finding a loophole to her marriage/inheritance situation, instead of sitting around trying not to get shot.

Maybe Lizzie had the right idea. Paris was better than the projects. And he couldn't keep asking her to wait. This time if she left, he'd follow and figure it out later. Although his time was ticking, it wasn't up yet. He needed money and a lot of it, quickly, to keep her in Chicago. It was either that or Gorilla Glue her feet to the pavement.

CHAPTER 44

Chase looked down at his hands, noting how soft his skin was wrapped around strong fingers. That always served him well in the past. He was always one shoulder rub and smile away from any woman he wanted—always.

Now, he was looking across a crowded apartment wondering how the hell he was going to save his remaining family. Hell, how he was going to save himself.

The hallway always provided a gauge to the feeling of the neighborhood. Sometimes there was laughter, sometimes fights. That was normal. When something went down, he never heard a peep from beyond the door.

Even the street was quiet. With the exception of the normal range of cars and buses, the block was quiet—no screaming, laughing, playing with children; no adults on the balcony hollering back and forth for whatever reason.

The silence was deafening, driving him crazy. He started tapping his fingers on the edge of the couch. Even the barely discernible tapping was better than the tension-driven quiet engulfing the neighborhood.

He switched on the television to fill the living room with white noise. NuNu was dead. And the rest of them were in the eye of the storm.

Seraphina approached him. Her tread was softer than it had been earlier. The roll of her hips, subtle. She was back to being the seductress. For once, he wasn't in the mood to be seduced.

He declared, "I need to find a way to get us out of here."

Seraphina froze. "It sounds like you don't have faith in your wife."

It always came down to this. Whether or not he believed in her. Believing in her was irrelevant. The facts were the facts.

He had to be careful though. The truth was as hard to swallow as a five-pound boulder sometimes. That was especially true for Seraphina.

"Someone has you in their sights," he gently explained.

"I control all the street security in these buildings," she replied. "Someone always has me in their sights."

The set of Sera's shoulders became more resolute. "If someone wants to come for me, let them come."

Chase ran his hands up and down his legs. As if he was generating energy to respond. "The problem is, they're coming for other people, too. Fine, if you're risking yourself. But you're also risking Hawk. You're risking me. Hell, you're risking Vincent."

If nothing else, Vincent should get her attention.

Sera lowered to her knees to look him in the eye. "Do you love me?"

Chase pinched the bridge of his nose. Heaven help me.

Sera pulled his hand down."No, do you love me?"

"What good is that love? I mean, really, what good is it if we are all dead." Chase demanded.

CHAPTER 45

Seraphina stomped her way over to Vincent's apartment. Damn, Chase. She wanted to slash someone for the doubt that had crept into his voice. His job was to look pretty and stay by her side. He still looked pretty, but NuNu's death had rattled him, even more than the fights he'd gotten into with Hawk when they first moved in.

One little execution and he was ready to jump ship, as if this was the first time a member of her team had been shot. Chase had never been privy to the early days when Seraphina was trying to establish herself, or even how she reestablished herself.

Vincent got her the job; but even with Vincent behind her, people challenged her right to have it. As if she hadn't served the Knights for years, she literally had to fight for her spot.

In the warehouse, the Knights created a circle around Sera and Blue. Blue was so black he was blue and was beefy enough to play on the Chicago Bears defensive line. Blue took a swig of water, swished it, and spit it out.

The Knights murmured among themselves, probably placing bets. All sound hushed when Vincent asked, "Blue, what's your weapon?"

Chuckling so hard his belly jiggled, he responded. "Let Little Bit choose."

Oh, she was going to enjoy easing a knife through Blue's ribs. Sera smiled, "Knives." However, instead of her throwing knives, she received one steak knife. They might as well have allowed them to fist fight. She would need to get close to cut him.

Sera didn't take her eyes off Blue. They weren't supposed to start before Vincent's okay, but she'd seen shady shit in her years. Blue swayed slightly and blinked a couple of times. Vincent stepped back, "Go."

Something was off with Blue, but he lumbered forward anyway. Sera waited till he closed the gap between the two. At the last minute, she ducked to avoid his shaky attempt to stab her, dropped to her knees, and sliced his right Achilles tendon.

When he went down screaming, she sliced the other one. To this day, Blue claims he felt faint during the fight. That would explain the slight sway. However, what it also does is give a reason for Vincent's pause. There was a full minute between weapon selection and Vincent's telling them to go. However, treason at that level would get Vincent killed. Sera never said a word.

The rumor of what she'd done to Blue echoed through the neighborhood. They'd had a longer run of quiet than they ever had.

Climbing the stairs to Vincent's second floor apartment, she did a Temptation-worthy spin on the landing. This was going to be fun.

Ninja was going to find out something in his search of the tenants of the condos across the street. She could feel it in her bones. Once they figured out whom it was, the game would change. She'd be back in charge. And whomever it was, would be hunted like a deer in Wisconsin. She'd personally skin them alive.

She gave his door a few sharp raps. He opened the door, and his gaze softened the moment it focused in on her. She hit him in the chest. "Stop that."

Vincent's expression became a mask of innocence. "What?"

"Giving me that look."

Throwing his head back and laughing, he teased, "One day you're going to be living here, tucking me into bed every night."

Seraphina's head whipped up, so she could look him in the eye. "The hell."

In the Midst of Fire

He leaned in for a stage whisper. "I won't even tell you I told you so."

All these years and he was still so sure of her, even with all the evidence to the contrary. One of the ladies in the building told her once, "Marry the man that loves you more."

Looking at Vincent, she could've listened. She wasn't attracted to him, but there were worse things in the world than to be married to someone who would move heaven and earth for you.

"Oh," Vincent teased, "was that some softness in your eyes as you looked at me? Oh, shit." He waved his arms in the air, dancing like he was at the club. "It's about to go down up in here."

Seraphina brushed passed him and came all the way into the apartment. His setup was slightly different from hers. Vincent still stuck with the red, white, and black Chicago Bulls theme. His walls were all white. Posters of Jordan and Pippen decorated the walls as though he was still stuck in the three-peat era, in a refusal to embrace Derrick Rose.

A massive 60-inch television was displayed prominently above a glass entertainment console, which held every video gaming system available to man, along with a myriad of tangled cords. His black leather seating with red pillows was set up in a "U" shape in front the television.

The room was a bit messy, with a few shirts in various places around the room, a pair of jeans on the couch, as well as lotion and a pair of socks. She hoped that meant that he dressed in the room and had not jacked off.

Vincent's teasing made Seraphina want to smile, but they had serious business to tend to; so instead, she glared at him. The way his smile widened led her to believe that her glare didn't have any impact whatsoever.

No one knew her like Vincent. Was it possible she made the wrong choice? No. Chase was her husband. But still, years later, he'd never have her back like Vincent. Now would he ever love her like Vincent. Vincent saw her, understood her, and loved her anyway. It was getting harder to say no to that.

Feeling restless, she roamed over to his living room window. She reached for the curtains that were flapping in the breeze. She whipped them open. "Dude, you need some light and air in this place."

Vincent scurried over to the window. "Girl, don't you know better than—"

A sickening thud forced her to whip around in time to see Vincent touch his chest and his finger come back sticky with a bright red liquid. The shocked expression must have matched her own.

"Vincent!"

He collapsed on the floor, inhaling shallow breaths.

She ran and slid into him, cradling his head in her lap, rocking back and forth as she screamed her pain, ending with, "No. No. No. No. No."

His shallow sporadic breaths were the indication that the arrow had pierced something significant this time. She'd seen death enough to know when it had opened the door and walked right on in.

She pulled away. "Gotta call the ambulance."

Vincent's breath hitched. "No. No," he commanded. "Stay."

Seraphina couldn't keep the tears at bay. They flowed down her face in rapid succession. She keened softly.

Vincent's eyes followed her movement. "Shhh. Shhh. Baby, being in your lap means I'm already in heaven."

She snorted out a laugh. "V, baby. I need you to stay with me."

"I love you."

Vincent's eyes fluttered and closed.

Of course, she knew it was possible that Vincent could die. But this was Vincent. He was supposed to have her back—forever. "I love you, too."

With his eyes still closed, his lips produced a ghost of a smile. "Yeah, kinda' figured with all the tears and shit."

"I'll find them, V," she promised as she gently rubbed his scalp. "We'll find them. I'll make sure of it."

Vincent blinked his eyes open. "Looking at you is a damn fine way to go, mon chère."

Sniffling, Seraphina replied. "We aren't French." Her heart might actually be breaking. It might actually bleed out. She wanted to clutch her own chest because of the pain that filled her heart. But that would mean letting go of Vincent's head. And she wasn't letting go of him, not so soon. Seraphina pressed her lips against his.

She tried to get out the emotions that were welling up and leaking from her eyes. "I . . . I"

Vincent's smile increased. "I know, chère. I know."

And he released his last breath.

CHAPTER 46

In the short time since Giselle last heard from Ninja, she kept expecting him to come knocking on her door, at any moment. With his computer skills, he could find anyone. Actually, she wasn't trying to hide. People hadn't realized that they should be looking at her as a threat.

Settling in the sand on North Avenue Beach, she watched a Latino family as they went about their day. The children were running ahead and checking back to make sure their two smiling parents were following.

Giselle scooped up sand in her right hand and let it sift through her fingers until there were only a few grains left in her palm. The action was a sure representation of the people who meant the most in her life.

There was a comfort in knowing parents were still behind you as you forged your way in the world. It didn't go away when you reached adulthood.

Giselle wanted to look back and see a parent somewhere in the mix, ready to protect her, even as she ran towards independence.

Her mother was like that. She was such a joyous presence in their lives. Giselle remembered that last day with her. A crisp fall day when they'd taken a trip to the circus, her dad had bowed out, but he was home.

Sunday was always family day, starting with an awesome breakfast together and ending with a fantastic dinner. While driving home, her mother was doing a mean recap of the elephant that balked instead of following the other elephant.

"Kids, that elephant was like, I don't make nearly enough for this. They pay me peanuts." Laughing, she added. "I wish I had a strike poster to give him."

Giselle and Hawk were laughing. Suddenly they whipped to the side and back in place as a car slammed into the driver-side door and spun the car around, sending it into a tailspin.

Their laughter suddenly turned into screams that sounded unnaturally loud, even to Giselle's ears. She pushed a scream past the fear that temporarily robbed her of her voice.

She slammed her eyes shut, praying for stillness. After they hit something so hard, her body elevated from the seat, fighting the seatbelt for escape.

Thank goodness the seat belt won. She peeked out of her left eye in time to see a pole bending toward the windshield. Another closed-eye scream escaped before she understood what the weight of the silence from her mother and Hawk meant.

As she dared to open her eyes again, her mother was sitting among shards of broken glass, whispering. Giselle couldn't see her front, but a pole had staked through the windshield.

"G? Hawk? Please. G? Hawk?" Her mother coughed out their names.

Giselle looked over at Hawk, taking in his shallow breathing and the crumpled metal, indicating exactly on what side of the car they had been hit. But the blood coming from her mother scared her the most.

"Mom? Are you okay?" Giselle managed to ask. Something was wrong, so wrong.

"G, why isn't Hawk responding?"

Giselle cried. "I don't know, but he's breathing. That means he's fine, right?

Hawk groaned.

"Yes, dear," her mother replied. "See, he's groaning. He'll be fine."

Giselle attempted to loosen her seat belt, but couldn't manage it. "Mom? There's blood. Are you okay?"

Her mother took a shallow, broken breath. "Shhh, baby. I'm really tired. I want to close my eyes. But I can't . . . not until I say this one thing." Her breathing became labored. "I need you to take care of each other—always."

"Mom. Mommy," Hawk whispered.

"I'm here, Hawk," Rose responded.

"I hurt, Mommy," he simpered.

"It'll be fine," she croaked. "Hawk, listen, you and Giselle have to take care of each other."

"Mommy?" he choked out, as he fumbled with the seat belt.

Giselle knew that her mom was really, really hurt—the blood, the glass, the breathing. From her position in the passenger seat, Giselle could see much more than Hawk. Her mother had always been in constant motion—moving, cheering, hugging. Never still. Never quiet. Never whispering in pain.

Giselle shushed him with a simple, "Listen to her, Hawk."

"Take care of each other," she commanded. "Say you hear me."

"We hear you, Mommy," they answered in unison.

Then a raspy, "Love. You . . . " echoed over the hum of the car's engine.

Giselle couldn't stop crying. She sat in their broken car sobbing to the point that she threw up. Hawk managed to break free and released Giselle from the seat belt's constraints, dragging her from the car. It was Hawk who grabbed their mother's phone and dialed the police, then waited the eternity it seemed to take before the ambulance pulled up.

Giselle was on the sidelines then, too, shaking with pain and fear as the light of their lives was extinguished. She watched Hawk, who was only a few seconds younger, take charge and demonstrate strength that she clearly didn't possess. Thanks to Seraphina, she possessed it now.

She fought and forged her own steel, came back to the block, lived on the outskirts of the Burnham Park Apartments, preparing herself to take Seraphina to the death, if it came to that.

She hadn't done a good job, though, of protecting Hawk. She had left him encased in the clutches of his stepmother, trying to play along with whatever game she was playing in exchange for Giselle's freedom.

Giselle could skip, walk, run, tour the Maldives, if she wanted. Hawk had maintained such a life in such a tight perimeter, it was like the rest of the

In the Midst of Fire

city didn't exist for him.

Though Hawk was the one who held her hand, even though his own was bloody from the shattered glass on his side of the car; now fifteen years later, he was still doing more than his share to ensure he kept his promise to their mother.

Well, that was changing; it had changed the minute she'd taken her first self-defense class. She'd kept her promise to her brother. Giselle was now in the game. And she was making the rules.

She owed her brother way too much. Liberating her brother from the clutches of Seraphina was the first order of business.

That woman had years keeping her foot on Hawk's neck, threatening him with the demise of his family. Her only reason for doing so, was to keep the two males under her roof. If she had to threaten people to keep them around, then is it really keeping them? People should want to stay.

Giselle slipped off her Nike trainers, pulled off the Nike socks, and dug her toes into the sand. Resting her chin on her knees, she watched the waves lap up on the sand.

A little girl, she had to be about four, was playing with the tide, running back and forth trying to outrun the water. Giselle remembered when she used to do that.

A shadow fell over her. Holding up her hand to her forehead to block the sun, her heart skipped a beat until that familiar face came into focus.

"What are you doing here?"

CHAPTER 47

The lights of a police car created patterns on the walls.

Seraphina!

Chase jumped up and threw on a pair of deck shoes. He scanned the block, praying to see her. Her diminutive body was nowhere to be found, but the police were swarming in front of Vincent's building. When she was angry, that would be exactly where Sera would head.

The building entrance was blocked by officers who were checking IDs before they let anyone inside. Chase paced the concrete. In his rush, he'd forgotten his cell. He couldn't even call her.

He wasn't a church-going man, but he began praying that she was okay. He approached the officers at the door and noticed Officer Scalero was leading the pack.

"Sera. Is it Seraphina?"

"Sir, we're only allowing residents into the building at this time," Scalero sneered, giving him a disdainful look.

Chase took a deep breath to try to calm down, so he wouldn't punch the smug officer square in the nose.

"Sera! Sera!" In this heat, enough windows were open in Vincent's apartment. She would hear him . . . if she could. "Sera!"

In the Midst of Fire

Scowling, Scalero moved closer. "Keep it down," he warned. "Seraphina!"

"She's fine," Scalero huffed, finally coming to the realization that Chase wasn't going away. "Your wife's alive."

Just then Sera flew from the building, blood covering the front of her clothes and staining her hands. He staggered back, as he took on the force of her weight when she landed in his arms.

"Vincent. They got Vincent."

Seraphina sucked in breath after breath, each one a bit deeper and a little more desperate. Chase led her over to a half-broken chair that someone had put in front of the building. She sat down and tried to regain her breath.

"It was so quick. I opened the curtain. He went to close it, and just that quickly they shot him. They killed him."

For some reason those words didn't fill him with the remorse that he thought it should.

"They shot into the apartment?" he finally said. "It's a miracle you weren't hit."

Seraphina gazed at him, her eyes dripping in sadness, even while she clenched her teeth in anger. "An arrow. One arrow through the heart."

Chase merely held her stiff form, as she glared at nothing.

As Seraphina's breath normalized, she croaked. "They're playing with me."

"Who?" He rubbed her back, trying to relax her.

That was the question of the hour. Who had killed both NuNu and Vincent in less than twenty-four hours? He'd watched enough television to know that's called escalation; and once killers escalated, it didn't get any better.

Sera's eyes took on a glint so evil it sent shivers down Chase's back. Slowly, she inched from the chair, her back bowed. Her hoarse voice started so low. "Someone over there. I'll find out who soon enough. And then I'll toy with his ass. I'll kill his sister, his brother, his dog, before I end his life."

Chase glanced over at the police, hoping they hadn't heard her outright declaration of murder. "Shhhhh, Seraphina. Someone may hear you."

Seraphina's eyes glittered with anger and unshed tears. "Hear this," she shrieked with her arms and fingers extended, as if she was putting a "root" on the whole neighborhood. "A five-thousand-dollar reward for information leading to the person shooting arrows on my block. Cash."

The groups of people that were milling around earlier suddenly shifted their attention to Seraphina. People whispered behind their hands, as they watched Seraphina put a bounty on someone in broad daylight. Some people were bold enough to laugh, if their shaking bodies were any indication.

The big, bad, knife-wielding bitch had finally gone all the way around the bend. The police engaged in conversation with each other, but their eyes were steadily focused on Seraphina. Chase pantomimed a gesture that signaled "crazy" to the officers. With the blood covering her clothing and wild hair, it wasn't a stretch. Chase grabbed Seraphina's hand, guiding her toward their building.

Seraphina kept right on talking. "I promise you. I will flush them out, then snuff them out." She snapped her fingers, "Just like that."

"Come on," he encouraged, grabbing her hand. "We're going home."

Seraphina dug her heals in, snatching away. "No, I'm staying here until someone gives me a name."

Chase grabbed her arm. "Sera. Seraphina?"

"No, I'm not leaving until someone tells me who the hell over there . . . ," she pointed at the condo across the street, "wants me dead."

"Come out, come out wherever you are," she sang out, then opened both arms wide. "Here I am. Broad daylight. Easy target."

The police merely glanced from her to the condos across the street.

Chase couldn't believe this. She was losing her damn mind right in front of him, jumping up and down screaming, daring someone to shoot her with an arrow. Even as he continued tugging her arm, a crowd began to form.

Scalero and Chase made eye contact, and he mimed that they were heading home. Scalero nodded.

Seraphina continued yelling, as he dragged her back to the apartment.

Her hysterical delivery was probably the only thing keeping her away from the police. Crazed Angel was one thing. Crazier, psychotic Angel? Hell, even Chase wanted to flee.

She was so hysterical that he wanted to slap her, but there was the small issue that she had lost her hold on reality and she liked to cut people.

Losing Vincent make her crazier than a cat chasing a laser beam. He shut the door.

"Why did you drag me back here?" she demanded.

"Do you want everyone to think you've gone crazy? What's all this?" he asked, waving his hands wildly in the air. "Whatever that display was, that's all it was going to do."

Seraphina lost her steam and crumbled to the floor. "He shot Vincent."

He wrapped her in his arms. "We'll find him."

She began rocking, weeping. "Vincent."

Chase held her as she continued to cry. Now wasn't the time to be jealous of the fact that she broke down for a man he practically hated. Although Chase did feel some kind of way about it, he focused on the bigger picture.

NuNu and Vincent were on the block more often. It was easier to track their movements. That's probably the only reason he was alive today. Chase wiped Seraphina's tears away. He brushed her lips with his own, but his mind was swirling with the knowledge that Seraphina was probably going to die.

And if he stayed, he would as well.

So as he held her tight and nuzzled her cheek, he had to question, was she worth his life? And with a heavy heart he realized, the answer was no.

CHAPTER 48

Giselle's lip quirked in a half-smile, as she answered Ninja's question. "You mean, here at the beach?"

His body stiffened,

Teasing him probably wasn't the best move to make. "Oh, here in Chicago?"

"Yes." Ninja bit out.

Giselle patted the empty space of the sand on her right side. "Would you like to have a seat?"

Ninja didn't respond; a vein at his temple throbbed a steady beat. Obviously, it was taking great effort to hold in his anger.

"Guess not," Giselle mumbled.

Ninja was quite imposing, as he looked down on her. Breaking eye contact, she turned her attention back to the families and children playing in the water.

Silence stretched on, but this time it was Ninja who filled it. "Do you have any idea what Seraphina will do when she finds out you're back in Chicago?"

Four years was a long time. Giselle was no longer scared of Seraphina. Fear would make her stupid. And she couldn't be stupid fighting

Seraphina. She had to be calm and ready. "I really and truly couldn't care less."

Ninja shifted, blocking the sun from Giselle's face, allowing him to see her clearly for the first time. "Does Hawk know?"

She thought back to when she had followed him to the beach. How he didn't even bothered to give her a hug, his own sister; whom he hadn't seen since the wretched day when they were jumped. He warned her that Seraphina was crazy; then told her to go away.

"He knows that I was here," she responded, putting her focus on the sun. "He doesn't know that I didn't heed his warning." She chuckled. "He's so used to me following his lead. So he probably assumes that I'm back at Lexington."

Ninja didn't move, didn't shift, nor did he chuckle along with her. The tension pulsating from him was more than enough. She sighed, "Chicago is my home. I should be able to come home, right?"

Ninja's gaze lowered to the sand. "Chicago was your home."

Giselle unfolded her frame until she reached her full 5 feet 9 inch height. Still a good four inches less than his, but it didn't matter. "Seraphina doesn't run the whole city. She controls one project. One. And she rarely leaves her neighborhood."

Ninja's dark brown eyes seared into hers. "Which would be fine, if you hadn't taken up residence across the street from the projects."

"Damn computers." Giselle threw a handful of sand only to have the wind whip it back at her. "The condo isn't even in my name."

"Our last call made me suspicious," Ninja explained. "Your reaction confirmed it."

Damn Ninja. "You do know that spying on people is an invasion of their privacy."

Ninja perused the beach. "What game are you playing, Giselle?"

Giselle wanted so desperately to reach up and caress his face; to kiss him. But the truth was, they were on two different sides.

Shecouldn't afford to be vulnerable to Ninja. At least no more than she already was.

"I just want Hawk free from all of this."

"Hawk is a grown-ass man," he snapped. "You don't need to risk yourself for him."

Giselle didn't know if Ninja understood normal family bonds. In the few conversations she'd had with Ninja, he never mentioned a brother, sister, mother, father, uncle, second cousin twice removed on his momma's side. Nothing. Even she had cousins. They were distant, but they existed. Hell, Lizzie had married one.

He certainly didn't understand twin bonds. He didn't know that being ripped from Hawk like she had been, had caused her physical pain.

If she had been thinking more clearly, she wouldn't have left in the first place. Well, that wasn't true. She would've left because Hawk asked her to.

She became an adult alone, without the companionship that would have brought solace. She had thought long and hard about the decision to come to the Windy City.

There were forty-nine other states, plus Puerto Rico, the U.S. Virgin Islands, just a whole world of places where she could have made her place in the world.

Truth be told, she couldn't imagine going anywhere else without Hawk. They had come in this world together. and they would traverse it together.

"Ninja, you're an island. Alone. I don't expect you to understand. But I do need to risk myself for him." Giselle eased her hand into his. "He's my brother."

Ninja blinked as though he was trying to erase Giselle's very existence from his mind. "And if your presence causes him pain? what then?"

"And if my presence frees him, what then?" she countered, pissed that she had to justify her decision. He was worse than Hawk.

Ninja turned his back to her. The muscles underneath his shirt bunched and released. A group of teenagers walked towards them. Two guys were carrying coolers between them, while the girls kept in step, their arms linked as they laughed.

Giselle marveled at their freedom, the lightness and confidence in each step. Was she ever that young? She wasn't much older now. That could have been Hawk and Lizzie.

Yet, it wasn't. Hawk's steps had been heavy since the day their mother died. She'd been so focused on reaching the next level, the next accomplishment, the next . . . hell, she didn't know. She did know, though, that she'd never been any member of that group.

The weight of her life like Hawk's would have bowed a weaker back.

She was so focused on the group that she didn't notice Ninja turn until he reached up, trailing his thumb along her chin. "You don't even know the half of what's going on."

Giselle leaned in to his touch and whispered, "So tell me."

Ninja snatched his hands away, shoving them in his pockets.

Giselle inwardly screamed. *No. Come closer. Touch me.*

"I don't know if I'll be able to protect you," Ninja murmured.

Giselle closed her eyes, luxuriating in the memory of his touch, fleeting as it was. The group of teenagers ran up to the water and squealed once their feet connected with that cool liquid. Hawk deserved to experience that. She remembered the feeling of freedom, the lightness, the laughter—all elements that surrounded her mother like a silk cocoon. Giselle's life was supposed to be like that.

Turning towards Ninja, she realized all the changes she made to herself. Her dedication to her mission changed her forever. She'd never be one of those girls. Daring Ninja to contradict her, she responded. "I didn't ask you to."

Ninja pursed his lips. "But you may need me to, and that changes everything."

Giselle's anger erupted. "What are you talking about? What does it change? Why are you always so damn cryptic? All full of secrets."

Ninja merely raised one eyebrow. He was subtly referring to the fact that she had snuck into town and moved across from the apartments, but that wasn't relevant to the conversation at hand.

"Shut up," she growled.

Ninja gave a barely perceptible smirk. "Thought so." He turned to leave. "Good luck."

"Ninja," Giselle said in a voice barely louder than a sigh. The normal person may have missed it, but Ninja paused. "It was good seeing you again."

CHAPTER 49

Hawk took a deep breath and closed his eyes. Closing his eyes was probably a risky proposition, given how the crew was dropping like flies. But keeping their eyes open hadn't kept some of them alive either.

From down the block, he witnessed Seraphina's meltdown and how his father dragged her back to their apartment. He laughed, causing all the gawkers on the block to stare at him before they returned to talking in hushed whispers. Hawk didn't care.

He'd come to the realization that he needed to be careful what he prayed for. For years, he had prayed that someone would take Seraphina out. Then she couldn't threaten Giselle or his dad. Then he'd be free.

There were a lot of ways to be free. And death was the ultimate freedom.

No one gave a shit about shit when they were six feet under. It would be his luck that as he was praying for Seraphina's demise, he was going to cause his own. That was some seriously bad luck.

His phone buzzed in his pocket. Taking it out, he looked at the number. He never answered his phone on the block. That caused questions and curiosity. He didn't need either.

Ignoring Lizzie by putting his phone away, his mind whirled. He needed a plan, a good one, one guaranteed to make her stay. He motioned Hitta over.

"Hey, keep an eye out."

Hitta nodded and Hawk headed to where he always went to think. That was one thing about being in Chicago. All he had to do was head east, and eventually he'd hit water. It was true when he was rich, and it was true today, when he was so far from where his family's life began. The lakefront was the great equalizer.

The closer Hawk made it to the beach, the more he could inhale air that reeked of seaweed, instead of stale weed and cigarettes, his shoulders relaxed. He'd find a way to get the elusive Ninja alone and get that paper. Ninja mentioned previously that there was more money in the drug game. It may be time for him to cross over.

Even through his musing, he could feel eyes watching him, different eyes than he was used to. He was used to female energy coming at him in waves. He would smile or ignore it, depending on his mood. This was different. He perused faces trying to locate the threat.

The threat was in front of him, wearing cream slacks and a matching short-sleeve blouse. Her hair was pulled back in a ponytail. Her lithe body matched her daughter's. Only her face was hard, as if it had been etched from the kind of stone that made up those new condos. And her hazel eyes could have cut diamonds. Lizzie's mom. She was pissed . . . still.

Smirking, he walked up to her as if they were old friends. "Mrs. Warner. Fancy seeing you here." He let his eyes wander from the top of that deceitful head to the bottom of her trifling toes. "You look," he paused for effect, because he knew it would piss her off even more, "healthy."

She could have avoided him, crossed the street. She had chosen not to. She took his family away, forced Lizzie into a marriage, and all in the name of her dollar god. And now, the tables were turned, because Tory was trying to take her daughter, her grandchildren, and his checkbook to Paris—leaving her here and broke.

"Hawk," Mrs. Warner acknowledged his presence. "You look . . . hood." From a distance, he was certain they looked cordial, but this was

In the Midst of Fire

the only woman in the world who made his fist itch to connect with her face. Well, and Seraphina; but Mrs. Warner was even more dangerous. You expect shit from the hood. Lizzie's mother was the most ruthless hood he'd ever met, but she hid it behind a fancy address and impeccable manners.

Hawk laughed and walked around her.

She grabbed his arm, "Wait."

He paused and turned to gaze at her. Yes, she had bags under her eyes. Hair roots were graying. But she still screamed understated money.

Hawk didn't know what she wanted, but it was her big mouth that ruined everything for everyone. "Yes?"

With a softened voice, she explained. "Listen . . . I may have been hasty."

Hawk folded his arms to keep them from striking out at her. How dare she talk about being hasty now? *Now* she wanted to apologize. "When exactly?"

Mrs. Warner pressed her lips together until they were a straight line. "When I encouraged Lizzie to marry Tory, I may have been a bit hasty."

"Why are you admitting it now?" he challenged. "Because he has the means to make sure you don't see your daughter or grandchildren again? Or is it because he cut you off; and until Lizzie gets her check at 25, you're going to be penniless?"

Mrs. Warner looked off in the distance for a few moments. "She still loves you, you know."

How dare she? How dare she mention things she knew nothing about. "I don't need you to tell me that. I don't need you to tell me anything."

Hawk rushed past Mrs. Warner and narrowly missed getting swiped by a cab, shifting into the far right lane to pass a stalled vehicle. The driver honked and Hawk jumped back on the curb. Mrs. Warner grabbed his arm, forcing him to face her.

"Listen," Mrs. Warner demanded. Her face, originally chiseled hard with hate, evolved into an almost serene look. The softness around her eyes, framed with long lashes, almost made Hawk gasp. The suddenness of the transformation from an evil bitch to a beautiful woman was so shocking that Hawk wanted to touch her face to see if it was real. She was a chameleon.

Mrs. Warner spoke of Lizzie with every word serving as a testament to the love she had for her daughter. If Hawk hadn't seen the other versions of Mrs. Warner, he might have believed this one.

"She's my baby and you . . . well . . . did what you did, and I may have gone a little crazy." Loosening the claw-like grip on his arm, she added, "But we can change this."

And here we go, the pitch.

"I can get you a job somewhere in the Warner Consortium."

Hawk shifted his weight back to his heels. "I'm confused. If you're able to hand out jobs like that, why don't you get one instead of leeching off your daughter all this time?"

Mrs. Warner's left eye twitched. "As I was saying, I can get you a good-paying job. You and Lizzie can move back in the house. The executor won't have an issue with that. And all will be well."

Hawk thought back to the conversation he'd had with Lizzie about her inheritance. She specifically said a baby at her age would mean she was cut off. Mrs. Warner was a lot of things. A stupid woman she was not; a liar, absolutely.

Something deep in Hawk's gut screamed deception. This witch. "You lied to her."

Mrs. Warner lowered her gaze, as if inspecting her Manolos. Hawk grabbed her arm, causing all the Northsiders to give them a wide berth.

One man stopped and demanded, "Hey. Whatcha' doing?"

Hawk released her. "Tell me," he growled, his gaze never wavered from hers as the heat from his eyes conflicted with the innocence emanating from hers.

Mrs. Warner opened her mouth.

"And it better be the absolute, one-hundred percent right hand on the Bible, God strike me down truth!"

Mrs. Warner closed her mouth, brushed her hair, already perfect, back with her hands and pretended to straighten her blouse. "Lizzie will always be taken care of. The level of support shifts, depending on a few things. But Lizzie will always be fine."

In the Midst of Fire

Mrs. Warner's dark brown gaze skittered around but came back to the activity in the intersection. The light dawned with a sudden realization of truth.

"You. You're cut out of the will," he exclaimed. "Her pregnancy made you destitute."

Again, Mrs. Warner snapped her attention back to him.

Hawk's heart lightened. "He must've really hated you."

Mrs. Warner kept her focus on the crowds crossing under the bridge leading to the beach. "Lizzie was a surprise . . . , to him at least. Oh, he married me and he loved his daughter. But our relationship was cordial at best."

Hawk stared for a half a minute before answering. "No."

Mrs. Warner snatched her focus from the crowd and put it back on him. "What do you mean, no?"

"No, I'm not going to help you make Lizzie your sugar baby anymore."

Mrs. Warner's serene mask fell, and evil shot from her coal black eyes. "Well, then we'll both lose, won't we?"

Hawk stormed past her. "I'll find a way to get my family back without your help. You, on the other hand, better have a damn plan or something because public aid doesn't cover Prada."

Now more than ever, he was determined to get his family to stay in Chicago. That crazy heifer wasn't going to win. And she wasn't going to live off of Lizzie for one more day.

He whipped out his phone, hoping to get to Lizzie before her mother could put a nasty spin on what happened. He couldn't believe his luck or Mrs. Warner's desperation. Either way, he thanked a God he hadn't talked to in fourteen years for handing him the key to the only thing that kept him and Lizzie apart.

He felt sorry for Tory, even though he had every intention of tearing the man's family apart. And he was very grateful because Tory kept Lizzie insulated. He made it possible for her to stay herself, without her mother's evil or his problems changing her.

The closer Hawk got to the beach, the more sand covered the sidewalk. He wanted to take his shoes off; but there was always something hidden in those grains, and he wasn't up for any surprises cutting his feet.

On the fifth ring, Lizzie whispered a tentative, "Hello?"

"Just ran into Mrs. Warner."

"My mother—" Lizzie replied, confusion etched in her tone.

"Is a liar," Hawk blurted, "a big one. Contact the executor of your father's estate—or the head of the law firm, a partner, someone high up—today, without her being on the line. There's something about your inheritance that you need to know."

Hawk heard a deep rumble in the background. Lizzie responded to the voice in the background, then uttered into the phone. "Listen, I don't have time—"

"On my life and all those that I love, you have to get to them, today."

Lizzie paused. "I'll make that happen."

He released the breath he didn't realize he wasn't holding. Then he stopped breathing, walking, thinking—fire took root in his scalp.

"What did my mom say exactly?" Lizzie inquired.

"I have to go," he whispered, and quickly disconnected the call. He reached around into the small of his back and felt the bit of steel he kept nestled there. Wrapping his finger around the base of his gun, he wondered what the hell Giselle was still doing in Chicago. And with Ninja.

CHAPTER 50

Chase untangled himself from Sera, and he found himself mesmerized by the curve of her ass. Reaching over, he grazed his fingers over that chocolate perfection. He remembered her complaining before about the cut of jeans and how it was impossible to find a pair that fit right.

To him, it was perfection. She could walk around all day, every day, in just a thong and heels, and he would be a happy man; with the exception of the fact that he could also very well be a dead man. That was the crux of their issues. In a perfect world . . . He sighed and ran his fingers through his hair. Why even bother?

He had hoped that Hawk would leave him to the life that he deserved. He had taken Hawk down, as surely as if he tethered his ankle to a rock and threw it in the ocean.

Giselle had managed to escape this hellhole. Hopefully, one day Hawk would be free. Today, Chase had to figure out how he, himself, was going to leave this place.

He took a few strands of Seraphina's hair in his fingers, letting the silkiness slide through his fingers. Today, the air was thick with anxiety. People were dying. Even residents in the project were probably betting on whether or not Seraphina would be next.

He had a very narrow window to make sure he wasn't next. If he left right now, this minute; if he just left everything, walked out the door and started his life somewhere else, Seraphina would kill Hawk. She wouldn't take kindly to being dumped.

He couldn't hide from the depth of her evil anymore.

And if they stayed, no doubt their new residence would be worse than their current one. It would be six feet deep and surrounded by dirt.

Chase laid back into the bed, watching Seraphina's breath rise and fall. She slept the sleep of the exhausted, or maybe it was the sleep of avoidance. Either way, her nap had a lulling, calming effect. After all of the trauma and tragedy, a bit of calm was welcome.

He put his hands behind his head and leaned back, listening to the sounds of the night. Someone's television was on way too loud, piping some police show through the apartment window. Children were still on the block. Some kids were yelling for Baby Bro to come on. Judging by the bass in Baby Bro's response, they needed to leave the baby off of the name.

Occasionally, a truck or bus would rumble down the street. This should be the time he felt the most restful, but instead he was restless.

Every arrow that flew might as well have hit Seraphina directly. Every arrow that flew at one of Seraphina's people caused her to unravel just a bit more. A semistable Seraphina was difficult enough to manage. This Seraphina was daring the world to kill her. The world obviously was uninterested in her offer.

If Vincent's death impacted her like this, the world had already won that game. One more arrow, Seraphina would be ready to be fitted with a white jacket and sitting in a circle discussing her feelings with a group of total strangers.

Even as she demanded respect and loyalty, she was losing the battle for sanity. She knew it, and everyone around her knew it. Seraphina was losing everything she held dear, including her already suspect grip on reality.

He eased out of bed to stare at the condos across the street. Unlike Seraphina, he wasn't entranced by the building. The building didn't shoot arrows. People shot arrows. They were no closer to figuring out who did the shooting than they were when NuNu was alive.

In the Midst of Fire

Chase shifted his focus, mesmerized by a plane inching its way across the sky. The beacon lights on the wings called to him. Planes meant escape, freedom.

He knew when he saw fake Giselle that he needed to make a change. However, needing to make a change and actually making a change were two different things.

He lounged around the apartment for years, so caught up in his feelings that he let Seraphina take over all the family finances, draw Hawk into her game, and treat him like a puppet instead of a man.

Beyond the television, Chase heard the faint strains of Roberta Flack's "The First Time Ever I Saw Your Face." Straining to hear better, soon he found himself softly singing the lyrics. It was the song the he and Rose danced to at their wedding.

He had heard it before over the years, but this time . . . this time it brought him to his knees. With Seraphina snoring, and the police from the cop show cursing, he collapsed and begged Rose to forgive him.

Forgive him for failing her, for not driving them to the circus, for not telling her every day how absolutely lucky he was to have spent one day in her presence. Forgive him for not providing for her children, for not being there, for checking out of their lives and for denigrating the love he and Rose shared, by treating marriage like a game to be played, instead of a commitment to be honored.

Chase knew that first and foremost. He had to forgive himself. He couldn't spend the rest of his life or Hawk's life or Giselle's life wallowing in all the things he should have done differently.

Touching his cheeks, he pulled his hand back and stared at the moisture accumulated on his fingertips. No, it was time that he was a father first.

He knew the time for him and Seraphina was over. He had to leave, but he couldn't leave without a place to go, without a plan. He needed help. Chase felt it was too embarrassing to keep in touch with his friends while living in Burnham Park Apartments, so he didn't have many options on who could help. He might as well have fallen through the earth's core, instead of a few miles south.

Unless . . . , Chase creased his forehead in thought. A light had turned on. Maybe, it was time to show someone else that unconditional love that Rose had shown him. It was time to make right a wrong. He just had to figure out how.

CHAPTER 51

The breeze whipped past Giselle, trying to push her further toward this man who had insinuated himself into her thoughts. She stood staunchly in place, even though she yearned to touch him.

And if she did, she wasn't positive she'd have the strength to let go. Letting go of her mom was bad enough, letting go of her dad, letting go of Hawk, it was wearing on her.

Before then, she'd never been without Hawk for a twenty-four-hour span of time. There were no camps, vacations, anything that separated them at any time. And she had left him, injured and bloody.

He had saved her. She saved herself. And no one had saved him. He was trapped in Seraphina's cage of threats. Giselle had every intention of busting that bitch open as soon as possible.

She shifted her focus back to the man who made her want to forget revenge and just sink into his arms. He did look good, standing there in black jeans, T-shirt, and jumpers—clean and crisp. But she couldn't get sidetracked messing around with Sera's right-hand man.

Ninja's shoulders tensed and rolled. She whipped around in time to see Hawk reaching into the small of his back. Damn! That was never a good maneuver. Swear to God. Men.

"Wait," she called out to Hawk, and broke into a sprint, deliberately putting herself in the line between Hawk and Ninja before they did something stupid.

She could feel the emotions coursing through Hawk's body before clearly seeing his face. He pulled his hand from his back, set, and prepared. She launched herself into his arms.

He crushed her rib cage while lifting her from the ground. Home. Felt so good to be home. "This is how our first meeting was supposed to go," she whispered.

The chuckle rumbled in his chest, followed by a deep inhale. "It took everything in me to walk away from you. Had I even glanced your way, I wouldn't have been able to do it."

Giselle pulled back and looked him in the eye, but he was already looking over her shoulder. Clearly, he had only been temporarily distracted.

Tension rippled, and she could only assume it was because Ninja was close by. She wondered how she was going to explain Ninja's presence to Hawk when she didn't quite understand it herself.

"Hawk, wow. Here you sit on the block day after day like you don't have a care. One week, there's a tasty treat with a son that's not your son; and the next week, your sister who's supposed to be in Pennsylvania is living across the street from you."

Hawk and Giselle paused and chorused. "What?"

Words and volume battled for supremacy, as they turned to each other. "What treat? What son?

"Are you crazy moving across the street?!"

They stared at each other, and Giselle felt Ninja's eyes taking everything in. Damn Ninja. Stealthy as ever.

She watched the little boy building a castle, scooping sand, and hoped he was digging a hole big enough for her to disappear. Wishful thinking, no way she could get around this question.

Giselle took a deep breath, dragging her big toe through the sand. "Yeah, the place across from the projects is owned by the Warner Consortium."

Hawk snapped to attention. "Lizzie knows you're in the city?"

Apparently, Lizzie kept good secrets, but it was obvious that Hawk did, too. "You didn't corner the market on Lizzie. She's my friend, too. And if that tasty treat Ninja's referring to isn't Lizzie, you'd better explain."

Giselle understood every emotion crossing Hawk's face. He didn't want to talk in front of Ninja. She touched Hawk's arm. "I trust him."

Hawk didn't look at her. Instead, he kept his focus on Ninja, who was standing wearing his signature smirk. Damn it. She wanted to smack it off. Hawk's temper was also percolating.

Turning, she narrowed her eyes at Ninja. "Stop!"

Ninja gave a slight nod, which was probably as submissive he'd ever been.

Hawk's head vacillated between the two of them; understanding flashed in an instant. "Oh, come on, Giselle. Ninja? Ninja!"

Hawk threw a few air punches and paced a full minute before calming down enough to add, "You know how many men there are in this world? And Ninja's the best you can come up with?"

Hawk's outburst caused people to gape at them. Giselle grabbed both of them by the arm and pulled them along to a less crowded area of the beach.

Damn, Hawk! The last thing she needed was him all up in arms for no reason. "We're not together."

Her brother stopped in the middle of the pathway.

Giselle focused on his eyes. "We're not."

Hawk leaned in, flattening his lips—a sure sign that he believed she was lying.

"Dude. She's been at Lex U," Ninja said with an ear-to-ear grin. "I've been here."

Hawk flickered a gaze over to Ninja and started walking again. "You didn't just meet up today."

Giselle wondered how much to tell Hawk. The joy and curse of being a twin is that they not only heard what you said, but they felt what you didn't say.

Lies between them would never work. The truth may send Hawk over the edge, but maybe if she eased into it.

"You have to promise to listen to the whole story and not fly off the handle."

Hawk eased back, his gaze still moving between Giselle and Ninja. With a clenched jaw, he nodded.

"Seraphina sent Ninja to Lexington."

Hawk flinched, as though someone had struck him, but his strides kept pace with hers. "Were you supposed to . . . well?"

Ninja shook his head. "She was just supposed to know that I could get to her."

Hawk stopped dead in his tracks. "Like NuNu?"

Ninja stepped in Hawk's space so fast that Hawk slipped on the sand. He righted himself before Ninja emphasized, "Don't you ever mention me and NuNu in the same sentence."

Giselle held her breath. They focused solely on each other. Giselle couldn't tell what telepathy they were passing, but they both settled down and continued hustling away from the crowds.

"We went for coffee and talked," Ninja continued. "She's different."

"Swear to God if you so much as touched . . . ," Turning towards Giselle, he snapped, "Do you know what he does? He eliminates people for a living. Did he tell you that?"

Giselle went to him, wrapped him in a hug. She couldn't help it. She had missed Hawk's overprotective nature so much. "God I missed you."

Hawk tightened his grip on her waist. "That didn't answer the question."

Giselle didn't want to let go. This is how she was supposed to have spent the last four years—talking, teasing, sharing her life with Hawk. How did she make it through college without him? She wanted to graft her leg with his and become Siamese twins. She wanted to do flips in the sand.

Instead, she gave him a few quick pecks on his cheek, which he tried to avoid. "Calm down, Hawk. He's only called to check on me a few times. He didn't even know I was in town. So it's not what you think. He's pissed at me, too."

Hawk lifted his eyebrows, but didn't continue that line of questioning. Giselle could feel him. This close she had no secrets from him. This close

In the Midst of Fire

he practically knew every thought in her head. He knew. Their connection was that strong.

He could let that go, but Ninja's other statement required a bit more explanation. Looking out of the corner of her eyes, she urged, "If the son is not your son, then whose son is it?"

Hawk made a few small stretching movements like he was uncomfortable in his skin. "I thought you've been in contact with Lizzie."

"Apparently not enough," Giselle grumbled. She spoke to Lizzie about once a month. And they talked enough for her to know that Hawk was still in the 'hood and he was alive, but she never mentioned anything more than that.

Hawk blew out a jagged breath. "Lizzie had a baby after she got married. " Glaring at Ninja, he continued. "Ninja saw us together once and assumed the child was mine. He didn't know Lizzie's married Cousin Tory."

Giselle grimaced.

Hawk elbowed her as discreetly as he could.

Tory being gay was the worst kept secret in the family.

Ninja had to have seen at least some part of the interaction between the two of them, but as usual, he remained silent.

If Ninja's supposition was correct, she had a nephew. And that would explain what kept him in Chicago, away from her. And it would explain how precarious his position really was. Was Seraphina above bringing Lizzie and the boy into the fray? Hawk wouldn't ever tell Ninja the true parentage of that boy.

She grabbed Hawk's hand. "Ninja won't tell her."

Hawk stared straight ahead, jaw tightening, "There's nothing to tell."

"I told you it was none of my business," Ninja insisted. "It still isn't."

"Tory's got plans," Hawk explained. "If they move to Paris, they'll be out of her reach. But they'll also be out of mine."

He took a deep breath. "If I find a way to make them stay, there's always the risk that Seraphina will find them and use them against me in some sick game. She'd kill my family so that I'll play the part of being hers."

Giselle thought that over for a few moments, sifting through all of their options.

Hawk squeezed her hand. "I don't know what to do."

Giselle understood the issue. She'd been working for years to make sure she was strong enough and skilled enough to do one thing. "Kill her."

Ninja and Hawk shared a startled glance before shifting their gaze to Giselle. She refused to meet their eyes. They could stare all they wanted. That conniving bitch was out of time.

In the Midst of Fire

CHAPTER 52

Chase stood outside a house he hadn't been inside in years. He couldn't stand there all day. In this section of Lincoln Park, neighbors called the police first and asked questions later. However, like Burnham Park, the police would have the alleged perpetrator in a squad car before they could get a good sentence out.

A man walked his dog across the street, casting curious glances in Chase's direction. Shaking his head, Chase walked up to the door. Blowing a deep breath, he pressed the bell.

At one time, he had imagined himself and the kids living there. But he had killed that dream and ended up with a nightmare. To resurrect that, he needed to be the best version of himself. He hadn't seen that version since Rosie had been laid to rest.

Looking through the glass door, he saw her before she saw him. Raquel Warner was a manipulator in her own right. She'd see right through any game he threw her way. Hell, given how they ended things about five years ago; or more accurately, given how he ended things, she may not even be open to this conversation.

He didn't have a choice. To save his son and himself, he had to try. He rang the bell and watched through the glass as Raquel walked to the door. When she rounded the corner and came close enough to really see his image, she froze. Her expression went blank.

They stared at each other through the glass. She managed to keep it tight all these years. That was a good thing. Chase wasn't particularly interested in being with someone he would have to roll in and out of bed on a daily basis.

He held up his hand in a wave. Raquel remained rooted where she was. He gestured toward the lock, and she trudged until she placed her hand on the door; and then she waited, almost as if she was trying to talk herself out of letting him in. Evidently, curiosity won out. The door swung open.

"Chase." Her voice was tense, arms folded under her breasts. He was going to have to be more than good; he was going to have to be damn near brilliant.

"Raquel." His gaze roamed the length of her body, allowing his face to register appreciation for what he saw.

She smirked, "Wouldn't your wife mind if you are looking at other women like they were a bottle of Gatorade after a marathon?"

Raquel was the antithesis of Sera. Where Sera was short, Raquel was tall and statuesque. Where Sera was a deep blackberry, Raquel had a honey-kissed complexion. Where Sera manipulated him to stay, Raquel walked away with her head high and destructive anger in her heart. Now he needed Raquel to want him back as desperately as Sera wanted him to stay.

Raquel tightened her grip on the door, eyes warily searching for his reason for gracing her doorstep. "You never change."

Chase smiled slowly. "I'm sure I have. I'm all about constant improvement." His eyes narrowed a bit and lips lifted a smidge higher, just enough for her to think about all the ways he could be better.

She broke contact first, lifting her head to watch over his shoulder. Her stance shifted slightly to the right. Gotcha'. If Chase knew one thing, every woman wanted a man to love them—unless they were into women, of course.

But they would hold on to that dream of love to the exclusion of everything else, until the dream was shattered beyond redemption. And only then, would they truly move on; and some, not even then. "May I come in?"

She shifted, blocking the door with her body. "There's no reason for you to be here."

Chase took two steps closer and leaned in. "Oh, there's always a reason for me to be here."

Raquel took a step back. "I'm sure your wife wouldn't agree." She tightened her grip on the doorknob. "You remember her, right? The woman you actually did marry."

Chase paused. Damn, the ghost of Sera haunted every conversation. "Couldn't forget if I wanted to."

Raquel looked up as if trying to remember something. "And how much was she worth again?"

Chase reached out to play with the fingers gripping the doors. "Jealous, are we?"

Flinching at his touch, she straightened her posture to her full 5 feet 9 inch height. "Go home, Chase."

As the door closed, he played the last card he had—truth. "I was wrong."

Although her body stayed still, her eyes searched desperately for an escape.

Chase stepped closer. "I was wrong to let you go." Sighing, he closed his eyes. That cost him. It was beyond time to make right by Raquel.

She hadn't done a thing to deserve what he did to her. In one fell swoop, his actions rippled through him and Raquel, Hawk, and Lizzie, and probably impacted Giselle in some way he never bothered to define.

Raquel's lips tightened, but she didn't slam the door. That was as good a sign as any. "Go on."

"You deserved better than I gave. I . . . I didn't know how to live without Rose. I didn't know how to put my heart out there." Chase's shoulders tightened in a painful knot. He reached up to massage the knot away.

Raquel scrutinized him as though each orb was a scale weighing his words. "And you do now?"

Chase slanted his torso forward until they were a whisper apart. He didn't touch her though. To do that now would be a mistake. "I don't know.

But I do know that you were and still are my best chance at happiness."

Tears began to gather in Raquel's eyes. "You don't mean that," she denied his declaration in a breathy whisper, even as hope sprang into her eyes. "You never did."

This time when he reached out to touch her, she didn't flinch. "And I'm your best chance at happiness." Viewing the incredulity in her expression, he said, "Let me help you. Let me prove to you that I think you are worth everything."

Raquel paused for a half-step, "I don't need you to make anything work."

Chase spent the last few days finding the angle that would allow him to slide back into Raquel's life. It had been hard. Raquel herself didn't spread her business around. It was by chance that he found out about Lizzie. Tory's brother was chatting it up at Chicago Cut and gave up all the business.

"Well, the way I hear it, Lizzie's taking her money and her son and moving with her husband to Paris." He slid his hands in his pockets and rocked back and forth on his heels. "And word is that you aren't invited."

An angry muscle in Raquel's jaw jumped repeatedly. "Same old Chase, working all the angles. He got a job there. That's all."

"No, the old Chase would've kept that to himself and tried to work the angle. I'm telling you up front and offering you a solution."

The hope dimmed until her eyes were glittering globes of sadness.

"Yeah, funny thing, for some reason people seem to think that you're being cut off."

"Not your business," she countered and gripped the door handle like she wanted to wrench it clean off.

"You should've let her marry Hawk."

This time Raquel stepped forward, forcing Chase to inch back. "And give you the pleasure of having access to my baby's money. Never. Not standing straight up or six feet under."

"And in your efforts to keep me away from your baby's money, you shot yourself in the foot," he asserted.

She squared her shoulders and proclaimed, "My daughter would never leave me destitute.

"From what I understand, your daughter doesn't have a choice." He leaned in again. "But it's not too late."

Raquel inched back, allowing him to step into the foyer.

He inched closer to place a kiss on her cheek. She leaned back and eyed him. He held up his hands in surrender and continued into the grand foyer of Raquel's house.

The staircase curved like a woman's body, with a chandelier illuminating each turn. Chase swept his hand towards the living room, "Shall we?"

Raquel tapped her toe against the marble floor. "No. We shall not."

Chase moved forward, admiring the smooth wood surface of the banister, rubbing his hand up and down the gentle curve.

Raquel cleared her throat. "And your proposal is what?"

Chase let the quiet build before he lowered the boom. "Let her marry Hawk."

Raquel sucked her teeth.

He must've really hit a nerve for that to slip out. Raquel made sure she was always put together to her own exacting standards. The pre-gold-digger part of her was showing. "That wasn't very ladylike."

"The fact that you're in my house and I haven't shot you yet is about as ladylike as I'm likely to get."

Chase scanned the area, admiring the hall in which they stood. "Yes, it's a lovely house. Do you get to remain here when Lizzie moves to Paris?"

Raquel merely stared at him. He returned her gaze.

"So, this house . . . " he began, "is owned by the Warner Consortium."

Raquel tilted her head. "That sounds like a statement and not a question."

Chase eased towards Raquel. "It was."

"Aargh. Come on." Raquel swept into the living room and smacked her hand against the wall, turning on the light. "Apparently, this is going to last a very long time."

Chase moseyed behind her. He loved watching her hips switch from left to right. The fact that she let him in was a sign of just how desperate she was. On a normal day, she'd never even open the door.

On a normal day, she'd probably find the hose or turn on the water sprinklers. Or possibly even wrap her hand around one of those fine pieces of weaponry in the gun cabinet.

The apartment he shared with Sera was reflective of what it was like to be "hood-rich." Everyone had leather. Everyone had big televisions. Everyone had some type of painting with a man and/or woman in some level of undress that was supposed to be seductive and pass as art.

This was true wealth: bookcases with collector's editions on the shelf, spines facing out; another shelf with one solitary plate; art properly framed, hung, and lit to show it off. Everything you see is different yet it comes together.

His will had to be stronger than hers. Although he did want her back, more than that, he had to fix what he'd done to prevent Hawk and Lizzie being together. It had to be about them. He couldn't remember how long it had been since he put Hawk and Giselle first.

She flounced down on the couch.

Chase leaned back into the subtle firmness of the floral print couch. "So, funny thing, there have been some strange things happening in my neighborhood. People getting shot . . ." he paused, but kept his focus on Raquel. Her impassive face didn't change, so he continued, "with arrows."

Raquel plucked an imaginary piece of lint off of her silk top. "Dangerous neighborhood. Bound to happen at some point."

"And I got to thinking. I know two people with the skill to make that happen; and lo and behold, they are the Warners, who own the building across from mine." He shrugged. "Funny, maybe not ha-ha funny, but funny nonetheless."

Raquel sank deeper into her couch. "And you say that to say what."

"That maybe you're taking aim at people in neighborhood."

"Huh," Raquel replied, a small smile played at the corners of her lips. "Interesting. You think that either me or my daughter happens to be running around the ghetto shooting arrows at the good little citizens over there. You know, taking from the poor and giving to the rich."

Chase leaned forward, pressing his line of thinking. "You're a crack shot."

Raquel confirmed. "I am."

"Your daughter could skin a chicken with an arrow."

Raquel inspected her nails, as if the turquoise color was the most interesting thing she'd seen in her life. "She can."

Chase patted her thigh. "One phone call and the police are all in your business, tearing your life apart."

"I understand if you feel you should make that call," she challenged, meeting his gaze head-on.

Chase felt the need to wipe his sweaty palms against his slacks. *Why wasn't she upset? Outraged? Anything.* "I don't have to if you let Hawk marry Lizzie. You and I can get back together and everyone is happy."

Raquel's oval face registered her disbelief. "Will we? Be happy? With my empty bank account? Or has the projects reevaluated your priorities?"

Chase edged off the couch and kneeled in front of her. "I may not have a lot of skills, but I can make my woman happy."

Raquel rose, taking two steps to the side away from Chase. "Well, thank you for stopping by."

Confused, Chase couldn't keep a strained squeak out of his voice. What the hell was going on? "What do you mean? You can go to jail."

Raquel chuckled, "I'm not going to jail." She strode past the artwork, through the living room, and back into the foyer.

He rushed to keep up with her determined stride. By the time she'd opened her door, she knew he'd blown it. He'd miscalculated something.

"Think about what I'm telling you," he implored.

She placed her hand on his back and almost pushed him out of the door. "I know what you're telling me. You think because I can shoot an arrow and my daughter owns the building that we're killers."

He couldn't believe his ears. He might not expect her to react like a crazy woman, but he thought she'd at least react.

Raquel leaned in towards him. Now her eye was twinkling. "You'd better check your glass house before throwing stones. Guess who else can shoot an arrow?"

"She was right beside Lizzie through every single lesson. And she's the one who snuck back in town and is living in one of the condos right across from you."

Chase paused, heart racing as he took in the blows that landed with every word dripping from Raquel's lips. "Giselle. Giselle is home?"

Raquel sneered. "Didn't even care to tell you? So if you're going to call the cops, make sure your baby girl, who has a way better motive than I do, isn't caught in the crosshairs."

Giselle was back in Chicago. "Giselle?"

Raquel grinned as she shut the door in his face.

His baby was home, and cared so little for him that she didn't even bother to tell him.

It had to be recent. Just like the shootings. Chase shivered. Marrying one was bad enough, but could he have sired a killer?

CHAPTER 53

The moment Giselle walked away from Hawk, pain shot through him. It wasn't like the time he'd put her on the train headed for school. But still he wanted her to just be there, by his side, Bonnie and Clyde—or Batman and Robin.

Unfortunately, she had errands to run, things to do. What could possibly be more important than spending time with the brother who'd swim across Lake Michigan and back to keep her safe?

He moved from the water in time to see Ninja walk in the opposite direction. Exactly what was going on with Giselle and Ninja? Granted, he didn't think it was physical, but it was much more than platonic friends.

Although clearly Ninja was walking on the path that would lead back to the parking lot, did that really mean that they wouldn't hook up later? Like five minutes from now, when Hawk wasn't around?

Skip trying to figure out Lizzie; he needed to follow Ninja to see where he was really going. And if he walked his Nikes into the wrong door on Sedgwick, there was going to be a serious problem.

As he followed Ninja, his phone rang. Lizzie. At first all he heard was the kind of crying that should be limited to when someone is in the confines of their bedroom. Sniveling, sobbing.

"Babe," Hawk whispered, his heart pounding as if trying to crack through his ribs. "I can't understand you. Talk to me."

Through the sniffles, he heard. "I'm going to kill her."

There was something in her voice that he hadn't heard before.

"Lizzie, sweetie. You can't kill your mother," he cautioned.

"Really? I can't?" her tone sharpened. "She's been killing me slowly for years. Like a parasite. Do you know how hard it is to love someone you can't be with?" She declared, "That bitch ruined my life."

Hawk increased his pace, but he couldn't get good traction in the sand. "I know it's been hard, but we managed. We can still manage. You don't have to go with Tory to Paris."

Lizzie was silent for a few seconds before ranting, "So you think this is okay? You think she can treat me any kind of way, and she should get away with it because she's my mother?"

A crash echoed over the phone. "What's was that? What happened?"

"That? Was her favorite vase, smashed to smithereens. Oops."

His blood chilled at the glee in Lizzie's voice. Her laugh had a maniacal tinge that pushed Hawk from a scurrying walk into a full-out trot.

Shifting the phone to his other ear, he inquired. "Where are you, Lizzie?"

"I'm at my dear old mom's house, of course," she replied, so softly he almost didn't hear it. "She's not here, though. Some of her prize possessions aren't surviving this visit."

Hawk broke out into a track-star-style sprint. Ninja turned on him before Hawk even got close. He didn't know how Ninja could feel other people in the midst of a crowded beach. Right now he didn't care.

Anxiety stole his breath as he tried to run and calm Lizzie down at the same time. "Lizzie, come on. You—"

"She sold my life for money. Money!" she shrieked.

By now, Hawk pantomimed driving and Ninja nodded. He figured that Ninja would have a car somewhere close. Giselle said he could trust him. He was banking Lizzie's life on it.

Ninja gestured to a Jeep Sahara parked right outside of the entrance to the beach. Hawk pulled Ninja toward the car and whispered an address.

In the Midst of Fire

CHAPTER 54

Chase strode into the apartment, walked into the bedroom to view those condos across the street. The lights were coming on and off in some type of random pattern, signaling who was and wasn't at home. He wondered if one of those lights belonged to Giselle. Was she was fixing dinner right now? Or was she, at that very moment, gazing at his apartment while he was seeking her.

He placed a hand on the cool glass, wishing desperately that he was holding his daughter instead. She didn't even want him to know she was home. Their separation hurt, but it was nothing compared to the fact she was here and no one knew it. What was the purpose of living across the street, if she had no intention of visiting her family? So it was more like no intention of visiting him. Well, Hawk had probably seen her.

Chase paced the length of the bedroom, noting where all of the belongings resided. Would he run into Giselle on the street? What would she say? What would she do? Embracing might be too much after all this time, but he would try anyway. She was his baby girl.

He stopped near the nightstand, pulling off the picture he kept taped, hidden between the back panel and the wall. "Oh, Rose. I've made so many mistakes," he whispered.

Yes, Sera was a mistake. He'd let her come between his family, severing them, leaving them bleeding. He should've gone after his daughter. He should've protected his son. He should've been a father.

"Who am I kidding?" he mumbled. "I haven't been a father to them since you died, Rose."

That much was true.

The twins took care of each other. Always. They'd tell him when he had to show up places, drop off, pick up; but the day to day, they handled themselves.

Once they got their driver's licenses, they didn't even need him for a ride. So he was simply . . . there.

He hadn't realized how vulnerable he was until Sera rolled in. He wanted to say she captured his heart, but he had given that to Rose so many years ago. Sera did fill a void—a gaping hole in his soul.

Chase sat down on the bed. The room was illuminated by the solitary lamp that had survived Sera's unlikely tantrum after NuNu was killed.

Taking a deep breath that was echoed by the creaking of the bedsprings, he finally asked himself, "Why do I stay?"

He finally had to admit that staying was easier than leaving. It was easier than starting over—again. Right or wrong, it had become the nucleus of his life; or maybe more like the black hole in his life.

Sure, he had moments of happiness, moments of contentment. But having known real happiness, he recognized when it wasn't there.

Chase left the bedroom and ambled into the kitchen. A bottle of tequila on the counter begged for his attention. Taking a glass out of the cabinet, he poured himself a couple of fingers of tequila.

As he tossed it back, out of the corner of his eye he noticed Sera's cell on the floor next to the bedroom. That was odd.

She'd never leave her cell, especially with everything going on. She was expecting a call from Ninja at any time.

Chase ran his thumb over the screen. He didn't recognize the last number, but the last text was a stinger:

"Don't forget to bring your best, bitch." – Giselle.

Chase's hands trembled as he dialed Ninja.

In the Midst of Fire

"Something's going on. Sera. My daughter, Giselle. Where would Sera go if she wanted to fight or battle or throw knives? Where would Sera meet up with Giselle?"

Chase's knees gave out, and he found himself clutching carpet. He didn't have time for that, not today. Today, he had to do what he hadn't done four years prior—stand by his daughter's side and fight.

CHAPTER 55

Hawk tried to concentrate on Lizzie, but hearing his dad shouting through Ninja's phone about Sera and Giselle tore his attention.

Another crash in the background made Hawk's heart rate spike.

Lizzie giggled, "And the worst part of it was that I believed her blindly. Just whatever she said, whatever she needed me to sign. I did it. How could she? She's my mother."

Her voiced thickened with tears as she whispered, "My mother was supposed to love me."

"Hang on, Lizzie," Hawk imparted. "I'm coming. Less than five minutes. Just stay where you are. Don't touch or break anything else."

Lizzie's crying increased in intensity. "She's my mother."

As Ninja tried to get more details from Chase, Hawk contemplated leaving Lizzie to go to Giselle. But Lizzie needed him. Giselle needed him more. After Giselle's comment earlier about killing Sera, Hawk knew her encounter with Sera was going to be more a homegoing than a homecoming.

Lizzie's psychological break . . . Lizzie's emotions ping-ponged between utter despair and a level of cold anger that chilled even Hawk to the bone. He hoped he would beat Mrs. Warner to the house or it was going to get real.

In the Midst of Fire

As Ninja pulled up to the house on Mohawk, Hawk hesitated. Ninja shoved him into the door. "I've got Giselle. You take Lizzie."

Still Hawk couldn't force himself out of the seat until he saw the cold resolve in Ninja's eyes.

Ninja pounded the steering wheel. "Every second you sit here is less time for me to find Giselle. Do you doubt that I can handle Sera?"

Hawk realized Ninja may be the only person who could. This time he was putting his own life in Ninja's hands, because if this decision led to something happening to Giselle, he couldn't live with himself.

The minute his feet hit the pavement, Ninja sped away with such force that the passenger door closed on its own.

Lizzie was still on the phone in the middle of a crying jag. He pushed the door open and called her name. Then he stopped when he reached the living room.

Through the shattered glass and porcelain, Lizzie's dejected form was balled up on the living room couch.

Navigating around the broken glass the best way he could, he pulled her into his arms.

Hawk closed his eyes and pulled Lizzie closer. "It's okay. It's okay," he crooned. "We'll be okay. Shhh. Shhh, babe."

For the next half hour, the evening shadows crept into the room; Lizzie wasn't sobbing or talking. She was just lying on the couch being held by Hawk.

Lizzie stared into space. "What happens now?"

Hawk tilted her chin towards him. "You get a divorce."

She couldn't meet his eyes.

Hawk frowned. This is what they've been waiting for. They could get out of there . . . together.

"So now that I have money again, I'm worthy of you?" Lizzie responded in a dry tone.

"Bull shit," Hawk growled, "I've loved you since day one."

Lizzie pondered that a few moments. "A few days ago, you wouldn't commit to our family, but now that I'm rich again, it's okay. How is that different from her?"

Hawk wanted to curse. But if he started in on Lizzie's mom, she'd start up again.

Lizzie extracted from his hold and tiptoed her way out of the living room. "Shit," she grimaced. "I didn't realize I did all of this."

A shrief from the door cause them to turn.

Unlike last time when Hawk and Lizzie confronted Mrs. Warner, this time Lizzie squared her shoulders and narrowed her eyes. "Mother, is there something you'd like to tell me about my inheritance?"

Mrs. Warner parted her lips, but Lizzie held up a hand and said, "Before you answer, please note that you didn't bribe everyone at my lawyer's office."

Mrs. Warner's mouth opened and closed a few times. Hawk put some distance between them, giving Lizzie free reign.

CHAPTER 56

Chase paced outside of the Burnham Park apartments as he waited for Ninja. Where could he be? Hitta, one of Sera's boys, walked up and nodded to him. Chase ran up to him and grabbed him by the collar. "Sera, where's Sera?"

Hitta wasn't known for his patience; but as he looked in Chase's eyes, he laughed instead of punching first and asking questions later. "Oh, shit. Sera finally stepped out on you, huh? I don't know where she is."

Chase almost started a fight that he'd surely lose if Ninja hadn't pulled up then and put on his emergency flashes.

Hitta swatted Chase's hands away as he turned. "What's up, Ninja?"

"Any word from Sera?"

Now Hitta sobered up. "Do I need to get the boys?"

Ninja pulled a bag out of his car and began to trot across the street, replying as he went, "I'll let you know. Just holla' at me if you see or hear something."

Chase nodded as if to cosign on Ninja's instructions. He knew his nod meant nothing, but it made him feel better. Ninja grabbed a few tools from his bag; and before Chase could sneeze, Ninja picked the lock on the condo door.

Glancing around to see who was watching, he slipped in the door behind Ninja. As they ran up two flights of stairs, Chase inquired, "You knew Giselle was here, in town. Even you knew?"

Ninja issued instructions. "First, pretend as if you belong here. Stop looking around like the police are jumping out of the shadows."

Chase hissed. "This is breaking and entering. We could go to jail."

Ninja turned. "If you utter one more word, I will shoot you, tie you up in one of these condos, and call the police myself. I can't look for Giselle and deal with you at the same time. So which will it be?"

Chase paused at the intensity in Ninja's voice. Where did that come from? However, he knew better than to object. So he trailed behind Ninja, as they picked the lock on the first apartment.

Ninja ran to the window. At least he took the time to explain. "We need a condo that gives an angle on NuNu on the street and Vincent's apartment.

As Ninja contemplated the view, Chase hyperventilated. His baby girl was a killer. He had turned her into a killer. Raquel was right. He couldn't go to the police. He didn't have the money for a lawyer. He had to get her out of town.

It took less than a minute before Ninja trotted out of the condo and up three more flights of stairs. He picked another lock. Before they made it all the way through the door, Chase knew they hit the jackpot.

The condo smelled like Giselle's favorite lilac fragrance. Ninja held up his hand to slow Chase's progress. Ninja pulled his gun from his ankle holster as he eased into the living room.

Chase took a step to follow, but Ninja merely shook his head and he cleared the rooms like Chase saw people do on TV.

As Chase peaked around the corner, he noted a well-maintained living room/dining room combination with an open kitchen. The floors were a dark, wide-planked wood that appeared to run all the way down the hallway where Ninja had disappeared.

Chase assumed Sera and Giselle weren't there when Ninja flicked on the light—and when he didn't hear any gunshots.

In the Midst of Fire

Ninja dragged him into the room and pointed to a stack of papers by the computer. "I need you to go through all this stuff and see if you can find a clue to where they went."

As Ninja went towards the bedroom, Chase closed his eyes. Four years. She'd been gone for four years. He trailed his fingers along the keyboard where she worked. He picked up a photo of her and another female. He figured it was a friend from college because he didn't recognize her.

Chase sat in the office chair and rubbed his forehead, hard. What had he done? The pounding footsteps of Ninja forced him to grab a stack of papers and pretend he wasn't caught up in his mind, instead of looking for Giselle.

As Ninja entered the room, Chase's hands shook as he flipped from one page to another and tried not to show how unraveled he was becoming at everything he had missed. He had blocked his mind to the pain of Giselle leaving. Nothing prepared him for the pain of her coming back. However, the thought of being responsible for Sera killing her, because he couldn't keep it together long enough to help with her search, was the motivating factor.

Ninja tore through stack after stack. Chase paused. Even if they found a name or address, who's to say it was the right one. Think. Think.

There was one thing he knew about his daughter. He shouted, "Ninja, is there a landline here."

Ninja released a sigh. "No and her cell phone isn't here."

Chase rose and searched the outlets until he found her charger. Giselle never wanted her phone to run out of juice; so when she was home, it was always plugged in. She constantly doodled or wrote notes on any piece of paper closest to the charger. And that's where he found, "Kingsbury."

Breathing slowly, he handed the paper to Ninja, who shouted, "Damn it, Giselle." The building on Kingsbury had little if any foot traffic. It was an old warehouse district that the Knights used to meet people they wanted to eliminate.

CHAPTER 57

Hawk watched the silent war between Lizzie and Mrs. Warner. Mrs. Warner hadn't budged an inch, disbelief transmitted from her eyes. "Who are you to question me?"

Lizzie puffed up her chest.

"I'm the one daddy actually loved."

Mrs. Warner ran her hand through her hair," she muttered. "Son of a bitch." Then, she turned on Lizzie. "I made sure you were taken care of. Your husband is good and rich. His name is on Gregory's birth certificate. You're set for life. And that's not enough?"

"But I don't love him. I don't," Lizzie argued.

"My God," Mrs. Warner exclaimed. "You're just like her."

Confused, Lizzie inquired, "Who?"

"Rose," nodding toward Hawk, "his mom."

Lizzie glanced at Hawk, but he kept his focus on Mrs. Warner. No one mentioned his mother anymore.

Hawk and Giselle didn't remember much, but they pooled their memories in a collection that gave a vivid reflection of the woman they yearned for with each new day, and with every new "Mrs. Glen," that passed through their lives.

In the Midst of Fire

Mrs. Warner collapsed onto the floor. Hawk moved to help her, but Lizzie held his arm softly, but firmly, keeping him in place. Lizzie tugged Hawk towards the stairs where they sat.

"God, everyone loved Rose." Mrs. Warner gave a grudgingly respectful shake of her head. "I was there that first day, by her side as she hopped in the Buckingham Fountain."

Lizzie grabbed Hawk's hand and brought it towards her heart. Hawk could feel himself shaking, but didn't know why. It was just a story, a story about the mother he lost, only that.

"I saw him first. How could I not? Chase Glen was gorgeous. He was tall and lean. You could tell he wasn't from our neighborhood, but with a man like that, you don't care." She raised her face to the light with a faraway look in her eyes. "Even then, he only had eyes for her. He never even looked my way."

Mrs. Warner paused and exhaled a long breath before continuing.

"Rose had the kind of joy that could only come from a life full of getting exactly what you wanted." Bitterness caused Raquel's voice to scratch.

Hawk took a deep breath as Lizzie put her head on his shoulder, sensing these revelations were hard for him to hear.

"Her father loved her to pieces and spoiled her so." Mrs. Warner folded her legs. "I barely knew my father. He worked constantly, trying to pay for those expensive schools my mother wanted me to attend. The rent on our three-bedroom apartment had to be through the roof. He never complained." Mrs. Warner ran her fingers through her hair. "I never saw him all that much."

A hauntingly soft smile graced Mrs. Warner' lips, "I didn't want Chase for his money, or because she had him. I believed he loved me, too, that he finally saw me."

Hawk returned to Mrs. Warner. "But why would you keep Lizzie's inheritance from her?"

Mrs. Warner banged her hand against the floor. "It's her fault. If her father had left the money to me, instead of her, I could've been Mrs. Glen." Using her nails, she scratched at the floor. "I couldn't compete with

Rose. Fine. But after Rose died, he was supposed to be mine." Tears ran unchecked down Mrs. Warner's face. "But he married another rich woman and then another rich woman."

"But he didn't love them," Hawk interjected.

Mrs. Warner raised her voice, ignoring his statement. "Finally, finally, it was my turn. And he passes me by again, and brings home that poor insipid little tramp instead."

"But what does that have to do with Lizzie?"

"It was Rose all over again. You and Lizzie. Your father and your mother. You're broke. Your father's broke."

Now Lizzie was the one trembling in anger. Hawk shook his head to clear it. "But she's your daughter."

Angry glee sharpened Mrs. Warner's gaze, "But there was no way your father was getting his hands on a penny of her inheritance. No way, was he going to live off my hard work. No way, was he going to get off scot-free again."

"And no way, you were going to let your daughter get the happiness that you couldn't land," Hawk growled through his teeth. "Say it. Go ahead."

Mrs. Warner shouted, "I did this. I saw my chance with Mr. Warner and I took it. I lied about birth control. I got pregnant. I ensured our future."

"No, you tried to ensure your future through me," Lizzie's voice trembled. "My God, it's no wonder why he never took you seriously." She took in a few choppy breaths. "Do you love me at all? Are you even capable?"

Mrs. Warner's gaze never met Lizzie's.

As Lizzie tried to use the back of her hand to wipe at her tears, Hawk kissed the top of her head. His phone vibrated in his pocket. Answering, tension crawled up his back and became two knots in his shoulder.

Ninja rushed through an update, but all he heard was Sera, Giselle, and Kingsbury. He shouted, "She going to kill my sister."

Hanging up, he yanked Lizzie's hand as he dragged her towards the front door. Hawk grabbed her keys from a table near the door. He was surprised when Mrs. Warner scrambled to her feet. Out of the corner of his eye, Hawk saw her grab a violin case from the decorative coat tree as she

In the Midst of Fire

ran out the front door. What was she carrying? a Tommy gun? He didn't have time to think about that.

All of them managed to hop in the car before he slammed it in drive and prayed that someone got to Giselle in time.

CHAPTER 58

Sera watched Giselle light a fire that provided the main lighting source for the warehouse.

Originally, it was a meeting place for hypes to share needles, but the Knights took it over. Protected from prying eyes, it was now the perfect spot for meetings of any kind. If someone saw a meeting, they immediately "unsaw" it and kept on about their business.

Giselle had lost a little weight. However, she was basically the same, same lean frame, same confident stance. Then Giselle turned, and there was a hitch in Sera's breathing. Something was different. A subtle lift of her defiant chin; evidently, little Giselle had grown up.

She left Chicago a little girl shrouded in innocence, protected by her brother, and then hidden in plain sight at the college. Now it seemed that Giselle thought she could take on Sera Glen.

Sera flexed her right leg and felt the binding of the three throwing knives strapped there.

When Giselle called earlier, Sera couldn't believe her luck. The phone hadn't been her friend lately. Frankly, every time it rang it was either bad news or the reminder of bad news. She had considered turning the ringer off, but then what? What if something happened to Hawk or Chase?

She'd never know.

What if the inevitable happened? What if someone was coming after her? Even a few seconds of heads up was worth weeding through the condolence calls that were still coming in nonstop. Vincent.

She leaned back against the wall. The thought of Vincent being dead drained her of all of her strength. Sometimes she didn't want to do anything but sit on the floor or lie in her bed.

And that's where she was thirty minutes ago. Then the phone rang. Sera checked the caller ID. She didn't recognize the number, but for some reason her thumb hesitated to swipe to send it into voicemail.

A niggling thought in her mind forced her to accept it.

"Sera."

"Stepmother."

Sera's nose flared at the sound of that voice. So the prodigal daughter had returned. Just her luck! Life was crumbling around her. She was barely holding on to her sanity and her man by her fingertips.

"Giselle, how are you, dear?"

"Well, Sera, I would say that I've been better, but I heard they're picking off your team like flies," she gloated. "So in all likelihood, I'm better than you right now."

Sera's forehead furrowed. *First volley.*

Giselle's harsh laughter caused Sera to stretch and flex her hand, yearning for the weight of her throwing knives. "Darling girl," Sera purred. "Why don't you come on home where I can keep you safe?"

Giselle's anger spewed through the phone lines. "Like I was safe when you sent people to beat up Hawk; or when you left me to NuNu, who wanted to do something far worse than rip my shirt off? Safe like that?"

"Everyone survives that," Sera declared. She listened closely trying to figure out Giselle's location through the background noise, but it was nothing extraordinary until she heard a shout on her block echo through the phone.

So little Giselle was home.

"You hurt us. You won't get the chance to do that twice," Giselle proclaimed. "You even sent Ninja to threaten me."

"What do you mean *threaten* you? He was only supposed to check up to make sure you were okay," Sera chided, unable to believe the girl's nerve. "If I want you taken out, I would've dusted off my formal clothes years ago."

"You held Hawk hostage."

"He has a key," Sera scoffed at her juvenile reasoning. "The door unlocks and locks from both the inside and out."

As they talked, Sera eased through the apartment to the bedroom window to look on the street. Mookie leaned against a parked car talking to some chick. It wasn't Giselle. She would have heard Mookie's voice through the phone.

"He was scared for me, for my dad," she whispered. "You think I don't know about the needle."

Sera shifted tactics. "So I'm the little evil witch who tore your family apart and forced them to do my bidding."

"Exactly," Giselle shouted, then took deep breaths trying hard to retain the control that she'd been taught.

"Really? Because the last time I checked, Hawk's a grown-assed man who's living under my roof, rent-free, and can come and go as he pleases," Sera explained. "Chase was always looking for some woman to take care of him. I did that. I'm doing that. And you accuse me of holding them hostage?"

Sera took a deep breath. "That's right. I stabbed your dad in the leg with a needle. And the next day his dick was so far inside of me, it damn near came up through my throat and choked me to death."

Giselle's gasp was exactly the reaction Sera had hoped for.

"And no one, not a friend or an enemy, came after you while you were in college," Sera exclaimed triumphantly. "Little girl, you might not like how things have turned out; but it seems to me your tantrum is misplaced, especially since you benefited the most from all of this."

"I benefited," Giselle shrieked. If she didn't figure out a way to shut down her emotions, she would never survive. "My brother's afraid to move off a block where people are getting shot with arrows. Arrows. What the hell is that? My dad is stuck in a dead-end marriage with a woman who was supposed to be rich, but turns out she's living exactly the same way he'd been trying to keep us from living all along."

"They had food and a bed," Sera snarled.

"And they'll have their freedom," she shot back. "It's time."

"I don't have any issues with you, Giselle. I suggest you go on with your life and leave the real problems to the adults."

"This is my life—my brother, my father, and me. You're but a temporary black void that will soon be closed. When I go on with my life, it'll be with my family beside me. And you'll either be dead or alone. Which one is worse for you, Sera?"

Sera closed her eyes, staving off the pain that shot through her heart. Either Giselle was the most intuitive person on the block or someone had been talking when they shouldn't have. "And you're bad enough to do that?"

"We'll see soon enough, won't we?" Giselle's voice had deepened an octave or two.

"Save that bass in your voice, dear, it's not impressive. I'll meet you at the tracks behind 1200 North Kingsbury."

Sera rushed to the closet to get her knives, mumbling, "Kids are more trouble than they're worth."

One thing was certain, two women couldn't rule one household. And Chase was her husband. Hers. Not her baby daddy. Not her boo. Her husband. Not some random man that showed up one night to leave the next morning. Man and wife. 'Till death do they part. And she was holding him to that. No matter what. Giselle had him for eighteen years. The rest of his life belonged to the woman with whom he'd taken vows.

Now a half hour later, she stood across from Giselle. The time it took Sera to collect her throwing knives allowed Giselle to get there first. As Sera strutted across the vast floor, Giselle turned to watch her approach.

Sera pulled a knife from the strap on her thigh and threw it across the room, narrowly missing Giselle. Even from the distrance, she saw Giselle's eyes widen in surprise.

That's right, dearie. You're going to get cut tonight.

CHAPTER 59

Giselle smirked as she inquired, "Miss much?"

Sera sauntered closer. "You grew a pair in college. Good for you. And I only miss on purpose, as you'll see soon enough."

Stepmother had no clue that Giselle was well-versed on how to take a hit and how to give one, too.

Sera advanced, swinging in short, arching motions, while Giselle contemplated the best way to disarm her, quickly. She tried to keep her eyes on Sera's face, but something must have tipped Sera off, because the minute Giselle reached down, Sera spun away, grabbing Giselle's hand, yanking her off balance.

The next thing Giselle knew, she was on the ground with Sera's foot in her ribs. *Get up. Get up. Get up.*

Giselle rolled over and leapt back to her feet. Sera slowly eased a knife out. "Oh, so you want a knife." Sera gave a mock bow. "I'm happy to oblige."

Sera threw two knives in quick succession, Giselle leapt out of the way of one, but the other plunged deep into her left thigh.

Giselle grunted, sucking up the pain, and ran towards Sera. She chopped both sides of her neck and did a combination that had Sera on the ground. Using her right foot, she stomped on Sera's hand until a crunch split the air. She kicked, stomped, kicked, stomped, kicked, and stomped.

Giselle yanked the knife out of her leg, tossed it in the air, caught it by the blade, and threw it into Sera's hand.

As Sera lay crumpled on the floor, Giselle crowed, "I wouldn't dare come back without knowing a bit about knife work."

Sera struggled to stand. "Just leave."

"And Hawk?" Giselle inquired.

Sera grunted. "Take him, too."

Focusing on the last family member, she inquired, "And my dad?"

Giselle blinked down at the blood soaking her pants leg. Taking the knife out had been a mistake. Energy was draining out of her with every drop of blood.

Sera's smile now reached her eyes. "Something wrong, Giselle?"

Struggling to get her thoughts together, Giselle tried to focus. She couldn't even clearly see her nemesis, much less respond.

Sera leaned down, laughing. "You're going to bleed out, little girl. Seems you didn't learn enough at that fancy school of yours."

Sera grabbed the knife with her good hand.

Move. Move. Move.

She needed to focus on something to keep her from passing out. The light from the fire pit was all she saw. She headed that way.

"So much promise." Sera raised the knife. "Literally, cut down in her prime."

Blackness was closing in, but Giselle tried to keep it at bay by sheer will. Giselle managed to turn over. She was going to look into the eyes of her killer.

Sera raised the knife.

She heard Ninja shouting, "No." At least she thought it was Ninja, but she was so delirious and the voice sounded so broken, she couldn't say for sure.

An arrow pierced Sera's chest. Her scream cut through the air like the knife she held.

She stumbled, falling back into the fire pit.

Fire.

The continual screeching barely registered as a flurry of people converged on her burning body. The smell of Sera's charred flesh choked Giselle. Someone tied something around her leg, and another person lifted her up and carried her out. A single thought registered.

Wait? Did she see . . .

Was that Raquel Warner? with a bow?

Why did she have a bow?

CHAPTER 60

Hawk ran into the building just in time to see his father crumble to the ground, his arm reaching towards Sera. The stepmother was screeching an eerie cry as the flames engulfed her. He ran to Giselle on the ground.

"Sis, it's going to be okay." He struggled to take off his belt. His hands were shaking so bad. He snapped them trying to get them to pay attention to the instructions coming from his brain. "Come on. Come on."

He couldn't do it twice. He couldn't be strong while one more woman in his life bled to death. His mother had been enough. He didn't have it in him.

Ninja, whose eyes were always flat, cold, and analytical were now shattered in a kaleidoscope of pain as he looked at Giselle.

Lizzie knelt next to him, helping to release the belt from a stubborn loop. She wrapped it around Giselle's legs.

Hawk nudged him. "We should call for an ambulance."

Ninja scooped her up and held her to him as he hurried towards the street. "Take Lizzie's Range. It'll be faster."

His voice softened, "She's lost so much blood."

Lizzie and Hawk didn't have enough time for anything more than a quick glance between them before they ran after Ninja.

Gently, Ninja eased her in the back seat and grazed her forehead with his lips.

"Get in. We have to go," Hawk shouted.

Ninja stepped back. "No. I have to clean this up," hitching his head toward the warehouse. "Then I'll have to disappear for a while. The real bad asses around here don't like it when you disrupt their system. And Sera being dead . . . security . . . is a disruption."

Ninja turned to look at Lizzie. "Your mom—in or out?"

Lizzie, who'd been staring at Giselle, snapped her attention back to Ninja. "In or out of what?"

"Jail."

"What?" she whispered, clutching a hand to her chest.

"I have to clean the scene, and seconds count," he repeated. "In or out of jail?

Lizzie closed her eyes for a moment before she said, "Out. She's my mom."

Ninja trailed his thumb down Giselle's cheek before shuttering his emotions behind his cool facade.

Hawk slid behind the driver's seat and pulled off. In the rearview mirror, Ninja ran back into the building through the rearview mirror.

"Giselle, I swear when you wake up, you'll have to tell me what the hell is going on between you and Ninja."

Lizzie smiled a little, as she glanced at the back seat. "You think?"

"Did you see that man?" Hawk roared.

Lizzie toyed with the wedding ring on her finger. "But he left."

"That's the most emotion I've seen him show in four years," his voice laced with awe, "and that includes the time I held a gun to his head."

Hawk whipped the car around and headed down Clark Street. It would take them three minutes to get to Northwestern. "Okay, here's the story. We found her on the street stabbed. That's all we know. I don't know how Ninja cleans, but I'd hate for something we say to get him in trouble. Keep it simple."

Lizzie nodded, casting another worried glance at Giselle, who groaned.

In the Midst of Fire

"Plus, I'd bet my I-Roc that any trace of Giselle being on the tracks when Sera was killed will be eliminated by the time we get to the hospital."

Just then a phone vibrated. Lizzie and Hawk shared a speaking glance that spoke of their anxiety. Lizzie unbuckled the seat belt and angled herself to reach Giselle's jean pocket and pulled out the phone. "Hello?"

Ninja's voice came through clearly, as if the cell phone was in Hawk's own hand. "Stop right now. Destroy the sim card and phone under the wheel and run over it.

Lizzie paused. "But it's Giselle's phone. What good will that do?"

"Giselle hasn't had a phone that I haven't put in her hand since freshman year. Get rid of it."

Hawk pounded on the brakes. Lizzie scrambled from the passenger seat, then placed the phone under the front tire. The Range Rover ground it into pieces. Lizzie jumped back in the car, and they took off.

Hawk glanced at Giselle over his shoulder. "Yeah, you definitely have some explaining to do."

CHAPTER
61

Weakness toppled Chase, as sure as dynamite in an imploding building. Even as the concrete floor of the warehouse bit into his knees, he couldn't find the strength to get himself upright.

Ninja maneuvered past his crumbled form, making it to the remains, and began beating at the flames. But even as the flames were extinguished, Chase knew as sure as the arrow piercing her chest, that Sera, his Sera, was gone.

Something inside of him broke. and he began rocking;. another wife, another life snuffed out in the quick snap of time.

Then he remembered he wasn't alone. Raquel stood, legs askew, hate still sparkling in her eyes and a justified smirk on her lips. "You wanted to kill her all along," he accused.

"I saved your daughter," she proclaimed, without an ounce of regret. "I believe the correct response is thank you."

Ninja tentatively tested the charred, smoking body for signs of life.

"You hated that I married her."

Raquel unleashed fury in a few simple words. "I hated that you loved her."

Chase couldn't believe his ears. "But we . . . but why?"

In the Midst of Fire

"After Rose died," Raquel snarled, "if you were going to love someone, why not me? I gave you everything in my heart; and no matter what, it still wasn't good enough. Money," she accused. "You were always chasing the dollar, ending up in this hovel, with her." Raquel bellowed, gesturing to the charred remains of Seraphina. "And not even caring, until my bow and arrow forced you back into my life."

Ninja rushed back in with his arms filled with containers of industrial chemicals. "I need both of you to get out. Now."

"Don't you dare order me." Raquel straightened her back to her full height.

"You're wanted for at least two other killings. I suggest you shut up and get moving."

"I didn't kill NuNu," Raquel huffed.

Ninja's pace didn't slow. "I know. Now. Get. Out!!"

Raquel drew her head back in surprise. "Wait. How? Did you . . . ?"

"Out," Ninja pointed towards the door.

Chase took Raquel by the arm, dragging her out and into the shadows.

Ninja dumped liquid on the pit to extinguish the fire. He poured chemicals from the colored bottle around the floor where Giselle's blood still stained the concrete. Choking on the rancid fumes, he continued until his coughing turned to hacking. He sprinted to the door and took in several gulps of air, then made his way out to his Jeep.

Chase shuddered uncontrollably.

"Just get into the car," Raquel ordered.

Ninja rushed back into the building and a few minutes later he was piling the collection of chemicals back into the car.

"What are you going to do with Sera?" Chase inquired.

Ninja leveled a stony gaze on him. "For all those involved, it's best if you don't know."

"But I need to say good-bye."

Ninja looked in his rearview mirror. "So, say it."

He glared at Raquel. "I can't. Not with her here."

She lifted her chin. "I saved your daughter."

"You killed my wife," Chase growled in response.

"Who was trying to kill your daughter," Raquel shot back.

"You killed NuNu to get at her," he continued "You killed Vincent to get at her. And you were going to kill her, regardless. Giselle just gave you a reason."

Raquel shrugged. "I. Did. Not. Kill. That. Man."

"He had an arrow in his chest."

"Okay. Okay. I was *planning* on killing NuNu. I went to kill him, but someone beat me to it. So I just stabbed him after the fact." She slid him a glance. "He attacked Giselle, tried to rape her."

Chase blinked in surprise.

"Lizzie told me all about it," she continued, as though she hadn't shared such startling news. "Tell him, Ninja. You were there. Tell him what NuNu did."

She stopped and tilted her head. "That's why you killed him, because he touched her." Enlightenment dawned in Raquel's eyes. "You killed NuNu. I was your alibi."

Raquel leaned back with a self-satisfied smirk.

Staring at the back of Ninja's head, he realized there was a lot that he didn't know, a lot that he hadn't asked. Now, he took a deep breath. "Did Sera send NuNu to attack Giselle?"

Ninja kept his eyes focused on the road as he responded, "Sera wouldn't go that far. And NuNu didn't need an excuse."

The young man met his gaze through the rearview mirror. "I'm dropping you at Raquel's. Whether you hate her or not, you are now each other's alibi. You were at Raquel's all night. Pay those servants of yours whatever you need to."

"I don't have money like that," Raquel shrieked. "I don't pay them now. It comes from the trust."

Ninja opened the glove compartment and pulled out a stack of cash. "Something tells me you're the kind of boss that will have to pay them heavily for their silence."

Chase closed his eyes, as Raquel and Ninja continued to go back and forth—Ninja in an eerily calm voice and Raquel twenty octaves higher.

Through the haze of his thoughts, someone shouted, "Chase."

In the Midst of Fire

Then someone mumbled softer, "Chase."

They were outside the back of Raquel's house. "We're going to the hospital to see Giselle."

Ninja paused, gave him a onceover. "As long as you both have your stories straight and show up together, I don't have a problem with that."

Chase yanked the money from Raquel's hands and handed it back to Ninja.

He took a deep breath, neither one of them had the right to keep that money. "Something tells me I already owe you a huge debt."

Ninja paused, "Not at all."

An array of emotions ran across Ninja's face. He didn't know a man like Ninja could have emotions. Chase held out his hand. "Nonetheless."

Ninja took it and shook the hand Chase offered.

Chase watched as Ninja peeled off.

EPILOGUE

Eighteen months later

Giselle stared out of Lizzie's apartment window in awe of her view of the Eiffel Tower. How many people could say that they'd been to that historic place, much less had it as their backdrop?

The Parisian apartment had huge cathedral windows that opened onto a Juliette balcony. The apartment itself held a kind of Parisian historical charm—bright white walls, plenty of fireplaces, and enough light to make her believe the sun actually rose in the living room.

She closed her eyes, enjoying the spring Parisian breeze, the chatter of a foreign language caressing her ears. Too few could say they'd lived this experience, but then few still could say they survived what her family had.

After Sera's "disappearance," Chase filed a missing person's report, which meant the police spent three straight days interrogating him until they finally had to let him go. He had an alibi; his alibi was a woman who hated his guts.

He did stick around Chicago for a while, but finally decided his life was haunted by too many ghosts. He joined them in Paris, and he got a job as a bicycle tour guide. It didn't pay much, but it paid. And his looks landed him some amazing tips.

Chase grieved. Hard. Still. Giselle asked him if he loved her.

"I don't really know," he responded. "I guess in a way. I definitely miss her, though. I didn't think I would miss her like this."

Giselle rarely heard from or about Mrs. Warner. After figuring out her mother was a killer, Lizzie packed and was on the first thing moving to Paris. She would continue to support her mother as long as she never stepped within fifty feet of Hawk, Lizzie, Greg, or the twins. Thankfully, that batty woman complied.

The one-year-old twins were an amazing pair who had distinct personalities. Grace was going to be the rough and tumble one always chasing after Greg.

Hilton, named for his huge head which made for a difficult birth, was more cerebral. Lizzie said he had better be smart, forcing her to push that noggin through her hoo-ha.

Giselle had forgiven her father. She had to. He'd spent years trying to make money a good companion. Every relationship for him included loss, disappointment.

Tory, Hawk, and Lizzie had a sit-down. Tory wanted to be free to be himself—the purpose of the move to France. Letting Lizzie go hadn't been a hardship for him. They were working through the complicated matter, but Gregory was happy and that was the most important thing for all of them.

Giselle and Chase sat around like cats, constantly licking their wounds, hoping something would heal them, anything.

Her phone vibrated with a number she didn't know. Her heart knew. Her heart soared and tears immediately began falling down her cheek.

Knowing that she never received calls from anyone who wasn't in her contact list. Would he dare?

"Hey, stranger," she answered.

"Hey there, Hawk's Lil Sis."

"How are you doing?" Giselle said, unable to hold back a smile. "See, I asked about you first this time."

"Well, seeing as how you've been hanging out with the people that you normally ask about first," he countered, "I don't know if this counts."

Blood rushed in Giselle's veins like white water pushing a raft down a stream. "It counts. Trust me."

Ninja only responded with a noncommittal, "Hmmm."

As silence stretched on the phone, "Did you know? about Raquel?"

Ninja waited a second before responding, "Before you, yes; from the beginning, no."

Biting her lip, Giselle pushed, "How?"

Giselle ambled from the window towards her bedroom. Soon her energy bubbled until she was dancing. She mentally calmed herself, matching Ninja's cool demeanor.

A bus rumbled down with a tour guide giving bits of history about the area.

"Who would want to get to Sera, but use NuNu first?" he explained. "The obvious answer was you."

"Like I'd go through all that work," Giselle drolly responded.

"True," he agreed. "The next answer is someone who loved you. Hawk was next to me when NuNu was hit the first time. Your dad wouldn't hurt Sera. But the building across the street was owned by the Warner Consortium."

"It could've been a coincidence."

Ninja sighed his impatience, "Do you know that rich people are the biggest gossips I've ever met. I mean, damn."

Laughing, Giselle teased, "It must be your charm."

"Or people really hated her."

As excited as she was to hear from him, she had to be realistic. He disappeared for so long.

This call could mean nothing at all, or at least mean less for him than it did for her. "So I wanted to thank you for sending me a new phone . . . seventeen months ago."

Ninja laughed; the sound of it shattered any pretend indifference. "You're welcome."

Giselle paused before asking the question she'd been avoiding.

In the Midst of Fire

"How did you escape? Why aren't you in jail? Or are you? With so many, umm, issues that you resolved?

The silence hung in the air, disrupted only by the sounds from the still open windows.

Giselle broke it. "I mean so many people went to jail afterwards. And your name wasn't even mentioned."

Ninja blew out a breath. "It took every ounce of discipline not to stay with you at Lexington." He clarified, "I learned that discipline in the service."

Giselle dropped the phone and scrambled to pick it back up.

"I thought you left college . . . I . . . you said"

"Well, the Marines were looking for a few good men. Computers are my specialty. Homeland Security tapped me at my brother's funeral."

Dumbstruck, Giselle tried to speak. "But you . . . "

"I told you I was a contractor instead of a rent-a-thug.

Giselle pinched her nose. "But all the people you killed."

"Tate?"

"No, the others."

Humor tinged his voice, "Did you see any bodies besides Tate's? You should learn not to listen to gossip."

"What about NuNu?"

"There are only two people who can tell that story, NuNu and I. In my eyes, it was self-defense. My bosses agreed."

Through the phone, Giselle realized French was being spoken by someone close to Ninja. This sneaky bastard.

She raced to the front and pressed her cheek against it. Sure enough, the same conversation was being played out in the hallway and on the phone.

"You know, Ninja, this is the first time that I've heard the same thing in the background of my phone that I'm hearing in the background of yours."

Ninja's voice deepened, "Well, Giselle, what are you going to do about it?"

Giselle felt overwhelmed by all the things her heart wanted to sing to and all the things her mind refused to say. They weren't really anything to each other before she came back to Chicago. They were even less now, but there was still something. If she didn't say anything at all, then what?

"I missed you, Ninja."

He paused, his signature way of drawing things out. "Then I suggest you open the door and let me in."

She pulled open the door to find him leaning against the wall. Giselle launched herself into his arms, holding him tightly. She felt his deep inhale, as he too tightened his hold. Who knew the hood had a happily ever after?

In the Midst of Fire

In the Midst of Fire

www.ingramcontent.com/pod-product-compliance
Lightning Source LLC
Chambersburg PA
CBHW031059270626
47155CB00027B/2811